SWITCH

N.M. CATALANO

SWITCH

Dedication

This one is for you, Mom. I think of you every day and wish I had taken the time to ask you all the questions I have now. You were an amazing woman; you touched so many hearts with your love and your strength and your compassion. When you loved, you truly loved unconditionally, extending our family to include so many. You were a bad ass and a saint. I just hope I can someday be half the woman you were. <3

Books

CONTENTS

I have been waiting all my life to see the glory of your face.

Now, I have found you.

~ Rumi

Chapter One

Elizabeth

"Marco, thank you again for everything today." I smile at the most seductive, beautiful, confident and delicious man I have ever seen sitting across the table with me.

"Elizabeth, don't thank me, I just wish I'd known sooner so we wouldn't have gone through everything."

We're sitting in The George, an upscale waterfront bistro restaurant, having a celebration dinner. I got divorced today.

"You're right. I know I should have told you sooner but our relationship didn't start out in a way that we exchanged personal information, if I may remind you." I look at him cocking an eyebrow, a smirk pulling at the corner of my mouth. I will never be able to think about that first night with Marco without my breath catching.

The day I met Marco started out just like every other day had for the past three years. Just a link in the chain in this thing called my life. Wake up, punch the clock, perform, go home, go to bed and wake up to do it all over again day after day. I was existing and not really living. I suppose I needed that time initially to heal, to forgive, and to let go of the life I thought I had and the life I'd envisioned I would have. When we're younger we have these fantasies of what life is going to be like when we grow up. I was recovering from a heartbreak of a life lost and a life I'd never have.

That day I met Marco was already predetermined by destiny. It was the day she'd already planned for me to start feeling again. On that day I was brought to the world of the living, not the one we go through robotically every day, but the life our souls yearn for, the living we hunger for, a life lived with passion.

"Ms. DiStefano, need I remind *you* that you didn't want to give me your phone number, did you?" He leans in closer with that sexual masculinity of his wrapping around me, caressing me with just his presence.

It's obvious by looking at Marco that he is an extremely sexual being, it oozes from him like his strength, confidence and control. Marco has an aura that promises sheer ecstasy, luring you to him like the serpent enticing Eve to the apple, forbidden and tempting. A woman knows her soul will be lost to him but the rapture she will experience is worth the price. He takes a woman into him with unspoken words of fulfillment, of fantasies, of things she hasn't dared to imagine, and she gives herself completely. Marco is a man who has perfected dominant sexual masculinity.

I sit back in my chair, thinking about his question.

"You're actually really thinking about your answer, Elizabeth?" The shock is written all over his face, not because he's cocky or arrogant, I'm sure it could be argued that he is, but because of our intense attraction to one another right from that first look from across the room at the bar where we first saw each other.

Marco followed me one night after a girl's night out and caught me before I fell on my knees and sprawled face first on the sidewalk. He propositioned me before he and I even made any introductions. And I went with him, no names and no idea where he was going to take me. All he said to me was, "Let's go, Elizabeth," and I went. This was clearly an impulsive action. The moment I laid eyes on him I knew I wanted to get lost in him. I wanted to get high on him and drown in his glorious seduction. I wanted the ecstasy to burn everything from me and take me to a place where nothing existed but us. He watched me from afar at the bar as if he were stalking me, baiting me, waiting for the right opportunity to come in for his kill. And I died happily that night, over and over again (and this is proof that impulsiveness does make for good decisions). It was the most mind-blowing one-night stand I'd ever had. It turned into many and eventually my ex-husband showed up and tried to kill me.

"Yes, Marco, I am thinking about it because I want it to be an honest answer, not only for you but for me too. You were with me these past couple of weeks and saw what happened when Santino found out about us."

He looks at me and I can see by his expression that he knows what I mean. "I understand, but all things considered, did you?"

I knew the answer even before he asked the question, I knew it that night when I first laid eyes on him, "Yes, I did, no matter what."

I feel so much for this man right now, his kindness, his genuineness, his I-don't-take-any-shit attitude, and his so-much-sexiness, and I know it's all there in my eyes. He leans towards me and places a gentle kiss on my lips.

As always Marco gets us the table in the corner against the wall allowing us as much privacy as can be had in a restaurant. I think he also prefers tables with tablecloths, like this one.

"You are the most beautiful woman I have ever met, Elizabeth," he says quietly and close to my ear, his breath whispering over my heated skin. His hand comes to rest on my thigh.

"Open your legs, Elizabeth."

Every nerve in my body has just woken up and is sizzling in anticipation of his touch. I have no control over myself, his words are my command and I do whatever he asks me because I know his only intention is to bring me pleasure.

Marco

My life was clear and uncomplicated until I met Elizabeth. She came stumbling in to my life, quite literally, and I was more than happy to catch her. I couldn't wait to get my hands on her and enjoy all of the erotic delights I knew I would find there. But she was different and proved to be a challenge. And I never back down from a challenge, especially one as delicious as she is. Her body was an oasis waiting to be discovered and I indulged in all of the forbidden fruits she had waiting to be explored. But she went with me that first night complacent in her decision not to see me again and I was damned if anyone was going to stop me from having what I wanted. And that challenge fueled my desire to be with her again.

I had no desire for a relationship, at least not one in the literal sense. It has been years since I was involved with a woman that way and the last one left me bitter and unable to trust women. To me they seemed to be conniving opportunists and I was not about to let myself get used again, except for sex. I love to make love to a woman. I also love to fuck them. I love their bodies and how they respond to stimulation. That is what gives me the greatest satisfaction. Driving a woman's passion until she is mindless, then bringing her to bliss. That's the greatest turn-on, her mindlessness because of you. And it gets me off, having that control. It's the best fucking aphrodisiac. And I never let my emotions get in the way of getting me off. Control. Over everything. I was always in control with the woman I was with in every way. With Elizabeth I lost control. It was frustrating but fucking hot as hell at the same time.

Then I watched as her life was threatened right in front of me. I thought my brain was going to explode as I was forced to just stand-by feeling helpless. I would never let myself or her be in that position ever again where I didn't have control. That's why I asked her to move in with me. But there was more to it that I wasn't being completely honest with myself about. I want more than just her body. I want all of her. I want her to belong to me completely. Yes, I know she would do anything I wanted sexually. That's not the question. But she's holding back. She won't give me her heart and her soul. And that is driving me even more fucking nuts. I don't know why. I have not wanted a woman so completely in years. But Elizabeth is different. She belongs to me; she just hasn't admitted it yet.

Right now Elizabeth almost has me losing control of myself, just that kiss and my dick is hard, she smiles and I get hard, and when she moans my name, I almost lose it. It's a sick satisfaction I want all the time, over and over again. I don't like to admit it but she's got me by the balls and I love it.

Those legs of hers uncross and I imagine them wrapping around my head and the image makes my cock jump and my mouth water remembering her taste on my tongue. Her pretty little ass shifts in her chair as she moves to open her legs for me and I almost groan out loud wanting to bury myself between them. My fingers slide up her silky flesh and brush against her panties, skimming the edge and pushing them aside.

"I can't wait until I get you home and put those clamps on your beautiful pink nipples, baby."

Elizabeth

That turned into one of the longest meals I've ever had. With Marco's hand stroking softly between my thighs, teasing me and keeping my arousal humming, and the thought of trying the clamps for the first time tonight, I thought I'd explode from waiting.

"Get the nipple clamps, baby." His voice is strained from his pent up desire as well.

We've just walked in the door of my apartment and we're all hands and mouths and teeth and tongues leaving a trail of clothes from the front door to the bedroom. The box with the clamps Marco gave me as a present tonight are sitting on the nightstand beside my bed. I walk over and take them out of the pink box they came in and hand them to him, my hand almost shaking with excitement.

He strokes the back of one finger across each tip of my breasts and the sensations shoot through me making my flesh bump up all over. A soft moan passes through my slightly parted lips and he lowers his mouth to mine catching the sound.

"I'm going to put them on now, love. Let me know when they're just right."

I look at him wide eyed. "How will I know?"

His smile broadens wickedly, "Oh, believe me, baby, you'll know."

He takes one nipple and holds it while slipping the clamp over the hardened tip.

My shoulders push forward and I grimace before I even say, "It hurts a bit."

There is a little gauge on the side of the clamp that he moves and…oooohh, that feels really good. He studies my face and smiles knowingly.

"Like that, baby," he says.

"Yes, Marco, just like that." It comes out low and raspy.

He takes the other nipple and places the clamp on it, adjusting the gauge and my eyelids droop with the stimulation.

"Lie on the bed on your back, hands over your head, and hold the head board."

I climb to the center of the bed, the chain swinging back and forth tugging lightly on my nipples and I groan with the feeling.

Marco follows me onto the bed straddling me and his balls tickle my sex. I bite down on my lip. All of these stimulations are heightened because of the constant arousal of my nipples. I lift up trying to rub myself against his hanging sac.

My body is screaming for satisfaction, throbbing with need, and if he doesn't do something about it soon, then I will.

Marco

"You're almost ready to come. Your heart is beating so hard, your breathing is heavy, your skin is flushed so pretty and pink, and your pussy is glistening it's so wet."

Elizabeth's eyes roll back and a low moan floats from her slightly parted pink lips. I haven't even touched her yet and she's on fire. This isn't going to take long, for either one of us.

I shift down between her legs and spread them wide, admiring the beautiful view. I hold her legs open, pressing down firmly on her thighs until I know that she won't move them.

"Keep your legs just like this for me, even when I'm inside you." I force myself to stay focused and move slowly. This is about her pleasure now, not mine.

I see the muscles tense throughout her body, even her inner walls. I know her pussy instinctively clenched at my words; I saw it, followed by a little extra of her juices flowing from her. I need to taste her. I lower my mouth forward while still holding firmly on to her legs and swipe my tongue from her ass all the way to her clit.

"Oh God, Marco…" The words are more of a moan, sounding guttural and deep.

"I know, baby." The sound of my voice is raw, reflecting the rising need in me. "Just let go and enjoy me."

Her body reacts and it's almost visible as she goes from being here to being in our erotic place of abandon. Her head rolls back, her mouth opens just a little and her body arches, jutting those beautiful breasts up with her nipples being bitten by the silver clamps. She has just told me without words, *Take me, I'm yours to do what you want*, and I intend to do just that.

I place my finger on her bare mound and trace the bone at the entrance of her sex, then slide down along the crease of her thighs. The whole lower portion of her body tenses as she holds on tight, fighting the urge to move into my touch. She's anticipating, begging for me to give her what she needs but I know it's not time yet. I want her ready to explode until she can't take it anymore. She wants that too, that's why she gives me the control to give her what she needs. My finger lightly glides across her moist skin down over the cheek poking out from underneath her and comes up between the two cheeks. I circle around her opening and her lips and come down the other side, repeating the same thing there.

"Please, Marco…" She's here but she's not. She's getting lost in her place of oblivious pleasure.

"Patience, baby." I'm getting lost there as well, getting lost in her and the drug of her pleasure.

Bringing two fingers to slide through her wet folds, one on each side, I bring them back up and take one to make circles around her hole imagining sliding into her, first just the tip, and it's all I can do to keep up this slow pace. I place my other hand on her flat stomach below the chain linking the clamps so that all I have to do is lift my finger to clasp it. My finger mimics my musings of sliding the head of my cock into her, I insert it just enough so that I can continue the circles inside her. At the same time, I lift a finger to tug on the chain slightly to pull on her nipples.

"Aaaahhhhh!" Her back lifts off the bed as she grips tightly onto my finger inside her and pulls on the headboard she's still clutching with her hands. I hold the chain and slide my finger all the way in, rubbing my thumb on her engorged clit as I do. Her legs and torso are rock solid straight, holding on for dear life.

"I'm going to come, Marco, now!"

"Come, Elizabeth, I want lick up your juices."

Still holding on to the chain, my finger buried in her pussy, I lay my tongue flat on her clit and rub. She's spread open wide for me wanting more and more as her first orgasm ripples through her.

"Oh, yes, Marco, please don't stop…"

She's coming but she needs more.

God, I love this shit.

I keep my finger inside of her stroking her walls, teasing that spot inside as I get her ready for the next one.

"Baby, I'm going to take off the clamps now. It's going to be a little painful but just hold on."

"Yes…" I can tell she's not yet to the point of mindlessness, but she will be very soon.

I gently unclip one clamp, then the other leaving my finger inside her, curving it and rubbing her there.

"Ooooohhh." Elizabeth inhales deeply as blood floods her nipples, and I can see the change in their color. I want to pull them into my mouth and suck on those little peaks but this is new to her so I let her feel everything.

I lean over her luscious body and hold myself above her with one arm as I begin to fuck her with my finger.

"I'm going to fuck you now, Elizabeth."

Elizabeth

I am a tumultuous ball of sensations. My desire is off the charts, and even though I just came, I'm horny as hell. My nipples are screaming in glorious agony, the throbbing shooting straight to my groin.

"Yes, now, please," I say but I want to growl instead.

With just those words I feel the beginning waves of an orgasm I know will make me scream, and I can't wait. I feel like an animal. I want him to fuck me, raw, hard and primal. Marco is staring into my eyes, assessing me I think, as his finger alternates between sliding in and out, rubbing and curving, then circling while his thumb flicks my swollen clit. His mouth claims mine hungrily, rough and demanding. He breaks the kiss and sits back and removes his finger. Taking his hard-on, he begins to slide it over my sex, teasing my clit, and rubbing the head against me.

"Now, Marco, now…"

"It's going to be hard and deep, baby," he grits out through clenched teeth.

He places his hands on the tops of my thighs, his thumbs almost holding my lips open for him, keeping my legs open and in place. I can almost hear my pussy yelling, *Yes, yes, yes, do it now!* and gulping and gasping for him. My hands are pulling on the head board and I'm mimicking the chant of my sex in my head, *Yes, yes, yes, now!* His mouth consumes mine again as he slams into me, burying himself all the way to the top, his balls slapping against my ass. I let out a gasp in his mouth and he answers it with a growl. Everything in me, all of my focus exists only at that place where our bodies feed off each other. It seems like I'm devouring him, eating him, chewing him with each thrust and I can't get enough. I growl back. His arms move to slide around my waist as they wrap all the way around and hold me to him.

He shifts my hips up to meet him, getting him deeper. I'm pounding him, meeting him, grinding into him, filling myself with him, trying to satisfy my hunger. His hands slide down to grab my ass cheeks and he holds them still and slams into me. I begin to fall, the mask of oblivion coming over me and I throw my head back to welcome it. I let go and just give myself over to him and let him push me over the edge so perfectly, with each thrust and each grind.

"Oooooh God, yes…"

"Yes, baby, yes," he purrs in my ear, raw and deep.

He thrusts deep and hard inside me and I feel him jerk and spasm as he throws his head back holding himself buried all the way in.

"Fuck, Elizabeth!"

He collapses on top of me and I lower my arms to hold him and lift my aching legs to enclose him, finally wrapping myself completely around him. Our heavy breathing coming in unison envelopes us in a chorus.

I stretch myself awake and instantly flinch with unfamiliar aches and pains. I hadn't realized a little, okay maybe more than a little, sex could leave you hurting in some unusual places. Especially when you held yourself rigidly still. It feels like a Charlie horse wants to explode in my calf and in my love handles. If this is any indication of things yet to come with Marco, I need to step up my yoga and start putting in some exercise.

"Uuugghh."

I roll over on to my stomach letting out a moan and flinch again at the mild tenderness of my nipples. A mischievous little grin spreads across my face as I remember the nipple clamps and a little ripple runs through me thinking how turned on I was last night. I felt like a beast let off its chain ready to devour. I open my eyes and squint at the bedside clock. It looks like an old-fashioned alarm clock with two bells on top with a hammer in between threatening to beat them and scare the shit out of you with the pounding noise. But it doesn't do that, thank God. I'm not a glutton for punishment and wouldn't torment myself every morning with that hideous and torturous way of waking up. Its noise is a soft melodic chime. I need no help in being a grouch in the morning. Seven a.m., good, I have enough time not to have to rush because I know I'll need extra time to get myself motivated and out of the morning-after-lovemaking sex fog.

I hear clanging in the kitchen then the creaking of the old original hardwood floorboards in my section of this historic mansion. Marco. My body comes alive and floods with warmth as tingles shoot through me at the thought of him. I'm a Pavlovian dog and am definitely trained to salivate at anything that has to do with him. He is that good.

"Hi, baby, I brought your tea. I thought you might like to have it in bed."

Do I detect a hint of amusement in his voice? My eyes dart to look at his face as he comes to stand at the side of the bed next to me. Yep, there is definitely a little smirk playing at his lips. He knows exactly how I feel, the sadist.

I'm laid out, spread eagle, face down on my king sized bed buck naked, tangled in the sheets and the silk red and gold comforter. I'm sure my appearance leaves much to be desired. My long brown hair must be a rat's nest and I didn't properly wash the makeup off my face last night. There is no doubt in my mind the homeless woman has taken up residence in my face again this morning with her psycho black-smeared eyes.

"Why do you always have to look so perfect in those boxers of yours, Marco? Couldn't you just once out of the kindness of your heart look like shit one morning?"

He throws his head back laughing so hard I think the tea and coffee he's holding are going to spill all over the floor. And if it does I'm not cleaning it up. He will, just for being such a good looking ass. I can't help but chuckle as well. The whole situation is pretty hysterical. Here I lie, the morning after, looking like I was rode hard and put up wet, another Southern saying, distasteful as it is, describing me precisely.

"Come on, move over and let me lie down with you. You are stunning, smeared makeup and all. You look like that because of me and I don't think you could be more beautiful. Now make room."

"Okay, since you put it that way. But I'm going to the bathroom first, no matter what you say."

"If you insist." There's that hint of amusement again.

I roll over, get out of bed and take two steps.

"My goodness, why do I feel like I've been beaten up? It's not like we did anything out of the ordinary."

He doesn't reply as I walk out of the bedroom towards the bathroom, grabbing my robe from the hook behind the door as I go. I still have hints of my lack of self-confidence regarding my body, hating the idea of what is jiggling behind me and any signs of cellulite as I walk away with my back to him.

When I get to the bathroom and close the door, I almost don't want to even look in the mirror. I know it's going to bad. *Suck it up, woman, you can take it.* I inhale and lift my face to look in the mirror.

"Oh, yuck," I groan at myself.

How can all of this on my face once have looked really good and now look like *this*? I hope he didn't get a really good look at me. And this hair, God. Grabbing a makeup remover pad, I begin a quick job of damage control. Once I do what I can there, I turn to taming the beast of my hair. Slightly satisfied with the efforts of making myself fairly presentable, I go back to join the disgusting epitome of morning loveliness. And he's cheerful in the morning as well, ugh!

"Hi, gorgeous, how are you feeling?" Marco at least has the decency to keep his humor in check and appears to be somewhat concerned. Maybe it was my comment.

I join him on the bed and lean over to kiss him good morning.

"Good morning, handsome. I'm sorry I'm not the best morning person sometimes." I smile sheepishly at him hoping to get rid of some of my stupid grumpiness with my self-admonition.

He kisses me in the middle of my forehead holding his lips there for a moment and I let it seep into me, warming me from the inside out, melting the frostiness of the morning grumpiness from me. It makes me smile. When he lifts his lips from me he pulls me close, cradling me in the crook of his arm, then hands me the cup of tea he's made for me.

"So how are you feeling this morning, Elizabeth?" The rumble of his deep voice reverberates through his chest, penetrating me.

"I'm good, excellent, but some muscles hurt in my legs and in my arms. It just shocked me really. There wasn't really anything unusual about last night, other than the clamps." I blush a little saying the c-word out loud.

"Well, that's not exactly true…" He's leading to something.

"Oh, would you like to tell me what that is?" My ears are perked up and I'm at full attention.

"Well, the position that you held yourself in last night was one that you, your body, is not used to. When you were at your most aroused you held yourself very rigid and were completely absorbed in what I was doing to you." What he's doing to me right now is bringing me right back to that place by talking about it. "So you were using your muscles, probably some you don't normally use, in a completely different way." He kisses the top of my head lightly and strokes my cheek softly with his fingertips.

"Tell me, did you enjoy feeling like you were restrained?" His voice is now sultry, licking me, heating my insides.

I feel myself flush as my groin begins to pulse.

"Yes, I did, very much." I don't trust my voice to speak any more loudly than barely just above a whisper. My mind goes into overdrive with images of Marco tying me up so I'm wonderfully helpless against the onslaught of attention he would shower my body with. Holy fuck, that is so sexy!

His hand slides through the flaps of my robe and begins to tease my already hardened nipples as I feel wetness seeping from me.

I am in so much trouble.

"Yes, you did. And you're thinking about what it's going to be like when I do tie you up and do decadent things to you." How can he make me feel like he's seducing me with only his words?

My heart rate has just accelerated and the aches and pains are now a delightful promise of erotic things yet to come.

"Marco?"

"Yes, baby?"

"What's the name of that gym you go to?" I decide I'd better start preparing.

Fasten your seatbelts, it's going to be a wonderfully bumpy ride.

His laugh is gut deep and fills the room, shaking me with its force.

"Actually, that's not a bad idea. The name of the place is Evolution. I'll text you the address later."

The wheels are turning in my head with all of these new images and possibilities. And all of the places this can lead. How am I supposed to concentrate on work now?

Speaking of which, I tell him, "As much as I'd love to continue this conversation right now, my sexual deviant, I have to get ready for work."

I rise up and turn to kiss him and he hugs me tight, kissing me deeply. I climb up to straddle him not breaking our kiss, pushing my body into his and grabbing handfuls of his hair, completely turned on by what he's told me.

Coming up for air, he's still holding me close and I can feel his arousal pressed against my sex. He says breathlessly, "You'd better go right now or you won't be able to for at least another hour."

"Okay I'm going…" I sit there trying to compose myself.

With one final quick kiss, he pushes me gently, "Go now, baby, or neither one of us will stop."

Getting up I say over my shoulder, "Kill joy," and chuckle.

There is an obvious bounce in my step now.

"You're much peppier now than you were when you first woke up, sexy." He laughs at me.

"It's amazing what a few little minutes can do, wouldn't you agree?" I turn to look at him, smiling seductively, and wink.

"Yeah, well, I'm going to make you some breakfast and you're going to eat it. I have a feeling that beast of yours is ready to go and it's going to need food."

"Yes, sir," I purr at him.

"GO, before I throw you down and fuck the shit out of you for playing with me."

I think I have just about pushed him as far as I think I can.

He begins to lift himself off the bed looking at me with a predatory gaze.

"Eeeek!" I squeal happily and take off sprinting towards the bathroom.

Marco

This is going to be fucking amazing! Molding Elizabeth, dipping her into submission, seeing her blossom under my control. The thought of it makes me incredibly and painfully hard. If we just had a few more minutes I would get in the shower and fuck her fast and hard, no fondling, no caressing, just push her against the wall and pound into her. It wouldn't take long. Last night was about her pleasure, right now I need release. I'll have to wait until I get back to the hotel and take care of it myself.

This sucks.

I get up and put on the rest of my clothes and gather Elizabeth's among the trail we scattered last night. I would have picked them up this morning when I woke but I was running a few minutes late myself. I'm not looking forward to going in to work this morning. Things haven't gone exactly as planned and I hope there aren't any more surprises waiting for me when I get there.

Going into the kitchen to start the spinach omelet wraps, I half expect there won't be enough ingredients in the fridge. I can't wait to move into my place, hopefully our place, so I can stock the fridge and cabinets properly. Maybe my interest in the kitchen is due to the fact that I practically grew up in a restaurant; my parents owned a Greek diner for years in upstate New York. Ah, it appears Elizabeth is getting better. Everything, and then some, that I need is here. Good girl, she's paying attention. Taking it all out, I begin to hum to myself as I start cooking.

I always get a little pull in my stomach at the first sight of Elizabeth. This time is no different, she just took my breath away when she came into the kitchen. She has no idea how beautiful she is. It's more than just her looks. It's her strong femininity, her sensuality, her being. All of these things intoxicate me. I saw it the first moment I laid eyes on her and I knew I would have her. She's dressed in a black and white lace skirt with a white jersey top, stockings and black patent leather pumps. Perfection. The hard-on that never really went away before is now screaming for attention again.

"Sit. You have time for a quick bite," I insist.

"Okay, but just quickly."

Why does she always have to test me? She is a stubborn, strong-willed, sometimes mule-headed woman. And I think it's so refreshing it stirs my blood.

I take the seat on the stool next to her at the black granite breakfast bar. She's got a great place, very comforting and soothing, old mixed with new, neutrals with pops of color, and hints of her placed intimately throughout her home.

"Have you got anything planned today after work?" I ask her as she's barely coming up for air between bites. I've got to say, when Elizabeth eats, she does it with passion. I guess because she is a passionate person.

Reaching over to my bottle of water, she lifts it to take a sip before answering me.

"Not yet but I have to get in touch with a friend of mine, Elsie. She invited me to a Halloween party." She looks at me guiltily and continues, "And we have to talk about costumes."

Wow. Why do I feel…jealous, insulted, offended and just plain like shit?

"Oh? You didn't mention a Halloween party." I try my best to keep my expression emotionless.

"I'm sorry, I forgot. It slipped my mind with all that has been happening around us."

She looks as if she feels like she made a mistake for not telling me until now but I can't blame her. She's a grown woman with her own life apart from me. But that doesn't mean I have to like it. Because I don't. What the hell is wrong with me?

"I know. It's fine. So I guess I'll be solo on Halloween." I'm acting like a child who's been told he can't go out and play but has to stay home and do his chores. This sucks.

"No, we can see each other afterwards."

There is a look of…pity in her face. No one feels sorry for me. Now I'm pissed.

"Elizabeth, please, I am more than capable of finding something to do. Go to the party with your friend, have fun and don't cut your night short for me. Besides, there are a few invitations sent to the company from suppliers and associates that I haven't gone through yet. I should make an appearance at one of those as good public relations" There's an icy tone to my voice no matter how hard I try not to let it show that reveals this bothers me.

"Fine." She looks hurt. Damn it.

I lean over to kiss her tight lips, wanting to soothe her after my irrational behavior.

"Oh, the mover is bringing my things up from Florida tomorrow. I was hoping you would go with me to pick out anything else I might need, like paintings and accessories, and some kitchen supplies."

Her mood visibly brightens and it makes me feel better. Seeing her happy makes me happy.

"I'd love to. When would you like to go?"

"How about Saturday? I'll have gotten a lot of stuff unpacked and put in place by then. The cleaners came on Monday to get the place ready. Friday night we can spend the night there." I can't help but smile thinking of having her in my bed. That bed…

"Sounds perfect." A light flush has crept into her cheeks and her lips are slightly parted. The idea arouses her but I think she's a little nervous as well.

"Good, I'm looking forward to it." Why am I such a sadistic bastard? I love it.

"Me, too." Her eyes are wide and it makes my cock twitch knowing she's thinking of some of the things I might do to her.

Elizabeth

Sitting next to Marco and looking into his face I can tell that something is bothering him. I've come to know this man. I can read his thoughts on his face, that poker face he shows to the world. The slight shifts in nuance tell me there is something behind that beautiful façade that doesn't sit quite right with him. I decide that, for right now, I'll give it some time to come out.

Chapter Two

Elizabeth

Did someone open the floodgates and let all of the people with problems out today? Holy crap, the phone hasn't stopped ringing. Working in a boutique agency as a representative of a major insurance company comes with its fair share of hysteria, especially from customers who have money...and too much time on their hands.

I finally have a minute to stop and take a breath so I decide to text Elsie.

Hey you, busy?

No, Miss Business Lady, you at work?

I can't help but smile. If there is any book you can't judge by its cover, it's Elsie. She is short like me with blue-black hair cut in a pixy style with long fringe bangs brushed to the side over one eye. She has a couple of beautiful tasteful tattoos and a pretty little diamond stud nose ring. And she is one of the most straight, professional, hardworking women I know. She has a pretty fierce right hook too; I've seen it take out a full-grown man. Elsie was the wardrobe coordinator for the movie *Safe Haven* when I worked on the project. That's how we met. She's about ten years younger than I am but she's driven and talented and takes her work very seriously.

Yeah, do you want to get together tonight?

Sure, here?

How about meeting for a piece of pizza or something, we're supposed to eat, right?

Oh yeah, food, right, lol. Sure, slice of life on market 5:15?

Smart ass, I'll see you there.

YOU started it, ok, later then.

Marco sent me the address for the gym, Evolution. I can take a quick trip there on my lunch hour to check out what they might offer for women. I already kind of know two people who work there, Brian and John. Checking the time, I see there's only another hour until lunch so I dive into the pile of quotes waiting to get done from this morning's madness.

Marco

"Christine, what's all this on my desk?" I bellow from my office. I come from an Italian and Greek household, we weren't a quiet family, and obviously some habits are hard to break.

Christine is one of the only two administrative assistants currently working at KMD Enterprises. She's my assistant and doubles as a receptionist when the other girl, Savannah, is out. We moved into the offices last month and once this multi-million-dollar real estate project breaks ground, the offices are going to be filled. Right now things are in limbo until the building permits are issued. I have no idea what the fuck is taking so long with the infrastructure permits. It seems like the process is taking longer than usual.

"Liana was by this morning and asked to go into your office to leave some things on your desk. She wanted to do it herself. You know how she can be," she says from the doorway.

I roll my eyes. "Yes, I know exactly how she can be, don't worry about it. Its fine. I'll mention something to her and Steve. Are either of them here?"

"No, Liana said she was going to the newspaper and Steve said he's meeting with a concrete company. Would you like some rocket fuel, Mr. Kastanopoulis?"

I laugh at her name for espresso. This is one habit I picked up from my parents and grandparents. I have a cup of espresso at the beginning of my workday, like they used to in one of those little white porcelain cups and saucers with the tiny spoons and a piece of lemon peel on the side. I forgo the lemon. Just give me some sugar.

"Yes, please, if you wouldn't mind."

"Sure thing, it'll just be a minute."

I sit at my desk and get settled. As I leaf through the papers Liana left for me, a scowl begins to spread across not only my face but my mood as well. I pick up the phone to call her.

"Good morning, Sir," she answers on the first ring with that smooth voice she uses when she's trying to be sweet.

"Don't call me that, Liana. What is all this you left for me?" I'm on the verge of getting very irritated with her.

"Now don't be such a grump. Those are appearances, annoying maybe, but in this town these types of things are necessary. You want to seduce people, and being at those types of functions will help do that," she tells me confidently.

"But emceeing at a Bid On a Date thing? Come on." Is she serious?

She lets out a short laugh before saying, "Just be grateful *you're* not the piece of meat that will be sold off, although from my meeting with them, that's exactly what they would have preferred. They called *me* wanting *you*. It won't be so bad, Marco, this year's theme is Men of Service. You know, military men, firefighters, police officers."

I let out a sigh and I have to agree with her, "I get it, all right. And what the hell is Sassy?"

She lets out a belly laugh and I can't help but laugh with her.

"It's a local prominent women's magazine. Typically, they just interview women but they've finagled some way to get you in there. My bet is so she can be alone with you. Now remember before you get all uptight, you will have commercial and residential units for sale. Women make up a large segment of business owners and homeowners. Just keep that in mind when she's undressing you with her eyes," she tells me and I can sense she's really enjoying my apparent discomfort.

"It's not going to be like that. I'm sure she's a professional," I reply, begrudgingly admitting to myself that Liana has some very valid points. "Okay, thanks, Liana, as usual nice work."

"Oh, Marco, what about the Halloween event for UE? This is a very important function for you," Liana adds before I hang up the phone.

I feel a tug of annoyance because I would rather bring Elizabeth with me, then answer, "Yes, RSVP for me, you and Steve."

"Excellent," Liana replies smoothly, and I have the distinct feeling I hear a slight smugness in her tone.

"And, Liana, one more thing: please leave whatever you have for me with Christine if I'm not here. She is instructed not to let anyone in my office. Don't put her in that position again. Do I make myself clear?"

"Yes, Master, I'm sorry. I just like being in your personal space."

"What did I tell you? don't call me that. You're very good at your job. And that's all this is, a working relationship."

"Marco, I'm a professional but don't ever forget what an asset it is having me on your side," she purrs with a hint of her demure seductiveness.

This is the opportunistic woman I know so well.

"Believe me, I realize it. That's why you're here. Bye, Liana."

I hang up before she can try to antagonize me any further but I can't help and give her the credit she deserves. She might be a pain in my ass, but she's very good at what she does, which is public relations and marketing.

Christine comes in with the little white cup filled with the thick black liquid from heaven.

"Here you go, Superman, get ready for lift off."

Why do I surround myself with women who love to harass me? Maybe because Christine is adorable and very competent. And I'm a glutton for punishment, I'm sure.

Elizabeth

Getting to Evolution on Wrightsville Beach took me longer than I had expected. When I walk through the door I'm enveloped in hot, sexy, male testosterone. Where the hell have these guys been hiding in this town? Obviously nowhere I've been. But in reality I haven't actually been anywhere for almost three years, unless it was in an office, grocery story, or movie location. And here I am surrounded by Wilmington, North Carolina's most delectable male specimens. One question plagues me though: Do I let the secret out to the rest of the female population in our little city, or do I keep this treasure trove all to myself? I might tell just one or two special female friends, maybe even a couple of gay male ones too, just to be fair.

A man's deep voice stops my ogling and I lift my jaw up from the floor.

"How can I help you today?" he says with a friendly and professional tone.

"Um, yes." Yep, I'm a little flustered. "Could you tell me, does Evolution offer any classes or instruction for women?" and I think, *they could teach us a few wonderful things.*

"Yes we do, Miss…"

"Oh, I'm Elizabeth DiStefano." I extend my hand to shake his and he takes it in his big calloused one.

"I'm Scott Edwards, it's nice to meet—" He's interrupted by someone shouting my name from across the studio.

"ELIZABETH!"

I turn and see one of the two hulks, the dark haired one, who was in my apartment the day Santino showed up. The only thing I remember from that day is Santino had me in a choke-hold and I passed out as Marco was coming towards us. When I woke up, this man and another mixed martial arts fighter from here had Santino pinned down on the floor, my door was broken in, and Mr. Jones, my landlord, was standing in the doorway looking flabbergasted. I was hoping I would run into one of them today. I've never been one for exercise classes, but I think being around men in this situation is better than being around women. He is closing the space between us with big steps that match his large frame, and he's wearing a panty-melting smile from ear to ear.

"Hi, good to see you, Elizabeth. Marco mentioned you might be coming by today. How're you doing?"

Of course he did, I think to myself.

"Um, hi, and it's good to see you too, under better circumstances. I don't think I ever had an opportunity to thank you for everything that day. I can't begin to tell you how much I appreciate everything you guys did."

I catch a glimpse of Scott, the guy behind the desk who greeted me. His eyes are darting between this giant and me, mouth agape, looking totally confused.

"Please, don't thank me. We were glad to help. I don't think we were properly introduced, I'm John Wolfe."

He holds out his big hand and I take it, my hand swallowed by his, laughing lightly. "Elizabeth DiStefano."

Scott cuts in. "It appears you two know each other."

John turns his head to him but keeps his slightly slanted eyes looking at me. I'm thinking he's probably Native American Indian with the skin tone, dark eyes, high cheekbones and defined features, and the beautiful long black hair pulled back in a loose ponytail. I can see him sitting proudly on a beautiful black horse at the top of a mountain in suede leggings and bare chested, an Indian warrior, with his hair blowing in the breeze.

"Yes Scott, she's a friend of Marco's."

"Oh, now I see."

See what? I wonder.

"I'll take care of her. What can I do for you today, Elizabeth?" he asks as he begins to lead me slowly through the studio.

John Wolfe is a bear of man, with a subtle confidence, radiating strength and control quietly but powerfully, with hints of underlying dark promises. I believe he does not take any prisoners but rather is offered sacrifices, willingly begging to submit down on their knees for anything he would do to them.

"Well I wanted to find out what classes you have for women. Marco gave me the name of your place and told me you guys are MMA fighters." I blush a little from the statement. I don't know why, but to be perfectly honest it's probably because I find the idea of these warriors to be sexy as hell. An image of Marco hot, sweaty and fighting sends a tremor through me.

He seems a little embarrassed, turning his face down to look at the floor as a shy smile plays at his lips. John is a contradiction packaged in his brawny frame. On one side he's menacing, rakish, with a hint of primal sexuality, on the other side he's gentle, kind, and a tad bit shy, and a trace of sadness. I can't help but study him. He's probably in his early thirties but carries himself very confidently as someone who has lived life and has dealt with its ugliness emerging scarred but immensely stronger. I know he's got to be almost six and a half feet with a body built like a brick shit house, but he moves quite gracefully for such a big man. I think he still has a little of that wild little boy in him that this big, secure, kind-of-intimidating man takes out sometimes when he wants to play with his big boy toys. He's wearing a gray gi but it's different from the ones I've seen before. That's more than likely due to the type of martial arts practiced here.

I survey the mirror-walled room. There are at least ten body-size punching bags lined up in a row. Fine specimens of men glistening with sweat are kicking, punching and round-housing on all the bags. Metallica is being pumped in to feed the aggression of the would-be warriors. On the other side of the room is an area with weights, a section with padded mats, a large cage which is, I'm sure, where they spar to practice for MMA fights, and a couple of smaller rooms, where John is leading me.

"Well, of course we have kickboxing, Jiu Jitsu, which is the form of martial arts we teach that's incorporated in MMA, and boxing. But I think something you might be interested in that we've recently started offering is a women's self-defense class. We've partnered with the Wrightsville Beach police department as a 'safe communities' initiative," John informs me with a relaxed confidence. He knows his business and he takes it very seriously, and it shows.

His almond-shaped eyes turn toward me but their gaze have a puzzled look to them as if contemplating something quietly to himself. Could he be remembering that afternoon in my apartment when Santino's arm was wrapped around my neck? Is he imaging how that might have ended differently?

"That does sound very interesting. What's covered in those classes and how often do they meet?"

I decide to let the look go and pretend it never happened. That is the past, and I have a feeling that John and I are going to become good friends.

"They're given Monday and Wednesday nights at six o-clock for two months and we cover some boxing moves, Jiu Jitsu maneuvers, and a little kickboxing. It's a mix that's molded to give someone with a smaller frame the biggest advantage over an attacker. Guaranteed to take down even me if done right. It's our job to make sure that every single woman will be able to protect herself," he says quietly in all seriousness.

Yes, John is very sincere about what he does. I wonder what he must have seen or lived through that gave him the ghosts he lives with.

"And I'm assuming that it will help to build muscle tone, strength and stamina?" I ask, remembering why I initially came here.

I blush as my muscles give their little reminder of this morning's pains from last night's games. I can't look John in the eye. I know he knows what I mean.

The corner of John's mouth lifts in a half smirk. I can tell he's trying to fight it but it's too late. It's already there.

"Yes it will," he answers simply.

He definitely knows why I'm asking.

Trying to regain some sort of propriety, but I figure why bother at this point, he knows Marco,

I ask, "Do I have to wait for the schedule to begin?"

"We're actually beginning a new schedule this coming Monday and we still have slots open. Brian and I will be taking turns teaching most of those classes. He was with me at your place that day," he informs me to identify who Brian is. "Why don't you come down on Monday, try it out, no charge, and see what you think?" he suggests.

His large body is now fully turned facing me with his arms crossed in front of his chest and his feet spread apart. He is a very intimidating force, with an air of dominance and complete confidence and control. Much like Marco, but each of them distinct. Marco is refined with hints of raw sexuality. John is primitive with a seductively dangerous heat. I'm sure he knows how formidable he can appear, but standing here talking to him I also get the impression he's humble and is not the type of person to flaunt his strength, both his physical and his character. He doesn't need to, it's apparent.

"That sounds like a great idea. And I suppose I should wear something like yoga pants and a tee?" I ask, forcing my attention back to why I'm here.

"Yes, nothing loose fitting though. We don't want you to get caught up in anything."

My phone alerts me with a text. I'm sure its Marco as he already called the gym earlier to tell them I'd probably be coming, and I'm sure he's wondering how things are going. I don't bother to check it because I'll be leaving in just a few minutes or else I'll be late getting back to work. With all the time I lost because of the problems brought on with the situation with Santino, I don't think I can afford to be careless.

"I'll be here then, save me a spot," I say smiling at him as I turn to walk back towards the front desk. I glance around the room and notice a lot of the men working out are looking at me. I take it they don't get too many women in here during the day.

At the door I turn to face John and Scott, who is still sitting at the front desk working. Scott keeps his attention on whatever's in front of him but I know he's taking in our every move. Maybe that's a trait of a good fighter, always knowing what's happening around him.

"Take a card, I'll put my cell number on it. Call me if you have any questions or problems."

John grabs a pen off the desk and scribbles his number on a business card, then hands it to me. I slide it into my purse, remembering John is a good friend of Marco's and the circumstances that initially brought us together. He came running without question when Marco and I were the Slice of Life, in my mind I see two lovers from that long ago time in the doorway. Their story was a tragedy that came to an end right here.

He was from a prestigious and well-to-do family on his way to the senate; she was a beautiful mulatto from the wrong side of the tracks. He enjoyed his whiskey too much and that night he'd already had more than he could handle. She was in hiding from him because of the beatings he had already given her. They loved each other madly but it was a destructive love and she was going to leave Wilmington before it was too late. He saw her from across the street exiting the building, her friend in front of her, and he rushed towards them. They argued and she informed him she was leaving. He pulled out a gun and told her she was not going anywhere and shot her right there in the doorway. He was never convicted, his family was too powerful, and he more than likely continued his career in politics. Some say they see her agonized ghost imprisoned in this spot for eternity. Love can make you do terrible things.

I love this tragic love story; it tells of passion so strong it is unbearable.

I walk in and scan the room for Elsie. It's beginning to fill up with the after-work hipster crowd who can't really afford to eat out at nice restaurants but can look like it here in this modern but simple upscale pizzeria. A little arm starts waving from across the small room and it's attached to my little pixie friend. An attractive Asian college aged girl greets me at the door, wearing the black Slice of Life t-shirt, at least she's not another typical Beach Barbie lookalike.

"Hi, welcome to Slice of Life. Just one?"

"No, I'm meeting a friend over there, thank you." Don't these kids know that people who do dine alone would prefer it if it was approached a little more delicately? Just wait, pay back is a bitch.

"Okay, enjoy yourself."

My friend and I shall enjoy ourselves. Don't judge me.

Elsie meets me half way into the room and wraps me in her slender arms in a tight bear hug. "Hi, Elizabeth! We have so much catching up to do, you don't have to rush off, do you?"

Elsie is so pretty and deceptively delicate looking. She looks like she wants to take on the world but you just want to protect her.

"No, Elsie, I'm yours for a while. I want to know what trouble you've been getting into, Miss Thing." I shoot her a sly smile knowing she's got to have a few tidbits up her sleeve.

She laughs and it sounds like a melody.

"Nothing nearly as exciting as your wonderful night of decadence," she says rolling her eyes with a frustrated look. "Have you seen Mr. Sex God again?" Her expression has changed from frustrated to excited expectancy in a blink of an eye.

The blush automatically covers me from the top of my head down my chest. Before I even say anything she's bouncing in her chair like a little girl waiting for the surprise she knows is coming.

"Ooh, ooh, tell me, tell me!" She's practically clapping her hands in glee. It's so cute it makes me laugh. Women can be raunchy, sometimes even more so than men, have you ever seen us at a male revue show? We're bawdy, sex oozing, screaming women that would rip the men apart if we had the chance.

"Yes, a *lot* has happened since the last time we talked. But I wanted to ask you if you wanted to join a women's self-defense class I'm starting next week. It's at Evolution gym in Wrightsville Beach. It's a place for MMA fighters," I ask.

Then I sit back and wait.

Her eyes slowly open wide as her pretty little mouth shapes into an O. She gets it.

"Are you kidding me? Being in a place full of big, brawny, sweaty, sexy MMA fighters? I am so there! How the hell did you hear about it…and why the fuck do you think you need self-defense classes?" She got everything. Just like that. Her eyes are slits glaring at me waiting for me to tell her the whole story.

"Let's get a couple of beers first and order," I say as I look up at the waitress who's approaching our table. Here's the Beach Barbie.

"Okay, but don't you *dare* leave anything out." She gives me that *don't try to get out of this* tone.

We order then sit back and get comfortable. I look around and notice the place is filling up. A small group of guys by the bar are looking at us and talking to each other. Every so often one of them motions toward us and lifts his chin so I know the conversation is about us.

"Okay, Elizabeth, talk!"

I focus on Elsie and lean in toward her so only she can hear me. The tables are a little close together and I don't want all of Wilmington to know the Life and Times of Elizabeth DiStefano and Marco Kastanopoulis, with appearances by Santino.

"Marco told me about the gym it's the one he goes to" I begin.

"So you guys are seeing each other," Elsie asks eagerly.

"Yes, he texted me a few days after that first night together."

"You didn't tell me you gave him your number."

"That's because I didn't think he'd really call. You know how guys are," I almost snap.

"Why not?" she asks as a matter of fact.

"Elsie, do you want to know what happened or not? I don't know why, I just did."

"Yes, I want to know what happened but I want to get the juicy details too. My life is so boring compared to yours."

"Well, I'll tell you this. He took me to dinner and then a show at Thalian Hall where we had private box seats. It was the sexiest, most sensual night of my life, even better…well, maybe…than our first night together. And I'm *not* giving you details, use your imagination." I give her that little bit of information to tease her.

"You suck!" she pouts.

I chuckle. "Yeah but you love me anyway. So we see each other for a little while then Santino finds out about us," I continue.

"How? And why is he still an issue?" she asks me, surprised.

"Long story…anyway, Santino showed up at my apartment when Marco was there."

"Are you kidding me?" She's shocked.

"Nope, there was a little bit of a conflict," *if you can call me getting choked a little conflict,* "and Marco had called a couple of his friends from the gym to come by. They showed up about that time."

"Holy crap, Elizabeth, I knew your life was interesting but I had no idea." She sits back in her chair taking this all in.

"Yeah, things have been pretty interesting. Well this morning while Marco and I were talking I decided that maybe I needed to start going to the gym. He gave me the name of his and since I kind of know a couple of the guys who work there I thought I'd take a ride over. I went today and they have this new program they've just started. I thought it sounds perfect, killing two birds with one stone, building some strength and stamina and learning some self-defense."

She gives me a sly grin. "You need to keep up with Marco, don't you, you kinky little thing you."

"Elsie!" If I thought I was blushing before I was wrong. My face is on fire now.

"It's cool. I wish I had someone to get my kink on with. I'm so tired of the plain, same old stuff," she sighs, and her breath puffs, blowing away her fringed bangs.

"Well come to the class with me and find yourself a great big toy to play with," I say, trying to entice her, wiggling my eyebrows.

"You bet your ass I'm going with you. When does it start?"

"Monday night, I'll text you the details."

Barbie comes with our food and we dig in. No dainty pretending-to-pick-kind-of-eating but the-hot-spinach-and-ricotta-pie-with-white-sauce-then-washing-it-down-with-a-long-slug-of-cold-Michelob-Ultra kind of feasting.

Two guys from the group who were looking at us approach our table as we both have mouths full of food. This is not a smart move on their part.

"Hi, ladies, we thought we could buy you a beer."

Elsie looks up at Mr. Smooth Talker.

Oh no, this isn't going to be pretty. I can tell by the look on her face.

"Didn't your mother ever tell you that it was impolite to interrupt a meal?" Elsie informs them pointedly.

"You don't have to be such a bitch," one of the men snap.

"Obviously I do because you're an ignorant asshole. Please leave," she replies coldly.

They look at her for a long second, not believing that she actually just ripped their dicks off and shoved them up their asses in thirty seconds flat.

"Do you need me to draw you a map? Oh sorry, you probably can't read," Elsie adds.

"Fuck you," Frick and Frack say in unison and turn to leave mumbling some string of curses as they go.

"Never, baby," she says to their backs as they walk away.

She turns to me and asks, "You didn't want them to buy us a beer, did you?"

I look at her and burst out laughing, "No! Holy shit, you just beat the shit out of those guys without lifting a finger."

"Well, that was rude, coming over and interrupting us while we're eating. I hate thoughtless people, especially good-looking guys who think any girl will drop her panties if they just smile at her. Fuck those arrogant assholes," she states, picking up her pizza and taking a huge bite.

"You're absolutely right. I hate guys like that," I agree.

After finishing our pizza we pile our dishes to the side and sit back contented with full stomachs. The waitress comes over and takes the clutter from our table.

"So what about the Halloween party? Are you going to come with me…as my date?" She winks playfully at me.

"I'd love to, as long as I don't have to service you afterward. I hate going out on a first date when my date thinks it's an automatic-get-in-my-pants-as-payment," I play along.

"Oh, no, baby, unless you want to," Elsie replies, her voice dripping with sexual innuendo.

The girls look at us from the table next to ours. Elsie and I blow each other kisses sealing our meaning.

"Maybe I will. I always thought you were hot," I tease her.

The girls' mouths just fall open.

Elsie turns to them and asks, "Would you like to join us?"

I think Elsie is missing that tiny part of her brain that's supposed to hold the filter that catches things before you blurt them out.

"Um, no thanks," one of them quietly answers. They turn back to each other silently.

Elsie returns her attention to me. "So what about a costume for you?"

I get a little embarrassed before I say, "Don't think it's stupid and if you can't help me with this, just say so. But I was wondering if you had any access to something like a medieval female?"

Here is that excited little girl again bouncing in her chair.

"Oh, yes, yes, I do and it'll be perfect for you! It's green and it will be beautiful with your eyes and coloring. You just need to get a corset to push up the girls so they wiggle their hellos at the top."

I catch her excitement now. "Okay, thank you. I can do that."

"Come over this weekend and you can try it on. I'll do any alterations if you need it. And bring the corset and heels," she tells me enthusiastically.

"Okay, perfect! Thank you so much, Elsie. I'm really looking forward to the party," I reply, genuinely happy to be going with her.

"Me too! We're going to have such a good time."

"I know."

"And I want to meet this mystery man of yours," Elsie informs me.

"Yeah, he said the same thing about you," I answer, smiling.

We finish up and say our good byes. Elsie leaves as I check my phone and see Marco texted me an hour ago and it makes me smile. I have butterflies in my stomach. Why do I still get like this just from his simple random messages?

Hi baby, do you want me to pick you up?

That would be nice, I'm at the Slice of Life on Market.

Ok, I'll be there in 5 minutes

Ok ☺

I slide my mini white pea coat on and shove my phone in my pocket. I look up and see the guys who came over to us earlier looking at me again. Their eyes are like daggers. I want to stick my tongue out at them but I just turn away. I take out my phone again and start going through all my messages to clean them out, keeping myself occupied while I wait for Marco. I'm lost in thought when two arms encircle me in an embrace. I instantly recognize everything about him, his smell, the feel of the weight of his arms around me, the soft tickle of the hair on his face against my cheek.

"Hi, baby, your friend's already gone?" he whispers, nuzzling my ear.

"Hi, Marco, yeah, she left just when I texted you."

I love the feel of him against me.

"Come on, Elizabeth, let's go home and get naked," he whispers in my ear.

Heat shoots through my body. As I stand I happen to glance at those guys again and their mouths are wide open, watching Marco and me. Their surprise is written all over their faces. I stand taller thinking, *Yes, this amazing man is with me.* Elsie was right. They are arrogant assholes.

When we get to my apartment Marco takes my keys from me and opens the door. He helps me with my jacket and hangs it up in the closet in the hallway under the stairs, stairs that aren't even in my section of the house. It makes for a cool looking closet though.

"I'm going to get a set of keys made for you, Marco," I mention.

He hesitates for a moment before saying, "We haven't spoken about you moving in with me again since that afternoon."

I knew this was going to come up sooner or later but I would have preferred later. I turn away from him pretending I'm fidgeting with something, not wanting to look him in the eye.

"I know. Why don't we wait a little while until you move in before we talk about it?" I turn back to face him and look into his eyes, placing my palms on his chest before continuing, "Okay?"

"Okay." He studies me, holding me gently at my waist. "So how was dinner with your friend, what's her name again?"

"Elsie. It was great. We had a really nice time. I asked her if she wanted to join me in the classes at the gym and she said yes. I guess you two will be meeting soon." I wonder what it will be like between these two strong personalities. I'm sure it will be interesting to say the least.

"I look forward to it. Did you talk about Halloween?"

I lower my gaze and start to play with his shirt, feeling a little bad that I won't be spending Halloween with him.

"Yes, she wants me to come over this weekend to try on my costume." My face shoots up to look at him as I remember something. "Oh, I need to go shopping. Before this weekend."

One of his eyebrows rises in question.

"Oh, what for?"

"I need a corset." I unconsciously pull my lower lip between my teeth waiting for his reaction, anticipating it will be interesting.

"I think you might need a few of them, but what's this one for?" He smirks wickedly at me.

"To wear under my costume, Mr. Bond. Elsie thinks I should wear one to, um, push the girls up so that they are, um, participating at the party." I cock my head to the side and give him a flirty smile.

"As long as I'm the only one to whom they will be formally introduced, I would love to go shopping with you. There are a few more things I'd like to get and I know the perfect store. We'll go on Saturday after we shop for things for the condo. Now, let's go take a shower before I push you up against the door and fuck you. I'm so hard it hurts from thinking about you in that corset with those creamy tops of your breasts pouring out asking to be licked." His eyes have taken on a heated glow and it sears against my skin.

The hints of arousal from down deep in my belly that started at the restaurant the moment his arms went around me rage into an inferno. His scent fills me and fuels the flames, rushing over me, and I feel my desire seeping from me onto my panties.

"Do it, take me now, hard and rough." My voice is low and breathy and he sees the challenge in my eyes.

His mouth comes down hard on mine, his tongue pushing my lips open, fucking my mouth deep and fierce. Like he's about to do.

He's rough and demanding, turning me around and pushing me against the wall. One hand pulls both of mine over my head, pinning them in place on the wall as the other yanks up my skirt. He glides his hand over the globes of exposed skin of my cheeks between my stocking tops and panties. Pushing my feet apart with one of his, he moves his hand to slide between my legs over my damp panties. He palms my sex and pulls my ass back to slam into his erection.

"Oh God, Marco…"

"It's going to be rough and it's going to be fast, Elizabeth. This is for me, baby."

"Just do it…now." I want this. Bad.

"Leave your hands right there." He has gone to some place primitive. I can hear it in his voice.

His hands rip the panties from my body one second, then he rams himself into me the next. Grabbing my hips, he pulls me back to meet his thrusts, deep, hard and needy. I push back on him with as much force as he pounds into me with, skin smacking, balls slapping, nails digging into the drywall. I want to scream out, *Yes, yes, fuck me, fuck me!* and I do, with my body.

His fingers dig in to my flesh grinding me against him and I'm almost there. I just need a little more. I feel him twitch inside me. I know he's so close. He pulls us back a little farther making me bend more at the waist. Bringing both of his hands around to my front, he slides them down over my sex, one hand over the other, pinching my clit between his fingers holding me, pulling me back onto him like this. And I go wild, slamming back on him and grinding into his hands. I shatter and it's wonderful. Wild and wonderful.

He holds me tight against him as he stiffens, I feel his back arching pushing him deeper inside me, and his hold tightens on my pulsing sex.

"Fuck Elizabeth!"

"Yes! Oh God…" My orgasm just won't stop.

Marco

Oh my fucking God! Sliding into Elizabeth holds the same satisfaction as diving into a refreshing pool of water after spending thirty days in the driest desert. I give in to the heady sweetness of it and lose all self-control. It's like this, every time, nirvana and decadence, and every time it blows my mind.

I need to feel more of her. I'm like a wild man whose only desire is to devour, my hunger for her is so strong. Both my hands slide to grasp her pussy, pushing her harder onto me. I can't get deep enough. Nothing is ever enough. My fingertips clasp that beautiful swollen clit and her walls clamp down on my already throbbing aching cock. It's like a live wire from her clit, up my arm, through my body, to my cock and balls, shooting jolts of electricity, making my balls tighten so much I think they're going to get sucked into my ass.

"Yes, yes, yes." She's going wild, coming undone.

And that pushes me over the edge. I snap, my cock jerks inside her and the skin on my testicles is so fucking tight I think it's going to crack. I come so hard, thrusting hard and deep into her sweetness, grinding her ass onto me with her clit twitching between my fingers. Finally with the last spurts of my cum inside her heat, I collapse onto her back still holding her throbbing pussy.

We need a minute to catch our breath, our gasps filling the small space in the foyer between her living room and bedroom. I smile to myself thinking it's a good thing she doesn't live in an apartment building.

"Let's go take that shower, baby."

Chapter Three

Marco

It feels so good to move out of the Wilmington Riverside Hilton. I've been in a damn hotel for over a month and I was starting to climb the walls. The new condo is fantastic. It's the top floor of a three-story renovated historic commercial building on the Cape Fear River with a wall of windows overlooking the river on one side and the city on the other. The exposed rafters and brick are a perfect blend of modern and rustic with the frosted glass partitions and stainless steel appliances adding to the appeal. The moving truck arrived today with my furniture and the rest of my things that I couldn't fit into my BMW 5 Series. The cleaners also came by and helped organize things such as the kitchen supplies and linens after the truck got here. They even made a shopping trip for me to buy household goods like soaps, detergents and paper items. It'll be ready for Elizabeth and me to stay here tonight.

But what I'm really looking forward to is having her in my bed. Tonight will be too soon to use the bed in all the ways I'd like to but at least it's here. And she will be in it. Tonight. I survey the inner spaces, walking the rooms and feeling them, trying them on for size with my belongings here. It feels good. The white modern leather sectional sofa looks great against the red walls with the oversized glass coffee table in front of it and the stainless steel halogen lamps go well with the brushed metal stools at the bar. But what really commands attention is the large natural wood dining table that seats eight. It has chrome legs and the chairs match the couch in white tufted leather. I can picture Elizabeth spread out on that table naked and looking delicious.

I walk to the master bedroom where I've gotten almost everything unpacked. My king-size bed is also made from natural wood with the four posters an open weave of braiding. There are black wrought iron scroll hooks attached to all four of the post tops. It's because of this piece of furniture that my options were limited to a place I could move into. The ceilings had to be high enough that it wouldn't feel claustrophobic in the room. This loft type unit was perfect and I was so relieved Elizabeth liked this one the best as well. We are going to make some wonderful memories here.

I realize I'm thinking of a future with her, of memories being made, of snapshots of time being frozen in our minds together and it fills me with…hope. Something I haven't allowed myself to have with a woman in a very long time.

There are a few packages I had included in the move before I met Elizabeth. If I'd known her when I was organizing the transfer, I might not have had them brought here. But they're here now. I guess I'll just keep them put away until I decide what to do with them. We all have pieces of our past as little symbols that will one day, far from now, bring us back to that special moment forever caught in time in that inanimate object and with it will come the feelings, the sensations, that little piece of eternity that time caught and will forever stand still in. This is what I'm looking forward to with Elizabeth, catching those moments and freezing them forever.

Tonight I'll bring dinner in from a restaurant. Its four o'clock and Elizabeth will be getting off work soon so I decide to text her to make sure she's coming tonight. I'm sure she's feeling a little nervous. I sensed it in her yesterday when we were talking. To be honest, I am as well. I don't know why but I am.

Hi baby, busy day?

Hi sexy, yes, it's been a bit hectic. Getting settled?

Yes, I wish we were getting settled but I can wait until you get here for that

I can't wait to get there ☺

Me neither, when are you coming? I'm ordering dinner

I was going to go home first

That sounds like a good idea, go home and drop off your car, I'll pick you up.

A slight pause. I feel her excitement and it sends a thrill through me. I love that I have this effect on her. She has the same effect on me and it surprises me every time I feel it.

Ok.

I'll see you at your place in about an hour then.

Ok xoxo

Elizabeth

I jump as Carol plops herself down in the chair across from my desk because I was lost somewhere else deep in thought. My dad used to tell me after he'd just about given up driving and I was behind the wheel that I was always somewhere so far away. It's true, I'm always drifting off to someplace inside myself.

"What are you thinking about, chica?"

"You scared the crap out of me, Carol. Warn a person so they don't have a heart attack."

"You were in serious thought. What's up, is it Marco?"

A nervous thrill runs through me. I have no idea why I'm so nervous about tonight, we've been seeing each other for weeks. Why should tonight be any different just because we're staying at his place? I have a feeling things are going to be different somehow, and I think it's going to be in a good way. I sit back and smile shyly.

"Yes, it's Marco. What else, a man of course."

"Of course, is there any other reason for our aggravations?" she says rolling those blue eyes of hers.

"Well, I'm not aggravated with him. It's just…"

"It's just what? Spit it out. I'm sure there's a whole lot more to that hunk of a man than meets the eye," she says, sitting up in her chair and becoming fully alert.

"Well, he asked me to move in with him a few days after that happened with Santino. And yeah, I get the guy thing wanting to keep me close out of some need to keep me safe." I pause before I continue. "But I think it's too soon. God knows I'm crazy about him, he's all I think about and I count the minutes until I see him, the whole kid crush craziness thing. He brought it up again the other night and I told him we needed to wait a little longer." I look up at her, chewing on my nail.

"You are absolutely right. It's way too soon, manly controlling need or not. But I think there's something more." She's looking at me, squinting her eyes with a look like she's trying to figure something out.

"I think there is, Carol. I think there is more to him that I don't know about yet."

"And honey, what you went through with Santino, you take your time until you find out everything there is to know about that man, hot or not. I don't think it'll be anything bad or that it will end the relationship but it's better to have full disclosure before it's too late."

"You're right, thanks."

The last hour of the week passes by in a rush, thankfully so, keeping my mind too busy to analyze and study every word Marco and I have spoken, each touch and each look. Trying to find anything to give me a reason for this nervousness I'm feeling. I come up with nothing, only what I experienced in those moments we spent together.

Each time I go back to them in my mind, my body follows, feeling those feelings again, reliving those sensations and emotions, touching me to my core.

Marco

Sitting in my car in front of Elizabeth's apartment I reflect on all of the things we've been through together in the relatively short time we've known each other. Looking at the front door I remember that night Santino came here, and rage automatically courses through me. I push it aside, not wanting anything to spoil my mood for tonight. I see her pull up behind me in her little black Nissan Sentra. It's practical just like she is. She smiles at me through the rearview mirror and I see her little hand come up and wave at me. I fucking adore this woman. I'm smiling from ear to ear like a teenager as I go out to meet her.

"Hi, baby, it's good to see you." Pulling her almost pornographically close, I kiss her deeply, not giving a damn who might be watching. She's mine.

With her arms around my neck and pressing her body into mine she replies, "It's good to be seen, Marco."

"Come on, we've got to pick up dinner before going home," I say through gritted teeth. The need to bury myself in her right now rears its hungry head.

I open the door for her to get in the car and we head to Circa 1922 to pick up our three-course meal along with a bottle of wine. This is the restaurant I took her to dinner that erotic night of the symphony. We've got to christen our new place right.

"Is Circa 1922 going to be our special restaurant, Marco? First the symphony, then the first night in your new condo?" she asks me. It is kind of coincidental that on two significant nights we're getting our meal from here and it makes me smile.

"That's not a bad idea, Elizabeth, it's kind of like our song, but instead we have our restaurant." I laugh out loud thinking, *But we're screwed if they close up.* Looking back at her I say, "I think we'd better find a song. It would have a much better guarantee of always being there, don't you think, babe?" I wink devilishly at her.

Her smile is brilliant, she looks so happy and it makes me feel so good that I have something to do with that. A resounding need to always make her happy builds inside of me, possessive and protective.

"You're right, Marco, I guess we need to work on that."

My building is fitted with those old fashioned commercial elevators with the slatted doors that have to be pulled down from the top. I assume it's original and I hope to hell that the mechanics to it have been replaced and modernized. Although I love being with Elizabeth, I wouldn't want to get stuck in a fucking elevator in a section of a building where no one ever goes to except Elizabeth and me. It's a little late to think about that now, but I make a mental note to ask the building management office about the upfitting, just to be on the safe side.

My apartment is the only one on the floor and I love the privacy. I already set the table before I went to pick up Elizabeth so I go right into the kitchen with the food when we get inside.

"Wow, Marco, this is amazing. It looks like you've lived here for a while already." She takes her jacket off and hangs it on the back of a bar stool and places her black Prada purse on the bar in front of it. Elizabeth looks around the open space and walks tentatively through it, sliding a hand along the edges of the furniture as she goes.

"This dining room table is magnificent." Her palm is resting flat on the lacquered surface, the gloss so high she can almost see her reflection staring back at her.

"Thank you. A tree came down during a hurricane close to my house in Florida. I asked the owner of the property if I had it removed could I keep it and they said sure, so I had this table made from it. It was a magnificent old pine that I guess was already on its way down before the storm. Come on, let's use it and eat."

Coming to the table I set the plates down of chicken Marsala and linguine with roasted broccoli. There are oysters Rockefeller as well that are meant to be served as an appetizer but the meal won't wait. For dessert I brought home New York style cheesecake sprinkled with a raspberry sauce.

"Grab the wine, babe, please."

"Well, Mr. Bond, you never do things halfway, do you?" She smirks at me as she picks up the crystal glasses with the bottle of Riesling.

"I believe if you're going to do something, if it can be the best, then the best it is. That's why I have you." I lean over to kiss her lightly as she sits in the chair and I push it in.

"You're going to spoil me," she says playfully.

"That's the plan, and I'm going to reap all the rewards. Don't fool yourself; it is for purely selfish reasons." Everything I do to her and for her she gives me back tenfold with her moans, her smiles, her gasps, with everything in her. And it's only just the beginning.

Yes, I am a very selfish man.

"You get what you give, big boy." She has the audacity to wink at me.

We laugh knowing full well what the unsaid meanings and innuendos are, biding our time until they come to pass.

The meal is delicious and the cake is a perfect finish to it. I clear the dishes and rejoin Elizabeth at the table. Our wine glasses are half full and I pick mine up to stare at this naturally seductive woman sitting across from me, twirling the golden liquid around the glass, my eyes fixed on her. I take a slow swallow watching her over the rim and I can tell she's beginning to squirm under my gaze. She raises her hand to unconsciously stroke a finger along the edge of her blouse over the tops of her breasts.

"What are you thinking about, Marco?" Her face flushes thinking about what that might be, and she should. When it comes to her, the thoughts that fill my head are always wonderfully very bad. I want to possess her like a precious gem but I want to fuck her like a whore right now.

Elizabeth

"Tell me about the surfer boy you were dancing with in the club the night we met, Elizabeth." His tone has taken on a titillating quality.

My face blushes remembering that dance.

"What do you want to know?"

"What did he say to you?"

The length of his finger is stroking his lip and his eyes are piercing me as if he can see straight to my soul. He's waiting for me to answer his commanding question.

I squirm a little in my chair under his scrutiny.

"He said he loves older women because we know what we want."

A wicked smile pulls on his luscious lips. "Tell me what you think you want, Elizabeth."

My heart accelerates with the challenge of his words and his penetrating look.

"I told him we want a man who knows what to do with us with his mouth, his fingers, with all of him."

Studying me intently he lowers his hand. My eyes follow it. He is now stroking the arm of his chair. He slowly lifts himself and comes to stand behind me. He lowers his face so that it is by my neck and his hands come around me to rest on the table in front of me, not touching me but close enough that I can feel his body heat and inhale his scent.

"Move your hair to the side." His voice is deep and sensual at my ear.

Without its barrier, his warm breath licks my skin making me tremble with its delicate force.

"That's better." It's almost a whisper. He pauses for just a moment and I can almost count his breaths.

"Now I'm going to tell you what you really want." His lips are so close to my ear I can almost feel them caressing it.

I have no doubt this man knows exactly what I want.

"How do you know, Marco?"

I'm panting. The wanting he's talking about is clawing for fulfillment.

"Because I'm the man who will give it to you, possess you, take you fully, worshipping you and you will melt, giving yourself to me completely saying please take all of me, knowing I will quench that insatiable hunger inside you. I'll give you more than you ever thought was possible."

Desire floods me with his words. My eyes roll back, my thighs squeeze tight, and a low moan comes from my parted lips.

"You feel like you could come right now." His tongue glides softly along the curve of my neck.

"Aaahhh, yes…" I hiss. I'm on fire.

"Do you want me to make you come, Elizabeth?" He's taunting me, his voice low and seductive.

"Yes, please," I almost beg.

"If you were tied to my bed blindfolded, I could watch you writhing and panting, wet, and it would be so beautiful. You are going to come just from a touch of my finger. Then I'm going to take you fast and hard, feel you grabbing me with your throbbing pussy as you're coming and you'll come again."

My aching breasts are heaving, screaming for his touch.

"Please, Marco…"

"Open your legs, baby." The command is firm but soft.

My legs part wide, my back arches, and my lips open slightly.

"Sit back and lift your skirt."

Oh God, if he doesn't touch me soon, I'll scream.

"Push your panties to the side, I want to see that beautiful pink pussy."

Holy fuck! The cool air on my heat is maddening.

"Mmm, I can smell you. Give me a taste of yourself on your finger, baby."

Fuck.

Fuck.

Fuck.

Running a finger through my juices, I raise my hand. His mouth closes around my finger, sucking my flavor off with his tongue wrapped around my finger and my sex pulses in reaction.

"Now I'm going to touch you so you can come. Then I'm going to fuck you."

My legs widen, my sex and ass are grasping in anticipation, and the cool air licks my clit. His one finger slides up my folds, gathering my juices, circles my clit then touches it and that's it. I shatter, falling, spiraling into that orgasmic high.

"Oh, yes!" My hips buck, thrusting back and forth, wanting more. Just from that one touch of his finger.

His hand comes up to grasp my chin firmly, wrapping around my throat, turning my head up and to the side while he holds his face just above mine, our breaths mixing together from our open mouths. His tongue slowly licks my lips teasingly, the tip of mine peeks out to taunt his, pointed and just touching it, wanting to coax it into my mouth so I can bite it. Still holding my chin, he grabs my lower lip between his teeth and sucks it into his mouth, and a slow rumble comes from deep in his chest. My hands grip the arms of the chair I'm sitting in tightly and my groin instinctively pushes into it, my back arches, and all of me reacts to his sucking as if getting sucked in too. Releasing my lip, he slides his tongue over my cheek to my ear and pulls the lobe, capturing it between his teeth.

"I'm going to fuck you now, baby." It comes out strained and rough.

My pussy is standing up clapping, shouting her approval.

When Marco says he's going to fuck me, especially right now, it's not dirty or callous or cheap. On the contrary, it's heady, erotic and intense, with a deep timeless hunger, a culmination of a need so old to bond, to bury, to drown in each other, to submerge into that mindlessness where two become one. He is going to take me and I can't fucking wait.

"Come, I want to undress you."

He takes my hands and pulls me up from my chair and leads me into the bedroom. When I see his bed I stop, totally entranced by it.

"It's so beautiful." It comes out as if I'm mesmerized, and I am a little bit.

"Thank you, it's going to be even more beautiful with you in it. Come here, love, I need to see you stunning and naked."

I walk to stand in front of him, my hands at my sides, waiting for him to do what he wants with me. My sex pulses and throbs with anticipation of what he's going to do, my mind flashing images and with each one my heart jumps and my breathing accelerates. He lifts a finger and traces lightly over my lips, across my jaw, down my neck to brush on top of my collar bone then come to rest between my breasts.

"Raise your arms over your head, Elizabeth." The anticipation is killing me but I raise my arms slowly.

He pulls my top over my head, folds it and places it on the floor next to us. His comforter is a big white down overstuffed thing that looks so comfortable, I just want to curl up in it and never leave. There are lots of pillows on the bed but no throw pillows. The whole thing is extravagant but not excessive.

"Turn around, love."

Next is my white lace pushup bra. He unclasps it and with a light stroke of his fingers pushes the straps down my shoulders followed with one single kiss on each. I feel his hands at the waist of my skirt, immediately followed by the tug and sound of its zipper. It falls and puddles at my feet. My breathing is becoming heavier now, the rise and fall of my chest makes me feel the ache of my breasts wanting to be bitten, sucked and pinched so much I almost moan out loud. I clench my fists with pent-up desire.

"Soon, baby, be patient," comes his answer to my silent pleading.

His fingers begin the agonizingly delicious tracing of the outline of my white boy short lace panties, starting from the top of the crack of my ass then slowly moving to the front, down my mound grazing ever so slightly over my clit. He continues across the hem at the top of my thigh, and over the globe of my cheek to finally gently slide between my thighs. I stand stock still resisting the urge to spread my legs further, bend over the bed, slide my panties to the side and say, *Put it in now or I'm going to kill you!*

Marco hooks both thumbs into the tops of the panties and begins to slowly slide them down my legs. He's careful now not to touch me with any other part of his body except what he needs to remove my clothing.

Bending over he's still fully dressed and is holding on to my panties with one hand, my skirt with the other. He says, "Step out, Elizabeth."

And I do. The only thing left are the stockings and heels.

His large hand grabs my right ankle in a tight hold. The thrill of it, being held as if restrained, sends shivers through me. I think he knows what's going through me because he holds me firmly just like this.

"Lift your foot, baby." His voice licks over me hot and gooey as he pulls off my shoe, then he does the same with the other foot.

Now Marco begins the slow process of rolling down my hose one leg at a time. When he's done he stands. Every part of my body is throbbing, humming with need, so hard I can almost hear the pumping of the blood in my veins.

"Turn around and look at me, Elizabeth."

Oh my God, he's going to see in my eyes how much I want him, how full of lust I am for him, the raw savage beast hungry for him. I turn and stand before him, naked, completely bare of anything, stripped of everything except my blatant desire. His fingers mercifully come to take each nipple between them. They almost sing out with the pleasure from his flicking, twisting, pinching. His mouth comes down to suck them in as they're held tightly between his thumb and forefinger. Without a word he steps back and begins to undress. As he pulls his white tee from his jeans, I watch as hints of his solid stomach become more exposed as the shirt is pulled over his head. He folds it and lays it with my clothes. He's barefoot so he undoes his pants and takes them off, setting them with the others, then next the boxers.

"Face the bed, baby." His tone has dropped and become huskier.

Coming behind me he pushes me down gently so I'm bent over the bed at the waist. Placing one hand between my shoulder blades he gently shoves my feet apart with one of his.

"Hold your arms over head, Elizabeth." I know he wants me to keep them there so I move them and hold them straight with the imaginary bind on them.

His hands begin to lightly travel over my ass, smoothing over my cheeks, down the outside of my legs, up the inside of my thighs, to stroke over my folds teasing my hungry sex. He repeats this over and over. I'm fighting the urge to wiggle my ass and push down on his hand, anything to get some kind of relief from the intense wanting I need filled.

Finally one hand comes to lay firmly on the top of my ass just where it begins to slope down at the bend. The other begins to let a finger explore my folds, spreading my juices around the hole, up through the lips, around my clit and back again. The incredible need is almost about to burst. But I think that if I beg out loud Marco will make the long torment even worse.

"Oooooooohh!!"

Finally he slides his one finger inside me. I instantly grab it with my walls, wanting more, needing more. I am right on the brink of shattering. One, two, three times he thrusts it and pulls it out. I grit my teeth. That torturous finger is sliding up between my cheeks to my back, soaked with my juices. He swirls around there.

My body involuntarily pushes back and he slides in just a little with my movement.

My mind is screaming, *Please, please, please, I need more, give me more!!!*

Back and forth he goes between holes, switching fingers, between one finger and two fingers, filling me in one place, then both. He feels my walls closing in on him, my orgasm building in intensity waiting for its chance to explode.

His fingers leave me and are replaced with the tip of his hard-on kissing the entrance of my hole. Just there, then sliding over my lips, to my clit, back and forth. Finally the head goes in.

Oh, God, yes, yes, yes. Mercy will surely come.

The head slides in and out, teasing at giving me more. I'm going to die right here, right now.

Marco's fingers dig into my flesh, the first sign of his seductive discomfort.

"Now, baby," he growls.

And he thrusts himself all the way in, holding me tightly to him. He begins the slow steady pace of rocking us higher and higher, harder and deeper, so good, so delicious. And I begin to soar, nothing exists except him, me and this.

Pulling my bottom off the bed more, he slides one hand around and down to my clit, taking it between his fingers. It must be pulsing in his hold as he's rubbing it back and forth. Oh, God, it's so good, so perfect, just what I need. And I begin to fall. His other hand holds me still by my hip, I can't move. He pinches my clit and slams into me.

"Aaaaahhhhh!!"

Every muscle in my body is taut with the explosion rolling through me, the orgasm so intense I scream out.

"Yes, baby, come for me, grab my cock with your pussy, I fucking love it!" he growls pinching and thrusting as I clamp down on him inside me.

His movements become harder, deeper, wilder and I feel him jerking with me.

"Holy fuck, Elizabeth!!" he roars as he buries himself with a final thrust.

We collapse on the bed and he pulls me to him. We lay there long moments panting, lost in the after effects of our passion.

"Woman, what are you doing to me?" he says softly in my ear.

"The same thing you're doing to me, Marco."

A shiver flows through me with the aftershocks of my orgasm. Marco feels it and pulls me tighter, nibbling on my shoulder, which only makes the trembling intensify.

"I couldn't wait to have you in my bed, Elizabeth. There are so many things I want to do to you here."

I don't say anything and only smile as his arms tighten around me as images flash in my mind with all of the possibilities yet to come.

"Come on, baby, let's take a shower and come back to bed."

He stands and pulls me to him, wrapping me in his arms. His kiss is deep, possessive and satisfied.

When he leads me to the master bath I remember how large it is with double square sinks set in a poured cement counter, a huge shower with double heads and body massage sprays, and a large soaking tub in the corner, big enough for two. I see on the counter toiletries for a woman, me, and I feel like bursting with his thoughtfulness. It always surprises that he never forgets anything. Not only does he not forget, but he thinks of things I would never have dreamed he would.

He turns on both shower heads and holds his hand under the water to feel the temperature. When it's just right he steps in.

"Let me wash you, Elizabeth," he says holding his hand out for me.

His eyes are dark with a heat in them. This man is delectable, a dark master who intoxicates. His long thick erection is almost fully hard again and the sight of it makes my loins jump. I take his hand and step under the spraying water. There are two sets of toiletries in here as well, women's and men's body wash, shampoo and conditioner for me and a different set for him. Marco picks up the women's body wash and squirts a stream into a shower fluff. It smells crisp and fresh.

"Stand here, baby, let the water massage you while I wash you." Could he spoil me anymore?

I stand in front of the body jets and he turns the knob. Immediately sprays pulse rhythmically all up and down my body and it feels like heaven. He begins to lather me starting at my feet, working his way up as his fingers play in the folds between my legs and never leave while his other hand continues to spread the soap suds all over my body. He takes two quick playful bites out of each butt cheek and it makes me yelp.

"Turn around."

I do as my body slowly turns to mush. His hard-on is fully standing now and I can't resist wrapping both my hands around it. I want to feel the velvety smoothness hugging his rock-hard shaft. My hands want to possess it, own it, know every groove, bump and line on it. I need to taste him so I drop to my knees and take him between my lips, wrapping him in the heat of my tongue and mouth. One of my hands continues its captive hold on his shaft while the other reaches between his legs to cup his full balls, squeezing them gently and running a finger over the wrinkled skin. I want to know every inch of this man. I am so hungry for him it hurts.

I suck him, kiss him, bite him, scratch him, squeeze him, fondle him and pet him. I feel him reacting as he hardens even more, oozing out onto my tongue and I pull my mouth back and flick the tip with my pointed tongue, pushing it in the hole on the tip of his shaft trying to tease out more. He puts his hands on the sides of my head and begins to guide me but I push them away.

"It's my turn to play now, Marco, put your hands on the wall."

I smile devilishly at him, daring him to challenge me. He looks wickedly inquisitive but he slowly puts his hands on the wall above my head all the while watching me. I lower my mouth again to continue the feast I was interrupted from.

I get lost sucking on Marco, carried away with thoughts of how much pleasure he has given me. With him in my mouth I can still feel him inside me, stroking me, filling me and it excites me as much as my mouth is pleasing him. My hips are gyrating and moving with each thrust of my head on his cock. A moan comes from inside me with all of my thoughts.

His hands come down and yank me up on my feet, then he lifts me wrapping my legs around his waist sliding that piece of meat I was just feasting on deep inside me. Pressing my back against the shower wall he pulls down a sprayer and places it in the crook of our hips, the jet is directed right where we're joined with my clit front and center. Holding the tube in place with his thumb he takes my hips in his hands and begins to move me up and down his shaft.

Holy shit! One, two, three times and I come. Hard! The force of the multiple jets of water dancing all over me was more than I could take. But it won't stop, the pulsing continues keeping my climax going.

"Marco, please!!" I scream.

"Please, what, baby?" he grits out between clenched teeth.

"I can't stop!" my voice is ragged.

"I don't want you to stop." He sounds raw and primal.

A rumble starts from deep in his chest as his thrusts become stronger, deeper, more intense. I take the sprayer from his hand and put it under us, so it's hitting his balls and ass between his legs.

"Aaaaggghhh!!!" The scream this time is from him as I rip his orgasm from him the way he did me. He holds himself buried in me with his head thrown back and his whole body rigid as he rides that wave.

He sets me down and pulls the sprayer from my hand as his mouth takes mine hard and fiercely, his arms holding me tightly trying to take back control.

"Well, Ms. DiStefano, you certainly are full of surprises." His tone drips with sarcasm

"Now, Mr. Kastanopoulis, two can play at your game, now, can't they?" I look up at him sweetly.

His body moves into mine ever so slightly and his expression turns wicked.

"Are you sure you want to play, Ms. DiStefano?" There is an underlying current to his words as the backs of his knuckles stroke my cheek and I feel a tinge of apprehension. I look into his eyes a moment and see that there is an unspoken meaning there.

"Yes, I do." My words are soft but sure.

The corner of his mouth lifts in a crooked smile and he looks very satisfied.

"Well then, let the games begin." A full grin spreads across his perfectly chiseled face.

Do I know what I've just gotten myself into? I think I do.

Chapter Four

Elizabeth

Fridays are always busy at my office, I don't know why but they are. Maybe because people want to get their queries submitted before the weekend, which might give them a sense of comfort that their situations will be taken care of. I'm just finishing up the last prospectus I've been putting together to present to Marco for his real estate development company. He and his company are going to break ground on a project under the Cape Fear Bridge that looks quite amazing. The plans call for environmentally friendly systems that have gained a lot of positive attention from both the residential and commercial sectors of this area. Although some builders have claimed to utilize these practices in the past, none have ever committed to doing it on such a large scale.

I've never been one to pay attention to what's going on in the news, local or otherwise, but since Marco came in to our office asking for our representation I have paid closer to attention whenever his name or his company's name,

KMD Enterprises, have come up. I will be ready to present what I've put together for him next week including long-range plans to fulfill his needs. Well, those in the professional realm at least.

It's three o'clock and I've been tired all day. Sleeping in a place I'm not familiar with always does that to me and since I spent the night at Marco's last night, even though I was snuggled up to him, I didn't get the best night's sleep. Carol comes strolling in to my office and settles herself in the chair across from my desk. I was so deep in thought I didn't see her come in and she scared the shit out of me. Again.

"So what's new with you, Missy?"

"Damn, Carol, you scared me half to death again!"

"I always do. I'm beginning to like it, though." She chuckles like a little girl. "What are you working on? It's been another crazy day. I feel like I haven't seen you all day."

I sit back in my chair and take my glasses off and rub my eyes, they're burning from constantly staring at the computer screen and from being tired.

"I'm finishing up the quotes for Marco along with some other things for his development we can help with such as prospective buyer information, things we can include at open houses, information for the commercial units…you know—stuff."

She leans forward in her chair and turns my computer monitor around so she can have a look at what's open. If it was anyone else in the office I would have given them a piece of my mind but Carol and I are partners in crime, so to speak. We could get in to so much trouble if we allowed ourselves to behave like the immature children we want to. One late afternoon when things had quieted down she came in the way she did just now and the conversation somehow turned to Eddie Murphy. She stood up and did about half of his Raw show. We both laughed so hard, we almost peed ourselves.

"Wow, that's impressive, quite a presentation you've put together. This will tie up the links between the building and marketing portions, branching out to all segments of Marco's plans from the different types of residential units to the business arena."

I can tell by Carol's expression she's sincere, she likes what I've put together. Carol's the senior agent in the office and the boss when the owner is absent, her approval and praise are very important and shouldn't be taken lightly.

"Thank you, I appreciate it. I wanted to make sure we presented answers to all needs of

Marco's project, immediate and long term, and identify all applicable situations."

I feel pretty good about what I've done. After the fiasco with Santino, my ex-husband, and having been required to take a lie detector test and a suspension here at work, I want to solidify my commitment to our office, the company and the clients. Marco has given me the perfect opportunity to do all of that.

"Well, Elizabeth, it's perfect. It's sharp, concise, informative and easy to understand without being minimalistic. Nice work. When are you going to present it to him?"

"Next week, I want to give it another once over before I take it to him."

"Sounds good." Carol pauses thinking for a moment before she continues. "You do realize how big having Marco and his project is to our office, don't you?" She looks sideways at me.

"I have a pretty good idea. But putting modesty aside, we do pride ourselves in catering to the needs of the elite. And this entire project is the top level of the elite."

"I read that upon completion, the KMD Enterprise project will cost a few million dollars." Carol's voice is low almost like she's telling a secret that she's not supposed to. "And I can only guess what that's going to translate over for us. This is huge, Elizabeth."

"You don't have to scare the crap out of me, Carol. I can only imagine the stress Marco's company is under with that kind of money, but he doesn't give any indications of it. He's cool as can be."

"Well, Marco's a professional. This isn't his first day on the job. He knows exactly what he's doing and I'm sure his whole career has been leading up to this."

"Yes, I'm sure it has."

Her innocent but obvious statement causes my mind to wander, wondering what Marco's life has been like. I wouldn't let him tell me too much personal information about himself because *I* wanted to hide my past. There is so much about him I don't know. I have no idea if he's ever been married or engaged before, how many brothers and sisters he has if any, if his family still lives in New York. The list goes on and on. I suddenly feel immensely guilty for being so selfish and stupid.

"Okay, boss lady, get out of here, I've got work to finish up and a big weekend planned so I want to bust out of this joint on time."

"Oh, yeah? What ya got planned?" She makes no move to leave but instead sits up in her seat and rests her arms on the edge of my desk.

I smile thinking of the upcoming couple of days.

"Marco and I are going shopping tomorrow. He's just moved into a new condo on the riverfront. His furniture is fantastic but he needs a few finishing touches. And," I lean in closer to her from across the desk, "I have to buy a corset for a Halloween costume for a party I'm going to."

"Oh, you and Marco going together?"

"Shopping, yes, to the party, no. I'm going with a friend I worked with on the *Safe Haven* set." I still feel bad about leaving him alone for Halloween.

"Okay…" Carol looks a little confused.

"She invited me to go with her right after I met Marco, before he texted me that first time. You remember that crazy text, right?"

"Yeah, it was unusual." She smiles and rolls her eyes. She was walking by my office the first time he contacted me and saw how shocked I was to hear from him at all.

"I'd already told her I would go before Marco and I started seeing each other and I can't blow her off…just for a guy, even if it is Marco."

"You're right; it wouldn't be right. So he's taking you to buy a corset?" Oh, that taunting little smile she gives me tells me what's going on in her head.

"Yes," I am definitely not going to tell her that he said he knows the perfect store for items like that and there are only two that I can think of, and I bet he's not referring to the one in the mall.

"Well, then I won't keep you. I'm not going to be the one to hold you up from taking care of our favorite client. I'll be sure to ask Marco if you're keeping him satisfied," Carol says slyly with a wink.

I instantly turn bright red as images of all the ways I want to do exactly that flood my mind.

"All right Miss Thing, don't you have some work to do?" I tease her.

"I'm going, I'm going, don't be so pushy," she leaves laughing as she does.

As soon as she steps into her office my phone alerts me with a text. Can't I get any work done this afternoon?

Hi baby, I'll pick you up at 6 for dinner, Café' Phoenix, pack a weekend bag

The whole weekend at Marco's is exactly what I need to get used to sleeping at his place and the thought of it makes me want to squeal out loud.

Ok, anything else I should know about this weekend?

Just that we're only getting out of bed if we have to

Sounds like a perfect way to spend a weekend.

Marco

"Damn!"

Everything, even the information on the computer screen, shook with the impact of my fist on the desktop. This is not what I want to find out first thing Friday morning. The building department for the city of Wilmington is holding up issuing our first set of permits to begin work on the infrastructure for the development project. Steve Mikelson, my project manager, said that the inspector told him he wants make sure we are in complete compliance with Occupational Safety and Health Administration division. OSHA's approvals are included with our applications. What the hell is this guy's problem? I know there is no way I'm going to find anyone anywhere near the building department on a Friday so I'm going to have to sit on this bullshit situation all weekend. Not getting the answers I want right now is going to drive me crazy.

I'm going to wear a path on the carpet from pacing the length of my office so many times. I'm so fucking pissed off right now I could rip someone's head off. Something is not right; I can feel it. All the paperwork was done months ago and has been reviewed, reviewed again, and reviewed a third time. There is no way even a pinpoint, not even an i missing its dot, was left open for discrepancy.

"How the fuck could those permits not be issued? It's impossible!"

Every day of delay costs thousands of wasted dollars. I have never left any chance of a possibility for problems. And this project in particular is brilliant, years in the making, and I took extra time in preparation to make sure it is perfect. How could this happen?

I don't even bother picking up the phone to call my secretary. I yell from where I'm standing, "Christine, bring me the copies of the building applications! And tell Steve to get his ass in here too!" The poor girl, I'm probably scaring the shit out of her but I don't care. She's going to have to get used to me. Every day's not going to be a picnic.

Five minutes later Christine comes in with manila folders piled high in her arms.

"I heard about the permits so I brought the other files as well, just in case you might need them too."

Now I remember exactly why I hired her.

"Thanks, Christine, you're the best." I smile appreciatively at her, at least someone knows how to do their job and more.

"You're welcome. But Steve is out of the office, I just texted him and he said he'd be back in about an hour."

I know she's bracing for my outburst.

"Dammit! Where the hell is he?"

"He says he's got a meeting with a contractor but he'll be back soon.

"Fine, I'll get started on them alone. Could you bring me some coffee? I'm gonna need it if I'm going to find this supposed needle in the haystack."

"Got a fresh pot already brewing."

I sit down at my desk flipping open the folder on top and smile up at her.

"You're going to spoil me."

"Just doing my job so you can do yours."

"You're a smart kid, and we're lucky to have you."

That compliment makes the quick-thinking, intelligent assistant blush.

"Thank you, and, um, there's one other thing…" I notice she's fidgeting. She's nervous about something.

"What is it?" I ask her, getting a slightly annoyed that she's not spitting it out, then I reprimand myself, it's not her fault I'm having a shitty day.

"Well, this morning when I came in, I didn't think there was anyone else here until I came back here to turn on the lights and Liana was at your desk looking for something. And, um…"

"Go on." My patience is slipping.

"I've seen her at Steve's desk as well when he wasn't here." Uncertainty is written all over her face. She's probably torn between feeling like a tattletale child and concerned if there is something to this.

Although I'm not very happy with this news, I'm not going to add to Christine's discomfort. It's my job to make her job as pleasant as can be.

"Thanks for telling me, you did the right thing. I'm sure she was just looking for something but," I pause, "with the project hopefully getting into high gear, why don't we keep my office door locked when I'm not here. Sound like a plan?" I ask her giving her a wide smile trying to soothe her frazzled nerves.

"Sounds good, will do." Her obvious relief is clearly evident on her face as she turns to leave.

Turning my attention to the stacks of folders, I am going to find where the problem is, even if it kills me.

I'm not even halfway into my second file when Steve comes sauntering into my office. His relaxed attitude used to grate on my nerves. I thought he just hung around all day looking like he was about to hit the waves, the eternal beach bum, but it's this nonchalant attitude that has gotten him the respect of his peers. Not all successful men have to look and act like sharks, and I think we complement each other very well.

It could be said that Steven Mikelson wasn't quite born with a silver spoon in his mouth but it got there pretty quickly. He came up with me from Florida, along with a couple of other associates. Steve's father John is one of the owners of the company I worked for in Florida and is a small silent partner in KMD Enterprises. He is the M. His family is from the same neighborhood mine is from but they moved down to Florida from New York when Steve and I were just kids. We got our first two-wheel bikes on the same day. Steve also went to NYU to get his degree. The only difference between him and me is that he continued on afterwards in building and construction certifications.

The D in KMD Enterprises is for Vinny D'Angelo. Vinny started the construction company in Florida back in the seventies. He is also a transplanted New Yorker from Brooklyn, and is a major investor in KMD. The affiliations that brought Vinny and John together originally can only be assumed, but the connections they have are astounding, from the local drug dealer on the corner to several senators and congressmen. Vinny built the empire from a small, local single-family construction company, to impressive multi-use communities with John as a major factor in its growth and evolution over a thirty-year span. Vinny saw opportunities for future expansion farther up the coast and approached me several years ago with his plans, asking me if I wanted to run a division. I immediately saw his vision and jumped on it.

"Sucks ass, doesn't it, Marco?"

"No shit, what exactly did the asshole building inspector tell you?"

Sitting back and molding to the chair, he looks like he's ready to pull out a joint and light it up right here. "He wasn't very precise with anything, actually. He skirted around not issuing our permits yet, never committing to a reason. He was neither accusatory or matter of fact, but rather like, 'I think I'm gonna sit on this a spell'."

I'm stunned; there is no way to explain it. I just blink at him, mouth open, shocked.

"Sit on this a spell, are you kidding me? Does he know how much his sitting is costing us? Can he legally fucking do this?" My voice gets higher and higher as I go on until finally when I get to 'this' I'm yelling again. I wouldn't be surprised if my eyeballs are popping out of my head, the veins on the sides of my neck are bulging, and my face is red from my blood pressure shooting through the roof.

"Yes, he can if he has a legitimate reason to do so. And he's pulling out OSHA, environmental regulations, public health issues, and building standards."

Right now I want to slap the shit out of Steve's *hey dude* persona. How can he be so laidback when everything is threatening to go to fucking shit?

"We sat with the city council months ago presenting our plans to them and went over this countless times. There shouldn't be any questions now."

"Well, he can do this and he is. I don't think it's actually because he thinks something is wrong in our plans but I think it has to do with him personally. I don't know if he needs to justify his position, if the city is coming down on him for something, or he just doesn't like you. It could be as simple as that." As he shrugs his shoulders, his last sentence hangs in the air like a stinky fart.

"That's ridiculous." I can't believe that.

"Ridiculous or not, that's what I think." He waves his hand at the pile of folders in front of me. "You can spend all week reviewing that pile of dead trees, but you're not going to find anything wrong. This is why I was out talking to local contractors and suppliers. You know how it is. If you want to know the truth go talk to the people on the street."

Steve's right. Sitting here across from him, I get the feeling something really wrong is growing and I can tell it's going to blow. I don't know when or how, but my instincts tell me somebody is responsible for this, and my instincts are never wrong. When I find out who it is I am going to enjoy making them pay. Now I need to decide where to begin. One thing that rings loud and clear in my head is the first rule Vinny taught me:

Never trust anyone. The second rule is the place to start is with the people. Money can get even the straightest guy to help you if you know how to talk to him. I knew even when I was a kid everything could be found out on the streets if you asked the right people, even information that had to do with politicians and the men who pulled their strings. It's time for me to make a few calls.

Chapter Five

Marco

I'm looking forward to a night with Elizabeth after the day I've had. I just want to get lost in her and not think about anything else. Worrying about the problems at work now is not going to get those permits issued any faster.

She gave me the keys to her place so I let myself in. Long shadows are falling over the rooms, the sun has already set and there are only a few lamps on throughout the apartment. I hear the soft chatter of Elizabeth's voice from the bedroom and it stirs the beast within me. I turn towards that direction hoping that she can't hear my footsteps. I want to watch her for a moment without her knowing I'm there.

I walk through the darkened rooms of this old Victorian house where the past and the present live together. I pass pictures of Elizabeth's family covering the white walls in black frames. One photo of her mother stops me. It's a black and white of her on the beach. She's beautiful, reclining and posed like a 1950s Hollywood starlet. I have a sense that she was a very strong and commanding woman and I don't know why but I'm certain the blood that runs through Elizabeth's veins has the strength of the matriarchs in her family before her.

"Be at peace, I will take care of her," I whisper.

I can almost see her smile in response, nodding her head in approval.

Continuing on to the bedroom, I see Elizabeth and warmth floods me at the sight of her.

"What am I going to wear?" she's mumbling to herself.

Elizabeth's standing in the doorway of the closet, her hands holding the door frame with one foot tapping impatiently on the bare wood floor dressed only in her heels, panties, bra and stockings, very pretty matching panties and bra. They're powder pink, shirred between the cheeks with little black bows at the top of the crease of her ass and at the bottom of each strap of the bra. I want to see what they look like from the front.

"Turn around."

My voice startles her and makes her jump. She pulls her hand to heart when she hears me.

"My God, Marco, you scared me."

"Let me look at you, baby."

I'm leaning against the doorway, one foot crossed over the other, admiring her natural sensuality, letting it wash over me and bathe me in its beauty.

Elizabeth's whole body reacts to my request, seeming to become more sinewy and sensual but she doesn't utter a word as I openly take her all in, soaking her up and my cock responds to her. Pushing myself from the doorframe I walk towards her. I place a hand under her chin and lift it up so she's looking into my eyes.

"Get me the nipple clamps baby. I want to dress you."

Her mouth opens slightly in my hand and I smirk at her reaction. It's priceless, shocked and turned on at the same time. I lower my mouth to hers and brush my lips against her soft lips before letting her go. I stand there and watch that pretty ass sway over to the nightstand as she retrieves the clamps. When she comes back she places a white satin jewelry pouch in my hand. She bought something to keep them in. That means she really likes them and that makes me very happy. Happy with the idea of where we can go from here. We are at the beginning of our journey together, one of exploration and fulfillment. I'm looking forward to taking Elizabeth's hand and guiding her in her own journey of self-discovery and realization. There is a vast unchartered path ahead of us and I feel honored that she has chosen me to lead her on that path.

Before taking the pouch from her, I slide one pink bra strap down her shoulder, slip my thumb into the cup pulling it down pushing her breast out and up. I fight the urge to pull that already taut pink nipple into my mouth and instead graze it with my thumb. I can feel the breath catch in her chest the exact moment her nipple pebbles even more. Sliding the other strap down her shoulder I free the other beautiful breast as well.

I finally remove the clamps from the pouch as I watch the heavy rise and fall of her chest.

"I am going to be so hard all night thinking about these clamps biting into your hard nipples, Elizabeth. If I don't fuck you in the restaurant, it's going to be a miracle." My voice is raspy with my pent-up emotions. I need release badly, not only from my desire for Elizabeth but from the frustrations of today. Tonight I'm going to play, and she'd be better be ready for it.

Taking one finger, I begin to make slow circles around her left nipple, not touching it but threatening to, watching it tighten and harden more and more in anticipation of my touch. I take one clamp and secure it comfortably on Elizabeth's waiting nipple and my cock twitches in my pants.

I think to myself answering my dick, *I know, I can't wait either but the waiting is good.* I place the other clamp on to the other naked waiting nipple. I'm such a sick fuck, I can almost hear it sigh in gratitude.

I look into Elizabeth's face to see if there is any discomfort there. Her lids are half closed, her pink lips are slightly open and I can see her tongue touching the back of her upper teeth wanting to lick something. I know if slide my fingers over her panties she'll be wet and I know I won't stop with just a touch of my hand. Now that the clamps are in place I can suckle those nipples with my mouth. I can't resist. Lowering my head, I flick my tongue over each captive bump then suck it between my lips and take it between my teeth.

"Aaaaaaaaahhhh!!"

"All right, now let's find you something to wear," I say quietly as I cover her breasts with the bra once again.

"I don't think I can make it through dinner, Marco."

Her voice is breathy and heavy with arousal.

"You can and you will," I say with a wicked smile before kissing her softly.

I walk into the closet and find a little black dress.

"Here, love, this should do just fine for dinner, put your hands up."

I pull the dress down over her body then pull her hair to the side, slowly zip up the back and bend to kiss her neck.

"Let's go, Elizabeth. I don't know how long I can wait either."

Elizabeth

Café Phoenix is one of the original Southern nouveau chic restaurants in Wilmington where the celebrities who are in town come to dine. Since our little city got "discovered", it's not the only kid on the block anymore but it's still cool as hell. She's like an old grand dame who sits regally in the knowledge that she can still kick everybody's ass and continues to be highly respected for it.

Marco appears to have garnered something of a reputation in town. When we enter Café Phoenix he's known by face and he's given exceptional service. I suppose it's justified considering his company will be investing millions of dollars in this area, which will benefit everyone in the long run.

We've just ordered when a slightly older gentleman approaches our table.

"Mr. Kastanopoulis, I wanted to introduce myself and give you a personal welcome to Wilmington. I'm Charles Greer, town councilman." He extends his hand to shake Marco's.

Politicians coming over to introduce themselves to Marco? Wow, I didn't realize the importance of the man sitting next to me. It appears that Marco is considered quite a big shot.

Marco stands and shakes his hand, a rigorous man's shake. "Councilman, it's a pleasure to meet you, thank you so much for coming over. Would you like to join us for a moment?"

"No thank you that's very kind of you. I just wanted to say hello and if there's anything that you need please don't hesitate to give me a call." He reaches into his jacket pocket and pulls out his business card, handing it to Marco. Marco doesn't even glance at it, just slides it in his pocket.

"I do appreciate that. I will remember it. Enjoy your evening, Councilman." Marco takes his seat again. As if dismissing him. Holy shit, did he just do that?

"You as well." He looks at both of us. "Good night." He turns and walks off.

Marco takes his napkin again and lays it on his lap. I'm momentarily stunned, not knowing what to make of what just happened.

"Councilmen coming up to introduce themselves to you?" I finally say.

"Don't let it fool you, Elizabeth. It's all about goddamn money, and I'm going to spend a lot of money here…a lot. The more money you've got, the more important you are. These guys, some of them, are just whores trying to get you to put them in your money-lined pockets. Not just for them but for the community, if they can get credit, and your money, they will suck your cock if you ask and then take it in the ass. In the end, it's what you can do for them with your money. The more you've got, the more you can do. Plain and simple."

He turns to me and there's distaste in his eyes because of the crooked system he's forced to be a part of.

"Come here, baby, tonight's about us, not that." His expression softens as his hand moves to my leg and comes to rest at the apex of my thighs. Barry White's deep voice whispers, "Feels so good…" the beginning words to *I'm Gonna Love You Just a Little More Baby*. The deeply erotic words he speaks to his woman fill the space between us as Marco seduces me with his eyes, with his featherlight touch under the table, with the light breath against my skin when he leans into me breathing me in, caressing me gently with the stroke of his lips.

The thoughts going through my mind are of satisfying this aching need shooting from my breasts straight to between my legs where I wish his hand would move to. The need threatens to consume me if I allow myself to give in to it. Marco has barely touched me. He dropped off his car and my bag at his place and we walked, which would have been perfect any other night. But tonight with the clamps nipping at my nipples and the chain swinging back and forth with each of my steps it only served to heighten my arousal. His hand would touch my lower back letting his fingers graze the top of the crease of my ass, or he would caress my cheek when he brushed a strand of hair behind my ear, or his breath would stroke my skin when he leaned close to my ear to whisper something.

At dinner every so often his hand gently touches the bare skin of my leg or my arm, and sometimes he makes tiny circles up the inside of my thigh stopping just at the hem of my dress. He is deliberately teasing me. He knows everything he's doing and what it's doing to me. And I am enjoying every minute of the exquisite torture.

On the way back from dinner the streets are beginning to become crowded with the barhopping crowd. Marco has his arm around my shoulders when we come up to one of the few alleys downtown. It's well-lit and both streets running parallel are visible through the alley. The blocks are not very deep.

"Let's cut through here, Elizabeth."

About midway through, there is a recessed doorway. Marco pushes me into it with my back against the wall, he separates my feet with one of his while stroking me over my wet panties.

"Your pussy is throbbing, isn't it, baby?" His cheek is against mine and the softness of his stubble remind my thighs of the feel of it between my legs.

"Yes, Marco, it has been all night." I answer him quietly but I'm screaming in my head for him to please give me some relief.

"Do you want to come right now, Elizabeth?"

My legs are spread so wide, if they were any wider I would fall down. I did this, I opened myself up as far as I could comfortably go to beg him to enter me, slip inside me with anything, please. I need it. My arms are straight at my sides, palms flat against the wall behind me, my back is arched pushing my sex out toward him.

"Yes, please, Marco, I need it."

I can hear people walking by on the streets, some so close I can hear their conversations. I don't care if we get caught. Let them see us, the thrill of it makes me want it more.

The only parts of his body touching me are the stubble on his cheek and the tips of his fingers between my legs, barely gliding over the wet cloth covering my lips, which he's stroking. My body is rigid, not moving except for the rise and fall of my chest from my panting.

"Take one hand and pull your panties to the side. I'll make you come right here."

I force a hand to move. It does so slowly, slithering over my leg to pull the silky pink fabric to one side. I can almost see in my mind's eye my sex puckering, searching for what it wants, like the mouth of a fish. The tip of his finger is making circles in my juices around my opening, my walls are grasping inside me trying to grab him each time he circles.

"I'm going to slide inside you now." His voice is low and the words are music to my ears.

One finger dips into me. I want more, I need more but I'm already so close to coming, my walls are contracting. He gives me some wonderfully needed friction making me suck in air between my clenched teeth. Sliding that wonderful finger in and out of me, he presses his thumb on my clit and I shatter.

"Aaaahhhhhhh!!" I can't stop the scream from exploding from my mouth, the need is too great.

He pulls his hand away from me but doesn't move his body. My orgasm is cut short leaving me aching for more. My head falls back in frustration and hits the wall behind me.

"We're almost home, baby. But I think you'd like me to fuck you right here, wouldn't you?"

Yes, I would. If we were standing in the middle of the police station I'd want you to fuck me right now. That's how bad I want it.

"You are so lucky I like you, Marco, or else I'd kick your ass."

He laughs so loud it bounces off the walls and sounds like it's swirling around us in circles, like a gust of wind picking up leaves playfully dancing and encircling us in its cyclone, promising to whisk us away to a land far, far away.

"It might be fun but right now I've got other plans."

He squats down in front of me bringing his face intimately close to my sex and inhales deeply. Holy fuck!

"You smell so good, Elizabeth. I love it. I can almost see your pussy dripping, it's so fucking hot."

My head is bent over and I'm looking at the top of his with my mouth hanging open. I'm speechless. That is one of the sexiest things anyone's ever said to me, dirty as it is. He leans his head back to look up at me and his mouth curves up into the most devilish grin. This man is so bad and he knows it, and he relishes every moment of it.

I am so, so screwed.

When we exit the alley I wonder for only a second if anyone heard my scream. I smile thinking, *Good, I hope they did. And I hope there will be a lot more screaming tonight.*

The downtown streets are more crowded with the younger barflies walking from here to there in a hurry with no real place to go. Why are they hurrying? Are they afraid to get there one minute later for that beer? Do they have to hurry to get that spot as another body taking up space in the bar? I chuckle at the ridiculousness of the whole thing, remembering when I wasted my time just like them. I think the constant arousal from the clamps on my nipples is making me high, euphoric even. I could get used to this, and that could be dangerous.

Marco has me pulled close to him with his arm around my shoulders and I've got mine on his hip. I love the feel of the dip of his hip under my hand. I tighten my fingers there as my gasp surprises me while I'm imagining those naked hips grinding against me. He turns his face to me and nuzzles into my neck breathing me in as well.

When we get to his building and in the privacy of the open elevator, he stands against the far wall, crossing his legs at the ankles with his fingers steepled in front of his face. Marco's look is piercing and hungry.

"Take your dress off, Elizabeth."

He did not just ask me to strip in public!

He waits. Patiently. Waiting.

I slowly raise my hands up to reach behind me and undo my zipper. The sound is so loud filling the space. I imagine it floating out between the bars of the door mixing with the squeaks of the cogs and pulleys of the lift.

I pull the dress over my head and the cool air brushes my hot skin causing goose bumps to rise all over my flesh. I'm not sure if it's from the air or my desire.

"Give it to me," he says, holding out his hand, his voice rough.

"Now the bra."

His eyes have become darker and intense. His body is more erect and demanding. There is no way I can refuse him.

Reaching behind me, I unclasp the strip of fabric and slide the material down my arms. My breasts fall, heavy with need, the chain from the clamps swings and lightly tugs on my nipples. I pull my lip between my teeth, responding to the stimulation.

Marco's hand is out, waiting for the bra. I place it in his hand as the elevator comes to a stop.

"Take off your panties, Elizabeth."

It's not a request. It's a demand. My eyes are wide, my lips are parted, and my breathing is heavy. It's the only noise filling my ears along with the pounding of my heart. I tuck my thumbs into the elastic of my powder-pink panties with the little black bows and slowly slide them down my legs. I'm a mess, totally aroused. I don't trust myself not to fall if I don't hold on to the wall as I step out of them. I stand and place them with the rest of my clothes in his outstretched hand. I'm standing in an elevator dressed in only my heels and nipple clamps.

Marco is perfectly still except for the flexing of the muscle on his jaw.

"You are the most sensuous woman I have ever seen, Elizabeth. You are beautiful."

I have no reply. My desire has escalated and I am consciously keeping myself from squirming in response to the pulsing between my legs.

Marco comes to stand in front of me, close enough to lightly touch the pink pebbles of flesh poking out of the clamps, then he strokes my lips causing my lashes to flutter with the exquisiteness of that light touch.

"When we get inside," he says, his voice a gravelly whisper, "I'm going to tie you to my bed and blindfold you. Then I'll take you on a journey of complete erotic pleasure."

Oh! My! God!

Chapter Six

Marco

She's mine. And I can't wait to have her bound in my bed. My cock is throbbing in the confines of my jeans just thinking about it. I study her expression looking for signs of fear. It's there, slightly, along with intense desire in her glazed eyes. I turn and lift the gate of the elevator thinking I can't believe my luck having this entire floor to myself.

Reaching my open hand out to her I say one word. "Come." And she will be soon enough, many times.

She places her small hand in mine and I feel it trembling. She is completely naked and bare. I am stripping more than just her clothes from her; I am removing her inhibitions and her boundaries, bit by bit, and with each piece put in the pile, she belongs more and more to me. I squeeze her hand lightly to reassure her then take her out to the front door of the condo. Once inside we stop at the dining room table and I stand behind her with my hands on her shoulders.

"I'm going to blindfold you now, Elizabeth," I say quietly, close to her ear, "then I'm going to lead you into the bedroom. You'll stand at the foot of the bed and I'll have you separate your legs. I'll tie them. Next you'll lean over the bed, then I'll tie your arms. Do you understand, baby?"

I'm stroking her arms, soothing her, letting her get comfortable with what's to come. I feel her body shiver with the light kiss I place on that curve where her neck meets her shoulder.

"Yes," her voice is low and raspy.

"Good girl." Another soft kiss. "Are you ready?" My hands have stopped.

"Yes."

Reaching into my pocket I pull out one of her stockings. I bring it, holding it between my hands, in front of her face.

"Look familiar?" I can't keep the slight amusement from my voice.

Her body trembles as if she's chuckling.

"Yes."

I hold the stocking still in front of her eyes.

"Do you trust me, Elizabeth?" My tone is serious. I want to be sure she's okay.

After a short beat she answers, "Yes, Marco."

"Good. If it gets to be too much, just say stop and I will. But that's it, no more. Be absolutely certain you want me to stop. Do you understand, Elizabeth?"

Her fists are clenching at her sides. I'm not sure if it's in anticipation or fear. It's probably both.

"I trust you, Marco." Her tone is firm and sure.

"Okay, love, close your eyes."

I hear her breathe in sharply when the nylon touches her skin, making my dick twitch, and I tie it behind her head. Fuck, this is going to be beautiful. Is it wrong for me to want to almost torture her with so much pleasure I'm not sure she can handle it?

Who am I kidding? She can handle it and more.

Keeping my hand gentle on her shoulder I move to stand in front of her.

"I'm going to take the clamps off now. It will probably hurt a little." I graze a finger over both nipples. She stands perfectly erect. I take the first one off and quickly move to the other, studying her face for signs of emotion. Her lips tighten into a firm line. After a moment I can see

Elizabeth relax as her lips open and she pulls her lower lip between her teeth and I can't resist the temptation to touch her mouth. Raising a finger to the corner of her lips she instinctively releases it allowing me to slowly trace them. Her tongue pokes to flick the tip of my finger, and she lets out a quiet moan as she does.

The sound of metal clinking from the clamps when I place them on the table tickles our ears and it makes her nipples pucker even more.

"Let's go, baby." Those three little words again.

I go ahead of her leading her slowly through the rooms. She's clasping my hand with both of hers in order to keep herself grounded. When we get to the bedroom I walk her slowly to the bed and stop her when she's just in front of it.

"The bed is in front of you, baby. Reach out and touch it so you know where you are."

I can see by the rising and falling of her chest she's breathing very heavily. She bends slightly to touch the bed with her hand. When she makes contact with it she jumps just a little.

"Okay, love?" I ask gently. I know this must be a little scary for her and I admire her immensely for being brave.

"Okay." Her voice is so soft I have to strain to hear her.

Placing my hands on her shoulders I trail kisses down each side, stroking her, soothing her, comforting her and I sense her responding, relaxing a little under my touch.

"I'm so proud of you. Thank you for trusting me. I'm going to put some music on." The remote is right at arm's reach so I don't have to leave her side. The sounds of Rachmaninov's *Piano Concerto No. 2* surround us, enveloping us in its sensuality.

"I'm going to take your shoes off."

I squat down behind her between her legs which puts my face even with her sex and I can smell the intoxicating musky aroma of her desire. Placing my hands on the outsides of her thighs, I press my cheek against the back of one and rub my face against her leg.

"Elizabeth, you smell so delicious, mmmmm." I slide one finger from the front of her pussy to between her ass cheeks then I suck her juices off it. "Delicious." I remove shoes off and put them to the side. "Open your legs for me, as far as you are comfortable."

I can hear her breathing now; she's holding on to the bedposts. I want to tie her arms there but tonight I want her ass in the air. She loves it when I play with her ass when I make love to her, and I intend to play with both of her holes tonight.

"Good girl, I'm going to tie your ankles now, love." I hold one ankle firmly with one hand to make her feel grounded, then I take the Velcro strap that's tied to a foot post at the end of the bed with the other and gently place it around her slender ankle. Her dainty red painted toes are moving up and down pressing into the carpet. I lower my head and kiss the top of her foot before releasing it, then do the same to the other foot. I slide my hands up each of her legs, over her ass, then up her back as I stand. I move my hands down her arms to come to rest over her hands where she's clenching the posts tightly. I press my body against hers and rest my cheek against her soft face. Her head dips back against me with her lips parted.

"I'm going to take your hands off now and I want you to lower yourself to the bed. Then I'm going to tie your arms." I wait for a moment and let her digest this. "Are you ready, baby?"

"Yes…" She's panting. Good.

I take her hands in mine and lower them to the bed keeping my hands on top of hers. She begins to lower herself and I glide her hands along the bed to where I want them. The arm restraints that are tied to the posts at the top of the bed are also Velcro so attaching them is very quick. I stand and look at her bending over the bed, open and glorious, her pussy glistening with her desire.

"You are so beautiful, Elizabeth." I begin to caress her, her legs, her ass, her back, with long sinewy strokes, softly, then I squeeze the round cheeks of her beautiful ass, pressing into her flesh, molding her to my hands, feeling her fill them. "You. Are. Mine." I lick her from the top of the crack of her ass all the way up her back to her neck.

"Ooooooh…" Her moan is deep and long and I feel her squirming under my touch.

"Keep still and just feel…" I begin to stroke one finger under the curves of the cheeks of her ass, up her sides then down between the round globes of bottom, through her beautiful pink wet lips to her clit. I take that swollen nub between two fingers and pinch gently.

"Oh, my God!!!" Her body tenses at the sudden sensations.

Palming her sex, I place the other hand between her shoulder blades and lower my face close to her ear.

"Was that good, baby?"

"Yes…" She's panting trying to hold on. She doesn't want to come too quickly. And I don't intend to let her.

I stand but keep my hand firmly on her back. Time to play with her.

Elizabeth

Marco is giving me exquisite torture and I am getting lost in its intense delirious seduction. This is so magnificent, just feeling, not moving, receiving more and more delicious sensations and stimulations. I feel like I'm going to explode. Oh God, yes!!

I am lying halfway on the bed, arms tied straight over my head and my legs spread with my ass up in the air and I feel like my sex is screaming *please come and get me.* There goes that little fish mouth puckering, begging for relief again.

I feel Marco shift down behind me. I hear a click then a slight thump. I'm surprised I can hear anything at all with my heart pounding so loudly in my ears. His hand comes to lay on my mound, cupping it with a squeeze and I almost feel my juices ooze out with the pressure, I'm so aroused. He moves his hand slowly back spreading my cheeks as he does. His hand is moist and just glides over me like velvet and the feeling spreads through me like a drug. While his thumb circles and presses my back hole, his finger teases my pussy, sliding in, circling, exploring. The hand from my back begins to travel down until it comes to rest on my ass and spreads my cheeks.

Fuck!

Fuck!

Fuck!

Two fingers slide into my sex and my walls instantly clench on them, pulling them in. He turns them, bends them, moves them in and out so his knuckles press against that spot inside me. That wave of desire is beginning to crest, carrying me higher. The hand holding my cheeks open begins to move in rhythm with the other, caressing, petting, teasing and I start to beg silently, pleading for more. He moves and now one finger is in my pussy and another slides slowly into my ass. And he stills. He doesn't move. My silent pleading becomes louder, stronger, hungrier. And I hug his fingers with all of me, demanding him to give me satisfaction, holding them tight, pulsing around him. When I finally let his fingers go, he begins to move, agonizingly slowly, fucking me with them in both holes. It is so sweet, I never thought it would be so incredible. I don't want it stop. I am close to falling. His movements become deeper, more deliberate, pushing me closer to the edge.

"Ooohhhhh…" I can't stop the moan that escapes me.

He pushes in as far as he can go. I want more, it feels so good. He senses my need and wiggles those two fingers as he thrusts. And I come, slow and sweet. Still pushed deep inside me, his fingers stop again and he holds them there as I squeeze them, trying wring everything out of him.

Marco removes his fingers and is on his knees behind me. He grabs the insides of my thighs and opens me up then buries his face between my legs sucking, licking, and probing me everywhere. The last of my orgasm shoots through my body telling me it's not finished yet. But he knows that. Sucking the last of my cum from me, he stands and pushes the head of his cock inside my still throbbing sex with his hands still holding me open. He thrusts just the head in and out making me yearn for more.

"Please, Marco…" I'm begging, I don't care.

"Tell me what you want, baby…" His voice is low and hungry.

"All of it, everything, everywhere, please…"

"Not yet, baby."

"Oh God, please…"

With just the head of his cock at my entrance he begins to tease my ass, pushing just the tip of his finger inside me, thrusting and twisting it slowly. I can't push back on him; my ass is as far back as it will go. My need is becoming intense, climbing higher and higher with each little thrust with his head and his fingertip. I want to growl at him, scream at him to fuck me, hard and deep. His other hand moves to my clit and he grabs it between two fingers and rubs it between them. Almost, I'm so close, just a little more, please…

Moving both hands to my hips he grabs me tightly, digging his fingers into my flesh. He begins to thrust the head of his cock harder, then stops like he's hitting a wall. I hear him growl as his hands pull me closer to him pulling on my restraints. I can tell he's holding himself back.

"Fuck me, Marco, hard!" I yell at him.

He slams into me, his hips slapping into my ass, I love that sound, the sound of our flesh smacking. He pulls back and only enters his head again. Aaarrrrggh! He's going to kill me!

"Yes! Yes! Yes!" I'm pleading.

"Fuck, Elizabeth!" He grits it out through clenched teeth.

One of his hands slide down to my front, his other still on my hip, and pinches my clit tightly as he begins to thrust deep, hard and slow.

"Oh, God! Oh, God! Oh, God!"

I shatter, explode, gush! Yes, sweet, sweet release.

His movements become harder, deeper, stronger, grinding into me, releasing my clit to rub my sex, deliciously stroking me and holding me to him.

"Elizabeth, God, there is never enough of you, baby…"

He throws his head back and tenses, burying his cock and I feel him spasming as he comes.

Marco

I have to get Elizabeth out of these restraints as much as I'd love to fall over her and lie here holding her for a little while with my cock still spurting the last of my cum inside her. My hunger for her so intense it's never fully satisfied. I squat and undo her ankles first, rubbing the marks to bring back the blood flow and soothe them away. Standing, I do the same to her wrists, rubbing and kissing them to ease the discomfort. It looks as if she was pulling on them pretty hard. I lift her and place her on the bed, not trusting her limbs to carry her after holding herself up like that. I go to the bathroom and come back with a warm wet washcloth to clean her.

I place light kisses over her face on her eyes, forehead, cheeks and lips as I gently wipe her body with the towel.

"How are you, love?" I ask softly.

She smiles up at me glowing and looking beautifully intoxicated.

"I'm good," she says softly as her smile widens.

I knew she was enjoying it but I wanted to hear it from her. I want to be sure she wants more.

"Tell me, do you want more?" I look intently into her eyes searching for what she might not tell me with words. They widen with all of the possibilities.

"Yes, I think I do, Marco…" It's barely above a whisper.

I kiss her deeply, letting all of the appreciation and happiness I feel pour into her with my kiss.

"Okay, I'll give you more, but not tonight," I tease.

"Thank God, I don't think I would survive." She rolls her eyes playfully at me.

"But we have some shopping to do tomorrow." I smirk mischievously at her, thinking of the list of purchases I have prepared in my head.

Her mouth falls open slightly at that implication, silent for a moment.

"Yes, we do. And by the looks of that smile on your face, Marco, I have a feeling it's going to be very interesting."

I can imagine the images playing through that beautiful head of hers of what I have planned for her.

Chapter Seven

Marco

We've fallen into the routine of me making breakfast because I enjoy it and I'm a good cook. Elizabeth has yet to cook for me. I think she's a little intimidated because I grew up in the restaurant business and she thinks I'm this great cook. To be honest, I am better than most people. Not only did I grow up in the business but cooking was a hobby of mine for a while during a very bad time of my life. It helped me to relax and be calm when everything was falling to shit around me. Now Elizabeth can enjoy the fruits of that.

Today is the usual spinach and egg omelets but I'm adding some potatoes on the side because I think we're both in need of a little more sustenance after last night and in anticipation of the day ahead. We have a lot of shopping to do for the house and for toys. I've decided already that I'm not going to tell Elizabeth where we're going and I'm definitely not telling her we're going to buy sex toys. I have a few in mind that I know she'll love but I'm very curious to see if she'll show any interest in picking anything out. She has surprised me with her desire for more. And I can't wait to give it to her. This is our weekend and I plan to enjoy every moment I have with her. That black cloud threatening to open up is not coming near us.

Just as I'm pouring Elizabeth's tea and my coffee, sleepy head comes out of the bedroom wearing one of my shirts and it makes me smile. I love seeing her in them.

Walking over to her I kiss her on the forehead, "Good morning, baby, did you sleep well?"

"Hi, sexy, yes, I slept so hard, it was fantastic."

"I'm so glad, I know you didn't sleep well the last time. Come on, let's have breakfast. I'm sure you're starved."

I walk over to the table and pull out a chair for her and wait for her to sit down.

"Get comfortable, put your feet up. I'll bring your breakfast and your tea." I kiss her on the top of pretty bed-head when she sits then I go to get our plates, coffee, tea and water.

"Drink some water. I'm sure you need it. I don't want you to get dehydrated." I wink at her.

She has a confused expression on her face. "Why would I get dehydrated?"

"As wet as you get, and as hard as you come, you would get dehydrated," I say enjoying the embarrassment on her face.

"Marco!" She scolds, turning beet red and swatting my hand.

"Eat up, we've got a busy day ahead. And you've got to go visit your friend about your costume for Halloween this weekend. When do you want to go?"

I'm wondering if she'll go alone or ask me to go with her.

"I don't know, I'll have to check with her and see when she's free." She raises her eyes to mine biting her fingernail and I know there's something she wants to say.

"What is it, Elizabeth?"

"Um, would you like to meet her?" She looks almost afraid to ask me.

"Of course I'd like to meet your friend. Just tell me when and where and we'll be there." I lean over and place a light kiss on her lips and I'm happy she looks relieved but happier she asked me to meet her friend. I was beginning to think she was hiding me.

"Now eat, it's gonna be a long day."

We look like newlyweds during the first part of the morning's shopping excursion, picking out paintings and photographs of local scenes in small little galleries and shops. Next we go to Pottery Barn for kitchen accessories. I need a new juicer and sea salt and pepper grinders. I enjoy both of these shopping ventures, as much as I love to cook. The sales lady keeps looking at me like, *I can't believe this guy is not gay*. We have lunch at A Taste of Italy, a little authentic Italian restaurant that started out as a deli but added a room with dining tables. This place is just like the delis in New York.

Frank Sinatra crooning *The Way You Look Tonight*. I look at Elizabeth and my heart swells. This woman intoxicates me.

"Dance with me, baby." I hold my hand out to her.

"Here?" She looks around warily. No one else is in the dining room so she takes my hand slowly as a carefree smile graces that lovely face.

I hold her against me pressing her body into mine.

I sing the words of the song softly into her ear, her cheek pressed to mine.

I dip her, just like they did in the old days when the song finishes, and her laughter fills the air. I'm going to remember this day for the rest of my life, a perfect snapshot caught forever in my mind.

We sit down to eat and I tell Elizabeth that next we're going to go look for her corset and some other things. I've been waiting for this since the moment she asked me to go shopping with her. I won't tell her where. I know by the glimmer I must have in my eye, she knows I have some surprises in store. She's like a little kid filled with excitement but at the same time her wanton inner slut side can't wait either. The two parts of her are incredibly irresistible.

As I drive up Market Street and go past the Harley Davidson dealership, she turns to me.

"I have a pretty good idea of where we're going, Mr. Bond."

I place my hand on her thigh, stroking it as a smile creeps over my face, my eyes never leaving the road.

"I'm sure you do. And what do you think?"

"I think we're going to buy more than just a corset, Sir." I don't miss the innuendo.

"Well you did ask for more. We'll see how much more you want."

When we pull into a parking spot at the Adam & Eve kinkfest, store I turn to look at her. Her face is flushed and she's biting her lip. She's turned on. This is going to be fun. I want to lick my lips in anticipation of everything we're going to do with all of these little toys of pleasure.

"Ready?"

She moves her face to look at me as a slow smile curves those pink lips. My cock hardens at her lascivious reaction.

"Yes," she whispers huskily.

"Let's go find some more then," I say as a wolfish smile spreads across my face.

Inside the second-story store the regular assortment of masks, vibrators, dildos and clothing are immediately visible. I guess it had to be on the second floor so that everyone couldn't see all of the sexual apparatuses on display if they were peeking in the windows from a first floor unit. The young salesman behind the counter looks up at us and smiles giving us a quick assessment before he greets us.

"Hi, let me know if you need any help." Smart boy, he can tell that I know what I'm doing but she is a bit nervous, so he gives us our space.

I answer him nodding, "Thank you, we will."

I turn to her and ask, "Why don't we start with picking out your corset?" It's more of a statement than question. It's best she starts with something she feels safe and comfortable with, and it will give her some time to get used to being around all of the paraphernalia.

"Good idea." There's a little relief in her expression.

Elizabeth picks out a beautiful red satin bustier with black lace overlay with demi cups that will make her breasts look beautiful, pushing them up and letting the tops quiver with her movements. My dick wakes up at the thought of her in it. I turn to the salesman.

"Can she try this on?"

"Certainly." He comes around the counter saying, "Right this way."

Inside the dressing room, yes I go in with her, she looks fantastic. So much so I can't keep my hands off her. I push her up against the wall and hold her hands over her head with one of mine, the other holds her still with my hand flat on her abdomen. My tongue traces the outline of the cups on her bare skin.

"Marco, we can't do this here," she whispers as she pushes her tits into my face.

"Ssshhh, baby."

I pull the half cups down letting her breasts pour out so her nipples are pointing at my mouth begging to be sucked. I pull one between my lips and teeth, biting, flicking, and sucking it as I roll the other between my fingers, twisting, pulling and pinching it and her hips begin to buck under my palm. I slide my hand down her panties, she's so fucking wet, and thrust two fingers inside her. Instantly she's riding my hand hard and fast.

"Mmmmm," I growl, "This is going to be a long fucking day." I release her with a final bite on each fleshy breast. She gasps at the slight pain and looks down at the marks. Looking in my eyes she can't fight the smile at the sight of my love marks on her.

"Get dressed before I fuck you right here," I say through clenched teeth, half hoping she'll dare me.

After we leave the dressing room I lead her over to the clamps. I want to get one for her clit. She will lose her fucking mind, I'm sure. The young tattooed and pierced salesman comes over to help us.

"Can I show you anything?" he asks in a casual tone.

I point to the jewel clit clamp. "Yes, we'd like that, along with this corset."

He holds his hand out to Elizabeth waiting for the garment. She turns scarlet handing it to him and I'm thinking, *If you're embarrassed about that, baby, wait until you find out what the rest of this is for.*

"And we'll take that black plug kit over there and the wireless plug." I direct him to the butt plug kit with anal beads and the vibrating anal plug, a little something for me when she has it in. He moves to that end of the counter and takes them out placing them with the rest of our things.

I look at Elizabeth. She looks like a deer in headlights with her little mouth open. I bend down to kiss her.

"Is there anything in particular you'd like, babe?"

"I think you're doing quite well so far, thank you," she answers me quietly.

I look back at the guy behind the counter. "Also, I saw beaded thongs, we'd like a pair as well."

"Absolutely," he says, glancing at Elizabeth to estimate her size, then he walks to retrieve a pack.

I take Elizabeth over to the vibrators.

"We'd like the G-spot and that one, and that lubricant," I tell him pointing to the flesh-colored larger vibrator. "Let's have those ben wa balls as well."

I look at Elizabeth again, studying her face. She's looking at everything I've picked out, and she's probably wondering what I'm going to do with all of it. I wonder if she thinks I'm never going to fuck her again because I'm buying two vibrators, or if I'm going to use them both on her at the same time. She knows how I am with her, how I want to make her get lost in pleasure, how I drown in her, how I lose myself in her and my only desire is hearing her moan and scream my name.

"Come over here with me." I tug gently on her hand and walk her towards the floggers.

"I'd like to use this on you. It can be very intoxicating if used correctly." I pause for a moment to let her get comfortable with the idea before I take one down.

"Okay." I can tell she's nervous and a little scared but she trusts me and agrees.

"You'll love it. I promise." I take one from the wall display, feeling the ends for their softness. This one should do nicely. It won't give too much of a sting if mistakenly used heavy handedly.

I approach the counter with Elizabeth and set the flogger down. "This will be all, thank you for your help."

Elizabeth squeezes my hand tightly as he rings us up, packs up our things and we leave.

Back in the car she's quiet, lost in thought. I'm sure her mind is going a mile a minute. I look at her and try to read her thoughts and gently squeeze her thigh.

"You okay?"

"Yes, I'm fine. It's a lot of stuff."

I chuckle. "Yes, kind of." My gaze scans her face and my heart warms. Her brows are furrowed and she's biting her lip. "Don't worry baby, we're not going to use everything at once. I want to give you more, this will help me do that." I pause and place my hand over hers holding it tenderly, "Do you trust me, Elizabeth?" I ask her again.

"Without a doubt."

Looking deeply into those hypnotic hazel eyes of hers where all the secrets of the world seem to exist my heart starts to talk.

"Pleasuring you, taking you to places where you lose yourself, where your body screams with unbound desire and every nerve ending in your delicious little body is on fire from my touch, that is what I want. That is what I was put on this earth for. I'm going to do wonderfully wicked things to you and you're going to love every minute of it."

She leans in to kiss me as her hand slides through the back of my hair pulling me closer, her arousal feeding into me with her kiss telling me she's mine.

Releasing me, she says breathlessly, "Let's go home so I can finish up with Elsie then we can start playing." Her smile is sinfully hungry.

This incredible woman never ceases to amaze me.

Elsie is the most adorable little thing, petite, feminine and strong all at the same time. When I walk into her apartment she looks me up and down, scrutinizing me. A smile erupts on her pretty face.

"Hi, Marco, it's good to finally meet you. Elizabeth's told me about how you two met and what happened at her place.," She discreetly leaves out Santino's name. She's quite a diplomatic young lady.

"It's a pleasure to finally meet you. We did have quite a beginning," I say, momentarily reflecting on our first few weeks together as the images speed through my mind. "So, you're going to be Elizabeth's date for Halloween? She's looking forward to it and the costume you're helping her with, I hear you're very talented. I'm going to go to the gym while you two take care of business. You and Elizabeth are starting a class there on Monday, right?"

Elsie's eyes widen and a mischievous smile tugs at her mouth. "Yes, I'm really looking forward to it."

"You should be, it's a great place and everyone there knows what they're doing."

I bet she's looking forward to it because of the guys, not the class. I'm well aware the place is filled with some of the most good-looking and built men in the area.

I turn to Elizabeth and take her in my arms. "I'll call you in about an hour, okay?"

Wrapping herself around me, she presses into me. She's wearing the beaded thong and I know it's been rubbing against her clit and pussy the whole way here. Her face is flushed and her mouth looks like it wants to be kissed and I want to stroke her folds to see how wet she is.

"Okay, have fun, don't hurt yourself, please. We have plans."

The naughty girl is looking forward to it, and my dick is very happy to hear that.

After warming up at the gym I get in the cage with John. He's bigger than I am and very good so sparring with him helps me to sharpen more defensive moves. Working out with him is helping me to get better, pushing me, challenging me, and knocking me on my ass a few times. He throws me a couple of jabs, I spin and try to take him off his feet by hooking him with my right foot. Back and forth, we punch, hand strike, and roundhouse kick. After three rounds, the usual length of a bout, we exit the cage together hot, sweaty and a little out of breath.

He takes this opportunity to bust my balls. "That was excellent, Marco. Pretty soon you might be able to kick my ass."

"What, and damage that handsome face of yours, John? That's all you've got going for you. I think I'll just keep taking it easy on you for a while."

We both laugh as we stop at one of the bags. He gets behind it and I start jabbing at it, left, right, left, left.

"Did Brian talk to you about anything he might have found out that might be happening with my project?" I ask him between hits, a little short of breath.

I throw a right upper cut and he barely feels it with the huge bag between him and my fist.

Brian Daniels was with John when he came to Elizabeth's apartment the night Santino showed up there. They have been friends since boot camp in the marines and John considers him the only family he has. These two men are incredibly loyal and generous, and have the ability to kill someone with their bare hands. When I arrived in Wilmington and found Evolution, they made me feel something foreign; a true friendship with no hidden agendas. We are the same, each of us a Dominant, but each of us unique.

"Not much, all he said is he thinks something's not right. He did say last time we spoke he was having lunch with someone to confirm the status of your paperwork before he talked to you about anything." He's pushing the bag back on me, forcing me to go into it a little harder. I attack it like a bulldozer plowing down everything in its path.

"Did he tell you who he was having lunch with?" I growl it out between jabs, my frustration and intensity are clear in my words and in my hits. I let my pent-up emotions flow through my hands like a powerful force exerting its strength on the object of its anger wanting to smash it and destroy it.

"No he didn't tell me. But he did say it was someone who would give him a definitive answer on your paperwork." His voice is tight. Even though he's on the other side of the bag he can feel the rage pouring from me, one hit after the other in rapid fire succession.

Brian Daniels' family owns a very large and reputable construction company here and have been in business for three generations. The company has now passed on to him, and he is very, very good at what he does, the best in the area. His friends and connections reach into many different facets of the community, forged over years, births, marriages, fishing trips, and sometimes a tall, cold glass of iced tea.

One final punch and I lift my head. The sweat is running down my face and body. "I fucking hope so." It's apparent I didn't get all my fury out because he can still hear it in my voice.

"I do too, 'cause I'd hate to be the one on the receiving end of that shit right there. That's going to be one fucked up individual when you find out who it is."

Turning my attention back to the bag, I start mauling it, taking out all of my frustrations about whatever the fuck is going on with my applications with the city. That feeling of foreboding is gnawing at me and it's making me fucking crazy.

Elizabeth

I'm so aroused right now, I could kill Marco for making me wear these beaded thongs! What was I thinking? I even contemplated going into Elsie's bathroom and masturbating just to extinguish this need. Every time I move, breathe, even speak, the beads rub my lips, my clit and my ass. I just want to keep shifting in my seat so I can come. If I didn't think I would scream from the release, I would.

Marco must know how on fire I am. He's barely touched me since he picked me up at Elsie's, just a flutter of his lips against mine or a light stroke of his fingers down my spine. Ever since we were in Adam & Eve around all the toys, my sex has been pulsing at the suggestion of satisfaction brought on with all of the vibrators, dildos, restraints and other naughty things. I have been wondering all evening what Marco's going to do to me tonight and it sends anticipated jolts of excitement throughout my body. When we get home we order Chinese food and he jumps right in the shower. But the only thing I want going inside me right now is him! And maybe one of those vibrators. Grrrrr! I'm going to die from horniness. I'm not waiting.

Entering the bathroom, I close the door quietly behind me. I turn my head to see Marco standing in the shower with water droplets cascading down the perfection of his firm golden body, the muscles bulging bigger after his workout at the gym. His fight for control is evident in his erection and the way he's standing, both arms resting on the wall in front of him and his head bowed. I stand quietly and admire how beautiful he is. The sight of his arousal fuels my desire, my insides coil and pull, making me gasp with the sight of his wanting me. This man is a primal beast lurking within the beauty of his controlled façade. The raw sensuality and power that pour from him are completely intoxicating, surrounding me, burning me, melting me so that all that is left is hungry desire yearning for his beast to take me.

He turns to look at me as I begin to undress. I still have the bustier on. Pulling the sweater over my head I lay it on the floor. Next I slide down the loose pants I'm wearing. Nothing tight could have been worn over the beads or they would have killed me, and I place them on the floor with the top. I reach to unzip the bustier, releasing my breasts, and I let it fall to the floor. Marco's jaw is tight, his muscle flexing showing his fight for restraint as he lifts his hand to me beckoning me to come to him. I pull my hair up and clip the mass away from my neck. I take his hand and come to stand in front of him under the waterfall. He runs a finger down my shoulder, kissing me lightly. My head falls back and I sigh heavily. A strangled growl rumbles from deep inside of his chest.

"I've wanted to see how wet you were all night," he whispers.

My legs open at his words and he runs a finger along the beads making them vibrate against my clit. I reach up and dig my nails into his arms.

"Oh God, Marco, please…" I beg. Just one more, please, and I'll come.

"I know, baby, I know." His voice is compassionate and firm. He runs a fingernail along the length of the beads resting on my pulsing sex, back and forth, three times. The vibrations echo through me and finally I fall over the edge, release humming inside me.

I slide the thong down my legs and taking the length of his shaft in my hands I wrap the beads around him and begin to gently slide them up and down his length.

"Fuck, Elizabeth," he growls between clenched teeth, throwing his head back, the tendons on the sides of his neck bulging, reflecting what's going on inside him.

As my hand slides slowly up and down massaging him, I reach down and take his sac in my palm and give his balls the attention they deserve. I love the weight of them resting in my hand, the texture of his wrinkled skin against my smooth flesh, and I can't resist the urge to fondle and squeeze them.

He grabs my hands and pulls them away. "That's enough of that. If you keep that up I won't last another five minutes."

Taking the body wash he begins to lather my body from top to bottom slowly and deliberately, his fingers dipping into all of my creases and folds, his lips and tongue stroking my smooth skin. His touch stirs the embers of my arousal, stoking them, bringing them higher and brighter.

Finally, he turns off the water. "Time to get out, baby."

He steps out first and gets us each a towel.

As I stand there drying myself I look at the exquisite specimen of man standing before me tying the fat white towel low around his sculpted waist. His eyes pierce me with a promise of satisfaction saying, *bring me your hunger and I'll feed you. I'll quench your need more than you'd ever imagined.* He extends his hand to me and I take it, letting out a quiet breath because I know he'll do just that.

When we get to the bed he removes our towels and tosses them on the chair in the corner. The lights are dim and the only sounds are the sounds of flesh on flesh, our breathing, and the pounding of our hearts.

Marco lifts me onto the bed and stretches his long muscular body over mine, his large hands travelling over all of my curves, mounds and dips. His mouth savors my breasts, pulling and flicking the peaks until I almost shout out in pleasure. Shifting his weight, he moves down between my legs and holds them open as far as they will go. When his lips close over my clit and his tongue thrusts inside me, the sensations are so magnified my need screams for fulfillment, throbbing and clenching inside me.

He turns me over and lifts my ass in the air. His fingers begin their dance over my sex, playing, stroking and plunging inside me. His attention is so precise in my pussy I almost think he can feel my pleasure. How can he be this good? He removes his hand and rests his torso flush against me. I feel his erection grazing my skin and everything inside me instinctively clenches at that contact. I hear a click then a thump on the floor before Marco's hand returns to cup my mound. His other hand comes to rest on my back hole with something soft and velvety—the lube. My hips buck in reaction to the visions of penetration of my ass. Marco's hand tightens on my sex holding me in place.

"Sssshhh, baby, be still, it's time for more, trust me." His voice is low and gravelly but soothing.

Oh. My. God! What is he going to put in there? I press back into him, my desire strong but my trust in him stronger.

He slides a finger inside my hot sheath while another sits at the entrance of my ass, circling, teasing, and pressing in rhythm with the other. I begin to rock with him, against him and I feel his finger pushing in, opening me up and another wave of hunger grabs me. I meet the thrusts of his hand, going higher, that sweet headiness takes over me. But I need more.

I feel Marco shift again as his fingers slowly leave me empty and wanting. Then his cock pushes slowly into me, back and forth, stroking my walls, thrusting and filling me, carrying me on that wave and I moan with it, it feels so good.

He buries himself deep inside me and places a hand on my back holding me still. And I feel it, the tip of something at the entrance of my ass. Marco begins to move, rocking, thrusting, gently plunging. Oooooh, yes, I can feel it sliding in, filling me, yes, moving with him entering me. His movements become stronger, deeper, more intense. I feel so full, so good and I start to soar.

In my head I'm saying, *Ride me, baby*, clutching him tightly within me.

I hear a deep rumble from Marco and it pushes me higher.

"Aaaahhh!" The scream rips from me the moment he turns on the vibrator in my ass making me shatter.

"Grrrrr, Elizabeth!!" Marco pounds into me, coming hard and fast.

My orgasm won't stop. I ride it with Marco, fierce and all consuming.

"STOP, PLEASE!" I can't take it anymore.

The vibrations stop, he removes it slowly and we collapse, two bodies exhausted and spent, crumpled together on the thick white comforter.

"Oh, my God, Marco…" My voice is weak but I'm totally satisfied.

"I know, baby. I felt the same way, unfuckingbelievable," he breathes out with his arms tightly around me.

A small chuckle begins to leave me, and I feel Marco's body begin to tremble with one as well before I hear it. We're both chuckling, then the laughter overcomes us and tears roll down our cheeks.

"Oh wow, that was intense," he says as he's trying to subdue his laughter. "I'm going to get a towel, be right back, my love," he says still chuckling as he kisses me on my forehead before he gets up to leave.

I hear the water running in the master bath as I stretch out and let the smile spread across my face and body. Yes, my body is smiling, it's glowing and it wants to dance wild and uninhibited under a full moon. I might have gotten up to do just that if my limbs weren't made of Jell-O right now. Marco returns with the warm cloth a minute later sitting down next to me to clean the lube and our juices oozing out of me.

"Marco?"

"Yes, baby?"

"Why do you always do this?"

He looks into my face, his expression so tender.

"It's my job to take care of you, love. And I enjoy taking care of you, now shush and let me do this."

Tonight I'm especially grateful for his attention, I am so spent I can hardly keep my eyes open. A yawn creeps up on me with that thought just to prove the point.

"Sleep, my love," Marco whispers in my ear. "But dream of me." That is the last thing I hear as I drift off, smiling, feeling so much joy, adoration and affection for this beautifully amazing man sent to me by the grace of God.

Marco

When I make love to Elizabeth it isn't about sex. Yes, of course that's what we're doing but it's more like the sex is a means to open her up to expose her soul. A way for me touch her essence, her being, a way for her true beauty to touch me and enfold me in its warmth and grandeur. It's celestial and I am humbled to being more than a mere man when she takes me there. It is the only time she is truly free with me. I'm greedy and I have to possess it but I refuse to admit I cannot truly have what is not given to me freely. So I take it every time I make love to her. It is then she gives me everything, everything that she is, all that she is unaware of. It flows from her endlessly and I luxuriate in it gluttonously.

"Elizabeth, I want to take some pictures of you."

I can see the shock in her face. She is stunning in her afterglow and I want to capture it, savor it, preserve it and keep it. I'm such a selfish man.

"Why do you want to do that? I hate pictures, Marco."

I can sense she's withdrawing and getting behind her safety wall, the place where she hides herself. I'm not going to let that happen.

"Because I want to capture your beauty, the beauty of your sensuality, your unmasked self. You're captivating, and if I can get even a glimpse of that in the photo it would be a masterpiece. One that I helped you to create in yourself. Will you let me do that, Elizabeth? Please."

She's silent thinking about my answer.

We're lying in my bed. It's the middle of the day on Sunday and the sun is shining through the sheer panels hanging on the window behind my bed onto her flawless pale skin. A faint horn from a boat blows in the distance mixing with the melody of the sea gulls. The auburn highlights in her dark hair look like a hint of fire embers that are smoldering within her. Her hazel eyes have specks of gold on the outside and a hint of blue around the pupils, such a compilation, much like herself, so many different facets to the woman that she is.

She's looking into my eyes, searching me, and I can see she's fighting with herself. She doesn't want to do it. I know she's afraid of her vulnerability. But she's enticed by the idea as well. I see a small smile tug on the corners of her mouth. And I can't resist it. I slowly lower my lips to hers, grazing them softly. Her lips are swollen from our kisses. I lightly run my tongue along them and her mouth opens slightly. I feel her breath mixing with mine. As always she lets me do what I want with her and I relish it. I love the taste and feel of her.

She whispers, "Okay."

"Thank you, baby." My mouth takes hers with the lingering fire from having just been inside her. She pushes her body into me dragging her nails down my back making me hard again.

"I'm going to get my camera. Stay just like that. You're perfect."

I go to my closet and pull down a box I haven't unpacked yet but I know the camera's in there. I turn it on to check if the battery is fully charged. My cock is rock hard thinking about the shots I'm going to get of Elizabeth.

"Look at you, Marco, you're obviously excited. You must really be enjoying this," she laughs at me when I walk back in bedroom.

"I am, baby. You have no idea how intoxicating you are right now. And you're letting me capture this moment. You're making me very happy."

"I can't believe I'm letting you, to be perfectly honest." I see the blush creeping across her flushed cheeks.

I sit on the edge of the bed and look into her eyes.

"Don't worry, I won't do anything to hurt you or give you any reason not to trust me. I asked you to let me do this because I want to capture your sensuality on film, see you open and exposed from making love with me. Even if just a small piece of it, I need to have it."

There's a long silence. Her expression is soft and very feminine, unguarded and open. And at that moment I know she is going to give me what I want, what I need, to be expressed in her pictures. The expressions of her soul.

"I know." Her voice is quiet but certain. "Just tell me what you want me to do for you."

My eyes move to gaze at her breasts showing through the sheet and I brush my finger over her nipples.

"I want you to think of us making love. I want you to relive that, feel those feelings, imagine my hands and my mouth on your body and show me what you're feeling."

Her eyelids dip as her mind and body go back to that place of passion we shared just moments before. Her lips part slightly and I see her tongue peeking out behind her porcelain white teeth. That lovely thick dark mane of hair of hers is fanned out against the white pillow under her head framing her in purity. There is a shift in her body that pushes her breasts out and my hand reaches out to caress her.

She begins to shift in reaction to my touch and I start to click away. Her eyes look at me with such affection it melts my heart. She's softly writhing, shifting and moving as if my hands and mouth are making love to her, tasting her, drinking her in. Her eyes are speaking to me, making love to me, beckoning to me like a siren's song and I get lost in them.

Her beauty is angelic. This moment, this thing we are sharing now is not human but spiritual. My soul is calling to hers and I know hers is answering. I hope I am able to capture this tiny moment, a small piece of this experience so I can drown in it again and again.

Chapter Eight

Elizabeth

Monday, but oh, what a weekend. I still shiver when I remember the decadent bodily delights Marco gave me. I feel the pleasure is still visible, written all over my skin. But it was a hell of a day at the office, nonstop since the doors opened this morning. I'm looking forward to blowing off a little steam. Tonight is the first night of the self-defense classes at Evolution gym and both Elsie and Janie said they were meeting me there. They have never met but I know they're going to love each other. Marco suggested he and I go together so he's picking me up in a few minutes. I wonder if he wants to go with me because of a possessive thing. I would be lying if I said I wasn't looking forward to watching him get in the cage and be all Neanderthal, getting sweaty and throwing punches with another guy. I can't explain it but I think it's sexy.

I was relieved when the day ended and now I'm sitting in the kitchen at the breakfast bar, I send both Elsie and Janie a text.

Hey, you still meeting me at Evolution for the class? I saved us all spaces.

Elsie – Are you fucking kidding me? And miss being surrounded by the sexiest men in Wilmington, yeah, I'm going!

Janie – If I thought I wouldn't be arrested for stalking, my ass would be parked outside that building 24 hours a day. Can I get there an hour early?

Is this today's version of women going to a male stripper show?

Yeah Janie, I think you can if you want but I believe you've got to work out and not just ogle.

Janie – As long as a big hunk of Adonis is working me out, I'll do whatever the hell he wants me to. Hurry your ass up!!

I'm waiting for Marco, he should be here any minute. You guys haven't met yet either, this is going to be a full night.

Elsie and Janie – I hope I get full!

Down ladies or we're all going to be a mess for class.

I hear the keys in the door. Marco must be here. I still get a little shiver of excitement each time I see him.

Marco's here, I'll be there in a little while.

Elsie and Janie – Hurry up!

"Hi baby." Marco comes up behind me and leans his arms on either side of me, resting them on the counter in front of me and kisses me hello.

"Hi sexy, so I get to watch you beat on some guy tonight?" I smile mischievously up at him.

He laughs deep and loud and it makes me laugh with him.

"Yeah, I guess you will. Do you like the idea of that, babe?" He's smirking at me.

"Why yes, Mr. Bond, I believe I do like the idea of that. Does that make me a bad girl?" I can't keep the innuendo out of my comment.

"Elizabeth, you are the best kind of bad girl and I would kick anyone's ass just to watch you watching me. Are you ready to go? And are your friends meeting us there?"

"Yes, I'm ready and yes, they're meeting us there." I hand Marco my phone to show him the messages.

He can't help but laugh at my horny friends.

"Well this ought to be interesting."

I don't miss the little smirk on his face. I stand to get my purse and a bag with a change of clothes, just in case.

"You look sexy as hell in those yoga pants, Elizabeth. Almost too good."

I come up and slide my arms around his neck, tilting my head up to him seductively.

"The only person I want to look sexy for is you, you have me completely captivated."

His arms slide around my waist molding me to him, and I can feel the contours and ridges of his body pressed against me. He's hard and strong, male and power, sexuality and control. Every fiber of his being emanates all of these, and if he wanted to he could destroy you or seduce you easily with just one look.

"And you are fucking exquisite bound and captive. Just remembering you tied and drunk on pleasure makes me crazy."

His mouth begins to drink mine, slowly, hungrily, completely and I feel myself falling quickly into that drunken stupor of pleasure again. His hands press me in closer, and I want to melt into him. Close is not close enough.

Pulling away from me he's silent for a moment as we gather our wits. I can feel how aroused he is by his erection pressed against me. I start to move to my knees. I want to take him in my mouth, taste him, swallow him, feast on him. But he stops me, holding me by my arms.

"Not now, baby, although I would love for you to suck every drop from me right now, but we don't have time. And the edge of frustration will be good for me in the cage." He smirks that devilish half grin at me, the one that says, 'Yeah, I'm a cocky son of a bitch but I can back it up.'

"And you too, you're going to be sparring with the real big boys tonight," he says teasing me.

"Yeah, do you think they can handle me and the girls?" I wink at him.

He throws his head back laughing, guiding me out of the apartment with his arm wrapped around my waist, taking my bag from me as we go.

"Oh God, according to those texts, I don't know if those guys know what's coming. This should be fun."

I text Elsie and Janie from the car to let them know we're on our way. They're waiting for us in the parking lot when we arrive. Elsie's already met Marco but Janie pounces on him with her effervescent personality as soon as we get out of the car. She's just like a grown-up ten-year-old.

"Well, finally I get to meet the mysterious Marco Kastanopoulis. Stalked my girl here, didn't you, that first night." Janie's got her hands on her hips, with a wicked little smirk on her face, tapping her toe like a mother scolding her naughty child.

Marco's not flustered one bit by Janie's show. "Yes, I did. And I would do it again, just like that. It's very nice to meet you, Janie. Elizabeth talks very highly of you. I wasn't sure if she was ever going to let me meet you."

"Come here, you big lug, and give me a hug. This is how we do it." Janie opens her arms wide for a big bear hug and Marco steps into them closing his arms around her and they both have big silly grins on their faces.

I can't help but feel so happy that they've finally met and they're hugging!

"So you two have already met?" I ask Elsie and Janie, looking from one to other.

Elsie chuckles a little bit before she says, "I guess we were both kinda excited about tonight. We got here early and we were hanging out. It wasn't hard to figure out who we were."

"Yeah, we were debating on going in and starting a little tour of our own," Janie adds laughing.

"Come on, ladies, let's go inside then." Marco takes my hand and leads the way to the gym doors.

When we walk into the gym, Metallica's *So Fucking What* is pumping through the speakers. Marco and I walk in first with Elsie and Janie behind us. Scott is at the front desk again completely absorbed in whatever he's working on.

"Hey, Marco, good to see you. Hi, Elizabeth, good to see you again, and you've brought company for tonight's class. Here's some paperwork that needs to be filled out before class starts," Scott says as he passes us each a packet of papers.

I take the packet and turn to face Elsie and Janie and they're both staring towards the inside of the gym. I turn to look and John's walking toward us through a sea of sexy sweaty male bodies. Tonight he's wearing gym shorts and a t-shirt with all of those muscles taking on a life of their own with each step he takes.

"Who's that?" they both whisper to me with eyes wide.

"I think that's our teacher for tonight, John Wolfe," I whisper back.

"There is a God," Janie whispers rolling her eyes to the ceiling.

"Marco, Elizabeth, good to see you guys! Brian told me you'd be here tonight, dude. He's just finishing up in the cage." John greets us and they do that whole cool male handshaking/slapping thing.

"Cool, I'll stay here with the ladies until they're ready to go for the class then I'll start on the bag." Marco's look becomes serious before he continues. "Did he tell you anything?"

"Yeah, man, he said it looks a little funny," he says shaking his head slowly. "He's gonna dig a little deeper, might take a couple of days but he's confident he'll find something." John looks a little disbelieving with whatever they're talking about. I don't know what it is but it sounds serious.

"That's what I was afraid of, God damn it! Okay, thanks man." Marco's brows are furrowed, he's obviously concerned about whatever they're discussing.

"And Elizabeth, who are your friends?" John turns towards Elsie and Janie, smiling that heart-melting boyish million-dollar grin.

"Hi, John, this is Elsie…"

Elsie extends her hand with her eyes never leaving John's face. "It's a pleasure to meet you."

"The pleasure is mine, thanks for coming out tonight, Elsie." John takes her hand and holds it in both of is. Do I see a little spark lighting between them?

"And this is Janie…" I turn toward Janie.

"Hi, John, so you're gonna teach us how to kick your ass?" She smirks at him.

John laughs, "That's the plan, Janie. And I can tell already that I might want to watch my ass with you."

She extends her hand to shake his. "Nah, I wouldn't hurt you too bad. And thanks, it's nice to meet you."

"When you ladies are done with the paperwork, meet me in the room in the back. Marco, I'll tell Brian you're here."

John walks off, leaving the girls to stare open mouthed at his retreating six foot six very large, very sculpted, very hot figure, with his long black hair tied in a loose ponytail reaching between his shoulder blades. Yep, definitely American Indian.

"Holy fuck, I think I've just died and gone to heaven. Built like a brick shit house, good looking and nice too!" Elsie, I believe, has just called dibs on John.

"I know, and if he looks like that I can't wait to see the rest of them." Janie is obviously keeping her options open.

I turn to Scott to ask him if he's got some pens and I find him standing there with his mouth open looking at us. I start to laugh at him. "What,

Scott? Haven't you ever heard women admiring men before?"

He shakes his head slightly smiling broadly, "I guess not quite so passionately."

Janie looks at him, puts one hand on her hip, the other on the counter and leans forward closer to him. "Honey, that wasn't anything. You'd better pull your big boy pants up because it's about to get real in here. Now how about some pens so we can get on with the show, huh, handsome?"

Elsie and I look at each other. Marco is silent behind me. I can only imagine what's going through his head.

Elsie turns to me and says, "I love her, can I keep her?"

"Only on the weekends, El."

Marco rests his hands on my shoulder and whispers to both of us, "I think she's pretty fucking cool myself."

My face wants to split with the grin breaking my face in half. I didn't realize it was so important to me that Marco like my friends. They have been by my side through a lot over the past few years, more my pillars of strength than even I think they realize.

"Absolutely, Miss, I am at your service." Scott hands Janie three pens, smiling widely at her.

"I will keep that in mind Scott, and I'll let you know when I need you." She smiles at him giving him her biggest flirty smile, then turns to us. "Here ladies, let's get the preliminaries done so we can continue on to the main event. It looks like their warming up for us."

"These boys won't know what hit them when we're done with them." Elsie looks wickedly through the room to where John is standing.

Marco smiles shaking his head, "You ladies are incredible, you've got bigger balls than a lot of men I know."

Marco

I knew it was going to be interesting and Elsie and Janie certainly didn't disappoint me. John's tough but if he handles a room full of women like *this* all the time, then he is one hell of a man. These women are professionals but they don't hesitate to tell it like it is when it suits them.

The girls finish their paperwork and we head to the back room where their class will be given. John's already there and a few other students have arrived.

I kiss Elizabeth lightly on the cheek.

"I've got the cage in about a half hour, I'm gonna grab a bag to loosen up first and find Brian. There's something I've got to discuss with him."

Her eyes become concerned. "Is everything okay, Marco?"

"Yeah, baby, just something about work. Have fun, okay?" Another light peck on her beautiful cheek.

"I will and you'd better watch out. I'll be able to kick your ass after tonight, Mr. Bond."

"I look forward to seeing you do it, babe. I'm a sick fuck like that, if you haven't noticed." I wink at her.

"I've noticed, but I would definitely call it sexy. Now leave so we can get this started."

Elizabeth gently pushes me from the room and I hear the girls laughing with her.

There's a free bag. I drop my things near the wall behind the bag and pull my shirt over my head. I've got gym shorts on, like John, which is what the typical attire is in the gym unless you've got a gi, which is mostly worn only during Jiu Jitsu classes. I start some stretches to loosen up before hitting the bag. I glance to the girls' class and notice that John has started it. He begins the class like a traditional martial arts class, showing respect and bowing to the students and they bow in return. Looking around I see the gym has started to fill up. I'm glad we got here when we did. I start jabbing into the air before I let go on the bag, loosening up my shoulders, arms and back. I love this sport, it makes me feel alive and the adrenaline rush is incredible. The bag is hard. It's unforgiving to my punches, showing me no give, which makes me have no mercy. I glance back at the class and see Elizabeth standing in front of John. He's got his arms around her, holding her tight. What the fuck?! I freeze, watching, feeling anger beginning to boil inside me.

Brian's voice comes from behind me pulling me from my jealous melt down. "Calm down, Marco. It's just demonstration for the class."

"Hey man, how was your fight?" I ask him, trying to act like what I was watching didn't bother me.

"It was good, I put him down in the second round." He looks towards the girls' class and John's still got Elizabeth in his arms speaking to the class. "You *know* it's just demonstration, right dude?" he asks, his voice laced with humor.

"Yeah, it's good." I shake my head, looking down at the ground. What the hell's gotten into me? I'm possessive, yes, but not jealous.

Brian Daniels is the quintessential handsome blonde man with striking good looks, in his early thirties. He has a formal but casual way about him and the uncanny ability to immediately put someone at ease. I think Brian's family had old Southern money back in the day, way back, and those genes have never been bred out of the family. He is as much at home in the gym as he is in a tuxedo.

I change the subject. "So John said you think something's up. What is it?" I couldn't wait to talk to Brian since he called me yesterday. I wanted our conversation to be face to face because you can get so much more meaning looking at and examining a person's expressions.

"Marco, I don't know what's going on but there is absolutely nothing wrong with your paperwork and applications. Everything is spotless in them. It's something else." Brian is serious. There is concern in everything about his expression and the way he's holding his body.

Brian and John served their entire time together in the Marines side by side. John's got the dark intense native look and Brian is the other end of the spectrum. He's the pretty-boy blonde with perfect facial features and sharp blue eyes. I'm not sure exactly what went down but they saw some horrible things while they were deployed and some serious shit happened. Brian's family is from here and he grew up here. John moved to Wilmington when they got out of the service because Brian's the closest person he's got in his life. John works as a personal bodyguard for the movie studio when needed, which has kept him pretty busy the past few years. They are inseparable. If I didn't know better I'd think they were lovers.

"What the fuck is it, Brian?" This information has just confirmed what my instincts have been telling me. I've seen shit like this in the past and it never ended well. A lot of money was lost. Strange things can happen in situations like this.

"I don't know yet, dude, but I'm going to find out." Brian's expression is determined and hard, etched with the same nagging frustrations that have been plaguing me.

"Just be careful, Brian. I've seen things like this before, if it's what I think it is, (and, God, I hope it's not), people have gotten hurt. It's just money." My concern is real. There is a lot of money at stake in my project, and I have seen people disappear in the past when this amount of capital has been involved.

"Come on, man, you make it sound like organized crime and shit." Brian lets out a soft laugh but it doesn't reach his eyes.

"I have a feeling this is a lot more than just the guy on the street or the fat inspector sitting in his office eating doughnuts. I'm just telling you to be careful. Let me know if you find anything out but don't be too pushy, okay? I've got some calls in to some contacts in different areas as well." I am completely serious.

"Yeah, no problem, you too. Now come on, old man, let's see what you've got." He grabs the bag on the other side while his words attempt to lighten the mood, brushing off my words.

I put aside our business and goad his cocky ass right back. "I've got your old man right here, asshole!"

I start laying into the bag while looking back in the class, and I see that big clown still has his hands all over my woman. I freeze. Elizabeth is physically attracted to John. It's nothing that she's doing or saying; it's how her body is naturally reacting to his closeness, the way it moves, the way it pushes her breasts out searching for the contact in response to that attraction, the way her thighs come together wanting friction from that pulsing in her groin. And the obvious flush spreading from her cheeks down her chest. Could this week possibly get any shittier? Yeah, it could I realize, my words of warning to Brian echo back at me. I'd better be careful.

When I get out of the cage later on, Elizabeth is waiting for me. She has a very concerned look on her face. I assume she watched the match and didn't like what she saw, which doesn't surprise me. It gets pretty raw in the cage.

"Hi, baby, how was the first class?" I barely peck her on the cheek because I'm a disgusting sweaty mess.

"It was really good. Is cage fighting always like that? You guys look like you're trying to kill each other. You do this all the time?"

Her eyes are searching mine. She is really worried. I can't resist holding her. Her genuine concern touches me deeply. All my thoughts of her attraction to John are pushed aside by the caring on her face.

"Come here, baby." I wrap her in my arms. "Yes, we fight like this all the time. It's the way it's done. Don't worry, there are rules in place for safety and I don't fight outside the gym." I look into her face and I see she's relaxing somewhat. "Come on, let's go home and get cleaned up."

"Um, well…" She starts to stall. I turn and see Janie and Elsie standing where another couple of guys are sparring and they're looking back and forth from the fight to us. They smile innocently and wave.

"What is it, Elizabeth?"

"The girls were kind of hoping we could, the three of us, go have some girl time for a little while. I can catch a ride with them…" I can see in her face that she feels bad for blowing me off.

"Of course you can hang out with your friends. Let's get your things out of the car." With my arm around her shoulders we walk over to Janie and Elsie.

"So you guys are stealing Elizabeth, huh?"

Janie, I believe the one with the bigger balls out of the two, attempts to put me in my place again jokingly. "Yes, you've had her long enough. It's our turn for a little while."

"Besides," Elsie cuts in, "we want to talk about you and all the men in here."

She got me there. I can't help but laugh at her blatant honesty. "Well, as long as I'm top on the list, okay."

We walk towards the door to leave and John and Brian catch up to us.

"Ladies, I hope you enjoyed class, and if you have an opportunity to practice what we went over tonight that would be very beneficial. Elizabeth, throw Marco's ass around a little; he needs it," John says.

"I gave him a run for his money already tonight," Brian adds.

"Ladies, this clown is Brian. Elizabeth, you might remember him. This is Elsie…"

"Hi, Elsie, nice to meet you." Brian says smiling.

"Pleasure…" She doesn't have as much to say to Brian as she did John. I guess I know what team she's on.

"And this lovely young woman is Janie… Watch your ass; she'll have you kissing it in a minute," I say smiling at her.

"Well, Marco, it's nice to see you learn quickly. Now I know why Elizabeth keeps you around. It's very nice to meet you, Brian." She shakes his hand laughing lightly at my joke.

"Hi, Janie, I am so happy to see your superb intellect. You and I will be great friends." Brian drips charm but the icing on the cake is the panty-melting smile.

"It appears these two lovely women have caused me to be kicked to the curb. You guys want to grab some wings and catch some of the game?" I ask the guys.

"That's what she told you; she likes me better now," John says.

The jealousy I felt seeing him with his hands on her and her body's reaction to her natural physical attraction to him surges up inside me like a boiling geyser ready to blow. I push it back, refusing to acknowledge it. Nothing happened and I am probably overreacting.

"Poor Marco, I guess we can sit with the old man for a little while," Brian says and I laugh.

"All right, assholes, I'll be right back." I turn to walk Elizabeth out.

"Thanks John, see you in a couple of days. Brian it was good to see you again. Take care of my old man, don't let him fall and break a hip." Elizabeth has to get on that Old Man Marco band wagon.

"You too, babe?" I pretend mock surprise at her description of me.

"I'm just looking out for you, Marco."

John, Brian and I are sitting in Carolina Ale House in front of one of the many TVs hanging on the walls with beers and baskets of wings in front of us. Half of our attention is watching the football games; the other half is on our conversation.

"So who did you talk to, Brian, anyone at the building Inspectors office?" I ask. This could make a big difference.

"Yeah, there's a girl I went to high school with who has worked there since she got out of college. I went in the other day to check on one of my projects and we had lunch together." He smirks at me to tell me that's exactly how he planned it.

"Damn, dude, you fucked her to get information?" John asks him, shocked.

"No, I didn't fuck her. I have too much respect for her, although she did give me her number." He gives us that shit-eating grin and wiggles his brows. "She said she reviewed your paperwork herself, repeating over and over that she could lose her job for contradicting the inspector, and that everything was perfect."

"So, what do you think?" I ask him wanting his professional and personal opinion.

"What I think is that someone is fucking with you, or just fucking you. I think that's obvious. The questions now are who, what, how and why. Do you know anybody you've pissed off?"

"The only one I can think of is Santino but I don't think it's him."

John says, "I've already checked any connections to him and it's as if he didn't exist here. What was he here, two, maybe three months? I doubt he'd have that much clout to have government documents held, even rejected, for no reason." He looks directly at me all joking aside. "The person you've pissed off has to have big connections to not worry about federal indictments, along with pulling the little guys, like the inspector, down with him."

I look at him, not saying anything. He has just verbalized my biggest fears. And if that's the case I could be screwed. Everything I've worked my whole life toward could be gone just like that, as easily with only one phone call to the right person who has the connections to make it happen.

"But you thought that already, didn't you?" John can read me like a book.

They both look at me with the face of war. These guys and their military experience could be very helpful, or very detrimental.

Elizabeth

The girls definitely enjoyed their time at Evolution. They are wild over John, Brian, Marco and all the other guys at the gym. We stopped at Port City Java downtown on Front Street to grab some smoothies. The guys are having wings and beer and we've got smoothies. What happened here? But I bet our conversation is a lot more interesting than theirs.

"Oh. My. God! You were not lying when you said you found the hottest men in Wilmington! Janie, did you see all those sexy beasts?" Elsie says, still on the high from the gym.

"You're damn right I did! And girl, I didn't think that man could be any sexier than what I saw at the bar the night you met Marco, but he is one incredibly sexy man. Holy shit, I can only imagine the sex. Is he very kinky, Elizabeth?" Janie just speaks her mind.

She didn't not just ask me that.

"Yeah, Liz, how kinky is he?" Elsie's eyes are wide anticipating my answer, leaning in closer waiting for me to give them all of my and Marco's sordid details.

I know my entire head must be red. My scalp even feels like it's on fire, it goes all the way down my chest, and I can't help but giggle.

"You guys really want to know?" I'll just tell them a little.

"Hell yeah!" Both practically pounce on me at the same time.

I lean in a little closer. "Well, Marco's just moved into this condo on the waterfront. He's got the whole top floor. Friday night he made me undress in the elevator on the way up and he tied me to the bed when we got to his place. It was unfuckingbelievable!"

"Holy shit! Why can't I find a man that's kinky like that?" Elsie sits back in her chair and pouts. Her pretty little cupid lips are all puckered up.

"When are you going to tie him up, is what I want to know." Janie says with a sly grin spreading across her face. She's always been a control freak.

"Probably a lot sooner than he thinks," I answer wickedly.

They look at me with shocked expressions. We bust out laughing all at the same time.

Chapter Nine

Elizabeth

Tuesday morning, I decide the presentation for Marco is perfect and today I'll bring it to him. All of the information he needs was ready last week but I wanted a couple of days to review it just in case anything else pertinent came up that would be beneficial to his company and to his prospective buyers.

Mr. Kastanopoulis do you have any free time today? I'd like to come by your office.

For you, Ms. DiStefano, I am always available.

Why thank you, Sir, I'll be by after lunch.

Come by at lunch time and I can have you for lunch, baby.

Why Sir, do you condone mixing business with pleasure?

Only with you, baby, makes the perfect work day.

Get back to work Mr. Kastanopoulis. I'll see you around lunch time ☺.

My mouth is already watering just thinking about you ;)

That man is incredibly, delightfully wicked.

Marco's offices encompass an entire floor of the Union Station building in the newest, extremely polished section of the downtown business district. PPD, Pharmaceutical Product Development, and the posh brand new convention center are its neighbors. You could say it's the Empire State Building of Wilmington. It really does have artistic details to its design. The whole corner, top to bottom, is curved glass windows, with the street level entrance as its focal point and silvery steel embellishments throughout the rest of its façade.

When I walk through the clear glass double doors of KMD Enterprises emblazoned with company logo, I don't find anyone at the reception desk. The décor is modern design furniture of stainless steel, mahogany and glass against white walls and gray carpeting. It is serenely chic. I hesitate for a moment wondering if I should wait for someone to announce me to Marco.

Maybe she's out to lunch, I think to myself so I continue down the hallway. The walls are lined with portraits of different buildings and communities. I stop to read a couple of the notes below the photos. They are names and dates, obviously of previous projects of Marco's company. Some are magnificently simple while others are quite evidently multi-million-dollar spectacular designs.

I hear Marco's voice coming from down the hall. It's followed by a woman's voice. When I come up to the partially open door I almost stumble. Who the fuck is that?

Marco is sitting back in his chair with his elbows resting on the arm rests and those fingers of his steepled in front of his face. I am so glad I wore my black form fitting pencil skirt with the slit in the back rising up to the bottom of my cheeks, and a body-hugging cashmere sweater. The outfit is completed by my black "fuck me" Jimmy Choos.

The woman looks utterly ravishing from what I see. She's in red from the top of her long shiny coppery red hair to her immaculate dress, leaning with her perfect ass and back to me against the back of Marco's desk, standing directly in front of him. Her hands are holding the edge of the desk in a very familiar stance. I know instantly he's fucked her.

"Mr. Kastanopoulis…" I purr from the doorway.

He turns his head quickly to face me. Does he have a guilty look on his face? I can't tell.

"Hi, baby." You're damn right, hi, baby.

I take a couple of steps into the office as the mystery woman slowly turns her head to face me. Isn't this just great? She's even more beautiful from the front with her pale cream flawless skin, red pouty lips, deep green eyes and a *yeah, he's fucked me* smirk on her face. It has not escaped me that she hasn't budged at all. Okay, bitch, it's on. I know my movements have instinctively taken on their most sensuous moves, this is a cat fight in its own right.

Marco is standing in front of me now, with his hands on my hips and mine flat on his chest. The contours through his expensive dress shirt feel so good under my palms, my hands reflexively grasp his muscles wanting to feel them. Marco wears his sexuality like his custom-made suits, perfect, precise and completely seductive. He smirks wickedly and lowers his mouth to mine kissing me gently.

I notice the she-devil still hasn't moved. She finally speaks. "You must be Elizabeth."

"I am."

Do I sound triumphant? Maybe a little.

"Elizabeth, this is Liana. She's in charge of marketing and public relations."

I bet she's quite good at relations.

"Pleasure to meet you," I say in my sexiest *fuck you* purr. Looking back at Marco I continue as if dismissing her. "You wanted me for lunch, Marco?"

His hands are still holding me by my hips, one of his eyebrows rise at my comment and the corner of his mouth quirks up with an *interesting choice of words* look on his perfect face. Fortunately, She-devil, the name suits her much better than Liana, doesn't see it.

"Always, baby."

My eyes turn to Liana obviously saying, *What are you waiting for? Leave.*

She slowly pushes herself away from the desk and walks toward the door past us. She looks like Jessica Rabbit in the voluptuous flesh. Stopping in the doorway and turning her face back to Marco and me, she says to him with a slight smile, "I'll be here when you finish with her, Marco," and walks out.

Oh no, she didn't!

He walks to the door and closes it and I stand there a little dumbfounded. He turns to look at me.

"Bend over the desk, baby."

My emotions are all over the place after meeting She-devil. I want to ask Marco when the last time was he fucked her. My blood is boiling. Instead of walking to the desk I close the space between us, grab him with both hands by his shirt and pull his mouth to mine.

You are mine, I tell him with my kiss.

I am instantly on fire, my sex is pulsing, my breasts feel heavy and I just want to devour every inch of him and mark him as mine. All the anger, frustration and jealousy I am feeling is turning into intense arousal pouring from my mouth in to his. Holding on to his shirt, my mouth still claiming his, I push him toward the desk. A growl comes from deep in my chest.

When his ass hits the desk I come up for air.

"I want you to fuck me hard and fast right now, Marco." My voice is deep and raspy as I begin to unbutton his shirt. I want to dig my nails deep into his flesh and leave my mark on him.

"I had every intention of it, love. After watching another man have his hands on you last night then you just left me to go be with your friends, I thought I was going to lose my mind. I was going to wait for you at your place but I didn't want you to think I didn't trust you."

"Why, Mr. Kastanopoulis, are you jealous?"

"No, Elizabeth, I'm possessive. You're mine. And right now I'm going to show you."

Before I can blink, he's got me bent over the desk with his hands gliding up between my legs coming to brush over my labia. The touch sends jolts through my body. He slides one finger under my panties and through my quickly moistening folds as I hear the zipper of his trousers come down. My hips move with that finger, pushing against it hard, searching for relief. I'm flat on my stomach on the desktop opening up more to receive him. He roughly shoves my skirt up and yanks my panties off, ripping them from me with one pull. Grabbing my hips roughly, he pulls my ass back to meet him and he's filling me, the head of his cock slamming my cervix making me moan in sweet discomfort. I'm pounding back against him like a bucking bronco, my hunger so fierce. I want him everywhere, in every part of me. Nothing is enough.

"Please, Marco, more, please…" I beg him.

"I know, baby," he grits out through clenched teeth.

The slapping of him against my ass becomes fiercer and more demanding as I feel his hands dig harder into me, sending my passion skyrocketing. I feel like I'm an animal going wild with need.

He pushes into me hard holding me against the desk, buried to his balls inside me. I love having him still inside me like this, my walls clamping down on him, sucking him, pulling on him and oh, it feels so good. One of his hands slides through my juices then comes to rest on my ass. His thumb pushes into my other hole and the stars begin to explode behind my eyelids. I moan deep and low in satisfaction.

He begins to thrust again, slow, long, deep with his thumb holding me still.

"Touch yourself," he demands.

My hand comes around and moves slowly between my legs, my movements reflecting the delicious languor I'm feeling, totally intoxicated by the sensations of him filling me completely. It's so wonderful.

I feel him twitch inside me, and it starts to push me over the edge. My fingers scissor and wrap around his cock sliding in and out of me. I wish I could see it, the thought of that is so beautiful.

"Aahh, Elizabeth, that feels so good."

My sex responds to his reaction. My palm rubs my clit as my fingers rub his cock sliding in and out of me. I shatter, my orgasm slow and intense like the movements of his hips moving against me, into me, carrying me higher.

"Oh God yes, Marco…"

He pulls me against him as he stiffens, buried deep inside me. And I feel him spasming as his hot cum pours into me.

"Grrrrrrr. You. Are. Mine." he says, thrusting with each word. He growls, his hands gripping me so tightly I know I'll have bruises. And the thought makes me smile.

He pulls out and bends, placing a fast kiss on each ass cheek before he slaps them.

"I should spank you because of your behavior. But she deserved it. She's a bitch but she's good at what she does."

Do I say what I want to say, ask him what I want to ask him?

"And what exactly, or should I say who, does she do, Marco?" There, it's out, my jealousy, ugly as it is, put right there on the table. I don't care. He needs to know I know he's had a relationship with her and I have to know if he's still fucking her. No person, man or woman, has such intimate body movements or places themselves in such familiar proximity if there hasn't been intimacy.

"She just works for the company, Elizabeth. That's all, baby."

He is dismissing it, albeit gently, but he won't admit it, at least not yet. I'll let it go for now but this discussion hasn't even begun yet. But I wonder, do we have to formalize that our relationship is exclusive? We've said words in heated moments of passion, like he said just now, "you are mine," but are they sincere? Initially he picked me up in a bar, well on the street really, and it continued and evolved, but to what? Maybe it's time to make the parameters clear.

"Okay, Marco, we'll discuss it some other time." I look into his eyes and he knows I'm not stupid. But more importantly, I won't be made a fool of.

"Now, Mr. Kastanopoulis, would you like to have lunch first or would you like to see what else I've brought you?" I regain my composure and put on my best professional voice after smoothing down my skirt.

"Let's see what else you've brought me first, baby. Can I taste it?" This man is completely incorrigible. I think he could fuck constantly if it were possible.

"Only if you want to lick my computer screen." I turn my head searching the room, looking for a door to a bathroom because I'm starting to feel oozing seeping from me. "Where is your bathroom? Your cum is going to start running down my legs and I don't have panties, thanks to you." My hands are on my hips and I'm trying to have a stern expression on my face but I can't help laugh at his expression. It's too priceless.

"Really, can I see, baby?" He looks like a nine-year-old boy asking his best friend to see his cool new bike, and it's adorable.

"No, you can't see it. Where's the bathroom? It's coming out!"

He walks over to me and grabs my hand leading me toward a door in his office.

"This way, but I'm coming in with you."

"No you're not, Marco, and you're taking me to get some panties before we go to lunch!" As sexy as that sounds, I am going to try to push all of this out of me alone because I know we'll be in that bathroom for an hour if he comes in with me.

"Come on, baby!"

"No," I chuckle and slam the door on his pathetically handsome pleading face and turn to check out the bathroom. I am impressed. This is really nice. It's spacious for an office bathroom and he's had it decorated quite handsomely. It matches the theme throughout the rest of the offices.

I come out of the bathroom when I think there's nothing left inside me after I've cleaned myself as much as I could. He's on the phone with a very serious expression on his face that stops me in my tracks, waiting until he's done.

"Vinny, I'm not sure what the situation is at the moment. But I do know what it's not, which helps a great deal." His tone is authoritative but calm.

"I have an idea of what is being attempted and I've got some people checking to eliminate any other possibilities. And to see if anything surfaces." He listens to whomever he's speaking with.

"I'll look forward to hearing from you, and I'll let you know immediately as well when I find anything out."

"Okay sounds good." He listens for a moment and smiles genuinely. Apparently whoever he's talking to is a good friend. I can tell by his expression.

He looks at me and his smile widens. "I can't say that I miss Florida. I really like it here. Sorry, Vin." He laughs at whatever Vinny said to him.

"All right, it was good talking to you, talk soon. Bye." He hangs up and sits back in his chair a little more relaxed, looking at me.

I walk over and sit in the chair across from his big mahogany desk.

"Mr. Kastanopoulis, are you ready for me?" I tease him, taking out my computer to show him what I've put together for him according to his prospectus and requirements.

"Yes, please, Ms. DiStefano, I'm all yours." I can't help but wonder if that is true and to what extent.

I pull up the presentation and show Marco what he'll need according to his timeline, the expenditures, any additional recommendations and what we can do in terms of marketing to his prospective buyers and what advantages there will be having us partner with KMD Enterprises during the buying/selling process.

And all of a sudden it hits me like a blow to the head. She-devil is in charge of marketing. I've presented marketing strategies. Holy fuck! I would have to work with that bitch!

I try to keep my countenance in check with this new realization. I think to myself, *I'm a professional. I can keep things separate.* Then my inner bitch kicks in. *As long as that slut stays the fuck away from Marco and behaves herself, I can.* This has just turned into a very shitty situation.

"This is amazing, Elizabeth. You've presented aspects we hadn't considered in this particular project. And the long-range prospective buyer targeting will definitely be advantageous with marketing. I love it. Although," he says and looks at me with a disgusted look on his face, "we might need to change the timelines." That's all he says, no reasons, no maybe nots, nothing.

"Oh?" I ask him hoping he'll expand on his statement.

"Yes." What a stubborn man. Just the like the first time we met, he answered a question the exact same way and I reacted exactly the same, frustrated and dying for more.

I'm not going to push him for an explanation right now. I'll let him relax and maybe approach the topic in a more comfortable environment where he might not feel the stress of the situation so much.

"Let's go to lunch, baby. Any suggestions?" He brightens up a little bit but I think it's more of a mask. This is the second time I've heard him mention a difficult situation and it sounds very serious. What is bothering Marco is serious enough that he appears very concerned, I think mostly because he is uncertain of so many things about it.

"Why don't we go to that little place Fork & Cork? They're supposed to be all about local and organic products." I have decided to do my little part in taking his mind off the situation. "And, Mr. Bond." I come over to his side of the desk and sit on his lap, which is one thing I have not done to a man in a very long time. "Maybe I can drop my car off at my place first, drive with you over to the restaurant then you can drop me off at my apartment so I can pick up a pair of panties before I go back to work." I snake my arms around his neck and lean into him.

"I think that is a great idea, Miss DiStefano. You are perfectly dressed to dine with me."

He does not miss my intentions at all and by the look on his face he likes them…a lot.

When we leave the office the receptionist is at her desk but She-devil is nowhere to be seen.

"Christine, this is my girlfriend, Elizabeth DiStefano. Elizabeth this is Christine, she puts up with my bullshit and helps keep me together."

"Don't worry, Christine, his bite is not bad. He's really a big softy." I laugh, looking up at Marco."

"Shush, Elizabeth, then everyone will think I'm a push over." He laughs with a playful sparkle in his beautiful dark eyes. God, this man should be illegal. His natural charm is so alluring and disarming, it's like the poppy fields in *The Wizard of Oz*. There is no way anyone is immune to it.

"Nice to meet you, Elizabeth. Enjoy your lunch, you two." She smiles and I instantly know she's a really nice person and that she doesn't take shit. Perfect for Mr. Tough Guy Marco. And the She-devil.

Fork & Cork is a small nouveau hippie diner, if that makes any sense, and is usually always packed. Today is no different. We have to wait a while for a table but the weather is great and I'm definitely not in any hurry to get back to the office.

About halfway through our lunch while Marco periodically strokes my leg, placing his hand on my lap, touching me in some way so that I'm constantly aware of the state of my undress, I ask how the project is going. And I wait almost holding my breath for an answer.

He sighs heavily, probably deciding on how much he's going to say, before answering.

"The building department has tied up my permits," he answers flatly.

I'm not well versed on the construction industry but I know a little about it. An ex-boyfriend had a painting company and I learned some things about it listening to him.

"That doesn't sound good." I give him a little more line hoping he'll bite.

"No, it sucks big time actually. After a certain point, every day will cost thousands of dollars on a project this size. And the biggest headache is they won't give me a reason. I don't know why." Marco sounds totally disgusted and he has every right to be.

"And what do you think, Marco?" I'm going in for the kill. He needs to get it out.

He looks me in the eye and leans in close. "You know, Elizabeth, I think someone is trying to bankrupt me to make me pull out of the project. I can't figure out who and why, especially here." He shakes his head completely confused and frustrated. "Someone wants to destroy me."

The reality of the possibility suddenly takes on a massive life of its own, dark and foreboding and immense. The power of it fills the room with a feeling of dread and finality falling on us with its heavy weight, as real as he and I.

"Wow, Marco. That's incredible. Not impossible, unfortunately, but really incredible. I wish I could say that couldn't happen because we both know that it can." I did not expect this. This is huge and unless he's got some big connections he's totally screwed if this is what's going on. My heart breaks for him. I want to hold him, give him some comforting words but Marco is a very proud man and he would abhor pity. I wouldn't want him to mistake my comfort for that.

"Don't worry, baby. This isn't my first day on the playground with the bullies. I might be the new kid in town but I'm also the baddest." That sexy powerful man is back winking at me telling me he's going to take this guy down. Go get him, babe!

Back at the office, after I go home and put on a pair of panties, there's a ton of emails to be answered, quotes to be done and phone calls to be returned. I sit back in my chair looking at everything wondering where to start. There is no way I can say my job is boring.

About four o'clock Carol comes strolling in. If it wasn't for her I don't know how I would feel about working here. She makes me like it.

"So how was the appointment with Marco?" She smirks at me. There is no way she could possibly know we had sex in his office!

"It was great. He was impressed with what I showed him, loved everything and all the ideas for long range buyer marketing. Remind me to talk to you about their marketing bitch." I pause reflecting on the news Marco revealed. "But there might be a situation."

She moves to the edge of her seat. That casual mood is gone.

"What's wrong?" The look on my face tells her it's serious. She becomes worried, Carol probably thinks he's gotten other quotes from a different company and he's shopping around.

"It's nothing like that. But I need you to not say anything to anyone." I move closer to her. "His permits have gotten held up in the building department and they've given him no reason for it. He thinks this could be really bad. If they get held up for an indefinite period of time, it would bankrupt him. After a certain point it will cost the company thousands of dollars every day. This could be really, really bad." I don't hide the deep concern I have about this situation.

"Oh my God, I see what you're saying." She sits back in the chair and takes the information in before she continues. "In normal situations that would sound absurd but with the type of project that Marco's company is doing, and the magnitude of it, it's completely plausible." She looks up at me after internally sorting through all of the angles. "That could be a very real possibility."

"I know and so does he. Please don't say anything to anyone. He's investigating the situation. The only reason he told me was because we might need to change the timelines on what we're doing for him." I'm torn now as to whether it was okay for me to tell Carol but I know if there is anyone I can trust, it's her.

"Don't worry, honey, I won't. And don't worry about Marco. He didn't get to where he is at his young age by being naïve. I'm sure he's got some secret weapons in his back pocket." She stands to leave winking at me with her little comment. She is absolutely right. I definitely feel better.

Chapter Ten

Elizabeth

Halloween falls on a Friday this year. I'm not really a fan of it, I never have been even as a child but it's a big party night. Although I am so far from being a partier it really is good for me to get back out in society sometimes. I don't know why actually but it seems like the right thing to do. I don't have to meet Elsie at the party until eight o'clock so I can take my time getting ready. She didn't tell me until tonight that the party is at the Wilmington Hilton Riverside, where Marco and I spent our first night together. That made me miss him. This is the first Friday we haven't been together in a long time, since Santino sent those allegations to my company.

Santino…holy shit! A thought creeps into my mind. Could it be that he is the one compromising Marco's project? This is a huge undertaking. Does he have the resources to do this? He was here just a few months and the only people I know of that he communicated with when he was here are my landlord Mr. Jones and my family. Is there anyone who could help him? Mr. Jones and Adriana. No. Not. Possible. But the idea gets bigger and bigger in my mind.

I'm standing at the bathroom pedestal sink with the straightening iron in one hand and the hair spray in the other, wearing only the bustier and a pair of thongs, staring at but not seeing my reflection in the mirror. The thoughts flow and evolve in my mind.

Since my dad died last year my sister has been half crazy with depression and she just might possibly be capable of anything, especially if Santino gave her even the slightest idea he is interested in her and wants to be with her. But would Santino do something like that? Is he capable of it? I don't know. The man I thought I knew wouldn't be, but I didn't think the man I loved would do a lot of the things he did. And one thing I've learned over the past few years is that you can't really and truly know anyone. Circumstances make people do things you would never dream they'd do.

What I have also come to realize is that I am absolutely content with my life and I no longer wonder if this is all there is. Most importantly I am content with myself, who I am, where I am and what I am doing. I have found what is important to me and what is just bullshit. What brings real pleasure and what will leave me feeling empty. Life has been a turbulent ride these past few years. Those I trusted betrayed me and I let down those I should have trusted and those who trusted me. One of the biggest things I've learned is that I have to forgive myself after truly feeling remorse for the wrongdoings I've done. It is then I am really free from the bondage of hate and anger toward others and I can forgive them as well.

And this freedom has allowed me to open myself up to living again. I think about Marco and smile at the thought of how lucky I am. Lucky because he didn't run, didn't think I was too much trouble with all my baggage and secrets. I don't know what it is that we have yet but I don't have to. Not right now. I know it's okay to appreciate the moment. Because if you don't, it will be gone.

What I feel for Adriana is pity. I feel sorry for her. Yes, I'm still angry with her, which is what's holding me back from forgiving her. At times I really do try because she's alone and she can't handle it. Which makes me believe that she would, if given the opportunity, be the first to approach Santino and proposition him to be with her. God knows she was insinuating it while he was here. And if he took that opportunity, is he capable of doing this to Marco?

There is no way for me to know.

Unless I call him.

Not yet. Let's see what Marco's people come up with first.

My phone buzzes with a text. Marco's face lighting up the screen pulls me from my thoughts and my up-and-down emotions.

Hi baby, you busy?

I miss him already, so much that I want to call off this party with Elsie. But I know I can't do that.

Hi Sexy, getting ready for the party. I miss you.

This is the first time I've ever really told him anything with personal sentiment. After all we've been through together already, the realization is shocking.

Me too, a lot. Don't be surprised if I come to you in the middle of the night. Not because of sex, but because it hurts to be away from you.

I'll be waiting for you in my dreams <3

Call me if you need me before then, love. And remember what I said about making sure I'm the only one the girls in your bustier are formally introduced to.

Always. Missing you, bye.

Until later baby, bye. M

This man makes my heart, body and soul sing…at the top of their lungs.

Seven o'clock, I'd better start my makeup. Finishing up my hair, I give it a final nod of approval. I've smoothed it and put some big loose curls in it. I've teased the top and loosely pinned that, pulled back two loose braids from the front and brought them together low in the back, weaving a gold chain through them.

The gown Elsie got for me to wear is drop-dead stunning with a little bit of a train and wide flowing arms. It's a deep-green velvet with a fitted bodice and gold trimming. The bodice is cut like a bustier pushing my breasts up so I don't think there will be a lot of bending over tonight. She was also able to find shoes from the wardrobe department, I think, or maybe they are one of her crazy finds at vintage shops, covered in gold fabric and tied with a bow in the front. Elsie also hooked me up with a brushed golden crown with semi-precious stones in a weave pattern that is simple but elegant along with matching big antique-looking jewelry of gold, rubies, emeralds and pearls. When I'm finally dressed in everything, I feel like I've just stepped out of a medieval castle. Elsie and I are wearing masks. She's Cat Woman and she made the costume herself, the Halle Berry version. She looks so incredibly hot in it, I'm relieved she will keep all of the attention on her tonight. Because she gets to wear a mask, I opted to wear one as well. Mine is a soft golden lace mask that ties behind my head with a ribbon. I've always wanted to wear one out. I'm not sure why, maybe because of the thrill of sensual anonymity it lends to the wearer and the viewer.

I've arranged for a car to pick me up tonight. I'd rather not drive just in case I decide to drink. I could walk but my feet would be killing me in an hour or so after I'd gotten there. It's an absolutely beautiful fall night. The temperature is still fairly comfortable and the wind is calm. The stars look so much closer and crisper and clearer at this time of year. From the car I see the Little Dipper and Big Dipper, Orion, and Mars. I used to wonder who else was looking up at the stars at the exact moment I was in a different part of the world. Was my soul mate standing there with his face tilted up to the sky wondering where I was? Thoughts like that still cross my mind, not necessarily the soul mate thing but the vastness of the universe and what we are when we are out of this body, when we are our true selves, our souls.

The drive there is only a few minutes as it's not far from my apartment. I decide I'd better text Elsie and ask her to wait for me in the lobby so we can walk in together.

Hi El, wait for me in the lobby, I don't want to walk in alone, yeah, I know I'm chicken shit.

No problem, I would be a bad date if I didn't, I'm almost there, c u soon ☺

When the car pulls up to the front door of the Hilton there are so many beautiful people coming and going dressed in elaborate costumes. And I thank God Elsie helped me with mine. Of course there are going to be beautiful people here; the party is being given by a movie production company. I think of the night I pulled up to this door just like this with the man who seduced me with just three words, and I didn't even know his name. The memories, all of them, flood me and my breath catches in my throat sending shivers through me. Tonight I let myself out of the car and I walk through those doors alone. Elsie is waiting for me just inside. She looks so incredibly seductively hot in that shiny black vinyl second skin and those sinfully sexy over-the-knee platform boots.

"Hi, Liz, you look incredible! Perfect, understated royal elegance." She beams at me.

My jaw hit the floor when I saw her. "Oh my God, El, you are the sexiest thing I've ever seen!"

She puts her hand on her hip, hoisting it up as she bends her knee and the light reflecting off the black vinyl looks like a wave of black water rippling over her sleek little body.

"Yeah, I look pretty fucking hot, don't I?" She smirks with her perfect red pouty lips and winks at me.

"Extremely, my dear, now let's go make those men drool over you." I hook my arm through hers and we find our way to the party, our heads held high and our asses naturally swaying because we know we look good.

The reception rooms are downstairs. There's a court jester and a police man, who is pretty hot and is probably someone in costume I presume, standing at the doorway.

"Good evening," the officer says, "welcome to A Night of Decadence and Dance. Do you have your invitations?"

"Yes we do," Elsie answers and reaches into her bodice pulling out the invitation. She smiles naughtily at him as she hands it over.

"And your name?" he asks with an obviously pleased smile on his face.

We could get into so much trouble tonight. I know it already.

"It's Elsie James, officer." She flirts with him.

"And is there anything else tucked in there, Elsie?" He is almost drooling over her. The poor guy is doomed.

"I don't think you need to worry about that. Hi Elsie, hi Elizabeth," says a familiar voice behind us.

We jerk our heads at the sound of that voice I know belongs to John. He's shirtless in all his beautiful six-and-a-half-foot glory, dressed in only suede fringed Indian style pants with his long black hair falling loosely over his wide shoulders and back. When my gaze finally makes it to his face, I see mixed emotions passing over it as he looks back and forth from Elsie to me. His eyes don't quite make it to our faces.

Mr. Officer clips in. "Do you know these two beautiful women?"

John looks at him. "Yes, and I'll be taking care of them tonight." There is an obvious double meaning there, but what exactly it is, I'm not sure.

The poor kid looks like his favorite toy has just been taken from him.

John stands in front of us to escort us in, extending both of his arms to us so we can loop ours through his. This is an excellent way to make an entrance to a costume party, on the arm of a huge shirtless gorgeously sexy Indian.

"Come, ladies, I'll escort you in, but I can't stay with you all night. I'm working."

Elsie is all flushed and timid smiles. She definitely has the hots for John and who can blame her?

"Oh, what are you doing?" she asks him, her voice a little high, and I want to giggle at her obvious shyness.

"I work personal security for the studio and because there are some big shots here they called me in. Brian's here too. They needed an extra pair of hands and since we still have our military clearance they brought him in tonight as well."

"You were in the service, John?" I ask him.

"Yeah, Brian and I were in the Marines together. And what's up, Elizabeth, no Marco tonight?" He turns and looks at me once we're inside, letting our arms go and facing us with his huge arms crossed in front of his chest.

"No, I'm Elsie's date tonight."

"I doubt highly you have trouble finding dates, Elsie." It's hard to tell if he's flirting with her but one thing is for sure. He can't keep his eyes off her. I don't think anyone will be able to in that black vinyl second skin of hers.

"It's the good dates that are a problem, John," she answers a little shyly. Elsie, shy? That is definitely a first.

"Enjoy yourselves, ladies, but behave, okay? I don't want to have kick anyone's ass tonight." He looks at us sternly but smiling. I have a feeling there is sincerity in that statement.

"Okay, Daddy," I say playfully, rolling my eyes.

"I'll find you later," he says before he leaves, looking us both in the eye.

"My God, Liz, that man makes me ooze from every part of my body," Elsie says as she fans herself when John is out of earshot.

"I know. He's just so much delicious man."

We finally look at the room before us. And we're both in silent awe of it. The studio must have brought in set designers because this is beautiful. It's done in a combination of glamour and spooky with the entire space cloaked in black and gold, smoke and bubbles, mummies, skeletons, bats, tombstones and everything else you can think of that symbolizes tonight's theme. They also hired the best DJ in Wilmington, DJ Milk from Pravda Club. I can only guess what he's getting paid when typically, a DJ makes about $400 a night. It's an open bar but this crowd is full of beautiful people. I doubt highly there will be any risk of drunken barroom brawling. Even some of the actors from *Under The Dome* and *Sleepy Hollow* are here along with some local celebrities like TV and radio personalities and high-ranking politicians and officials. Anyone who would have a significant affiliation with the movie studio, or who is just a big name in the area, is here.

And at that precise moment I see the newest big shot of Wilmington, Mr. Marco Kastanopoulis, dressed as a gangster in a black double-breasted suit with big shoulders and a black hat. And who is standing close to him sliding a hand sheathed in an elbow-length white silk glove? She-devil Liana dressed as…I can't fucking believe it…Jessica Rabbit, the Hollywood S-curl flowing hairstyle, the long body-hugging red dress with the heart-shape neckline over her breasts that are pushed up so far they're almost pouring out. This is too…perfect? Do I look a gift horse in the mouth or do I take this opportunity to watch Marco for a while to see exactly how he acts with her? Why thank you, Fate, I think I shall accept your little gift, quite appreciatively as well.

"Do you see who I see, Liz?" Elsie elbows me lightly, obviously having seen Marco the same time I did.

"Yep."

"And do you see who he is, um, with?" she asks hesitantly.

"Yep." Silence. A little more silence. Elsie is apparently waiting for me to say something. "That is, as I affectionately call her, She-devil, otherwise known as Liana. She's in charge of marketing and public relations at his company." Another pause. "And I know he's fucked her." That last statement falls like a boulder on top of us over the loud thumping music.

"Yeah, I thought so too, but I don't think in a while, not from the way he's reacting to her. He looks like he's got a boundary line drawn and she is obviously trying to break through it." Elsie's brows are pulled together behind her black vinyl mask showing the workings of her observation.

"You're probably right, but I think I won't make my presence known quite yet, just in case. Do you agree, my darling date?" I turn to look at her with my chin up, ready for an interesting evening.

"I think that's a great idea, darling. Come let me get you a drink. We both could use one. And I'm sure the camera guy, the young one who fell in love with you, is here. You can always be a cougar tonight, babe." I can see her wink under her mask.

"Hmm, I could, couldn't I, or I could see what a Marine is made of. Have you seen Brian around?" I am so full of crap.

Although both Brian and John are hot as hell and each the epitome of a man's man, there is no one I want but Marco. And if I catch him even doing the slightest thing that could be construed as suggestive with that woman I will walk right over there and cut his dick off, put it in my pocket and walk calmly away.

Elsie laughs out loud as she leads us to the bar.

"No, not yet but I'm sure he'll come around very, very soon. It could be fun."

And a thought occurs to me. "You know John knows Marco is here, and he didn't tell us."

"Yes, but I didn't see him run over to Marco and let him know we're here either," Elsie points out, ever the devil's advocate.

"I suppose you're right." But it doesn't escape me that he is Marco's friend, both he and Brian, and that's where his loyalties would be.

Yes, it's going to be a very interesting night indeed.

The party is packed, the music is fantastic, and there is a buffet catered by one of the best organic local restaurants in the area. Elsie and I have kept an eye on Marco and Liana from the bar, which is a good distance across the room, sipping on killer smoky drinks. They literally have smoke coming out of them.

It doesn't appear as if Marco showing any intimate familiar interest in Liana. I didn't think he would. He might be kinky but he's honorable, but she is most certainly putting it out there that she wants him and would take him right here in this room full of people if that's what he wanted. I can't help but see, along with everyone else who isn't blind, that she's rubbing her perfect curves all over him every chance she gets. Initially I wanted to go over there and rip every strand of natural red hair out of her head but then I just started feeling sorry for her, that she is that easy she has to beg for it even though it's clear he doesn't want her.

It looks like Liana is working the room, chatting with different people and bringing them over to Marco to introduce him. It seems she's making connections for him or for them. Some he just shakes hands with and a few words are passed. Others sit with him for a while and chat. There is another guy there, a handsome casual and relaxed guy dressed up like a biker. He doesn't look like a biker type though, the complete opposite actually, very laidback and nonchalant. He must be an associate of Marco's; he appears to be part of their team.

"What do you think, Elsie?" I lean my head over to her and ask as we're leaning casually against the bar as if we're watching some kind of sporting event or just waiting for a bus, not taking my eyes off them.

"I think this is totally a working gig. The bimbo's been bringing people over to His Highness and he's been holding court. The other dude is his sidekick. You see how they take turns talking? They work off each other." She looks up at me pulling my attention from the scene I've been intently observing. "I think it's all good here, babe. We can relax."

I let out a breath of relief. Thank God, I would have hated walking in on something. I'm afraid to admit how much I care for Marco, afraid that I let myself fall too far too fast with blinders on, not only giving him my body but my heart and soul as well. And the last time I did that my life was shattered. I'm not about to let anybody do that to me again, not even Marco.

"Time to really start partying, Elizabeth, let's dance," Elsie shouts at me over the music and pulls me onto the dance floor. We're moving to Rhianna and Chris Brown teasing each other in the song *Birthday Cake* when a pair of arms come and rest on my shoulders.

"Hey, Elizabeth!"

I recognize that man's voice, so I look at Elsie for a clue. She has a cat-that-ate-the-canary kind of smile on her face. Well then, at least I know he's safe and not some douchebag. I think. I turn my face slowly to see it's the young camera guy from the *Safe Haven* set Elsie was talking about earlier. I turn in his arms and hug him back. It really is good to see him, and I'm happy he is still definitely his adorably sexy self with his gauges and tasteful tattoos. He asked me out for drinks every weekend during the movie project and I never went until we wrapped. We had a couple of drinks one Friday night, and he told me how attracted he was to me and how much he wanted to make love to me. The funny thing is one afternoon before that after he'd come into the office for something, I can't remember what it was, I'd gotten this crazy thing in my head. I knew he liked me and I have to be honest I was attracted to him as well. I kind of started this poll in our department. "Who do you think is good in bed from the crew?" I guess I was feeling a bit aroused from all of the sexual energy going on between him and me. No one picked him, except me of course, and I was surprised because he definitely was and still is sexy.

"Hi, Damien!" He's dressed up tonight as a doctor and I almost find it hysterical.

"Don't tell me your name is Dr. Love." I laugh at him.

"I just want to be your gynecologist, Elizabeth, always have," he replies with a devilish little grin.

I sense him before I hear him.

"She is not in need of your services, doc."

I can feel him whenever he is close, pulling me to him with this electricity between us. Damien and I both turn our heads to look at Marco. He looks angry standing there with his jaw tense and his fists clenched.

"Come on, baby, dance with me."

I can hear Elsie shout to Damien as we walk away, "Boyfriend," in explanation.

Marco takes my hand and leads me away from Elsie and Damien, turns me around and pulls me to him holding me close as Chris Brown exclaims he wants to fuck Rhianna. He places a hand flat and low on my abdomen, moving my hips as his other hand pulls one of my arms around him. I begin to move, grinding, bumping, stroking him. It's obvious that's what we want to do to each other right now; angry, hair-pulling, teeth-biting, nail-digging rough sex. The frustration and jealousy between us come out in this sexual dance of possession and there is no mistaking we belong to each other.

The next song is Nicole Sherzinger's and Fifty Cent's *Right There*. He answers my push, and I move into his pull, I belong to him and he's mine, and he knows how to work me, very, very, very well.

When the song is over Marco pulls me from the dance floor and leads me to the bar.

"Give us two of your specials tonight," Marco tells the bartender. Then he turns to me, mouth clenched and eyes glaring.

"Who was that and why did he have his hands on you, Elizabeth?" The anger has simmered just a little but has not disappeared. *Good, how do you like a taste of your own medicine?*

"That was an old friend I worked with a couple of years ago," I say smoothly and noncommittally. He can think whatever he'd like. I'm not giving him anymore, not until he tells me what I want to know about She-devil. "I didn't know you would be here tonight."

His eyebrow shoots up in surprise and I can't help but smile. I try to make it innocent instead of letting the satisfaction I'm feeling show.

"And is my being here creating a problem for you?"

Oh, he is getting pissed again.

"Actually I had wondered that very thing myself. Are you here with anyone?"

Realization slowly shows on his sinfully striking face.

"I told you that I was going to accept a business invitation. I am not the only one that is part of that company. Liana and Steve are here as well."

I continue to look at him, waiting for more.

"Elizabeth, I'm not fucking her," he says adamantly.

"Fantastic. Then are you having a nice time?" I coo at him. He has removed his jacket and is wearing suspenders. I slide a finger slowly up one of them, over his shoulder and lean into him raising my face to his as I do.

"It's fine, but will be much better if you keep guys from touching you. It makes me insane," he says pulling me tightly to him, molding me to him as his mouth takes mine possessively putting his final claim of ownership on me.

When we come up for air I tell him breathlessly, "I've got to get back to my date."

He looks up over my head still holding me to him and searches the room. His eyes stop and a slow grin spreads across his face.

"I think Elsie's in very capable hands, baby, two sets as a matter of fact. I know they will take very good care of her."

It sounds like he knows a secret that he's not quite willing to share so I follow his eyes and stop when I find Elsie. Both Brian and John are with her, one on each side, looking as if they are…claiming ownership of her as well. And Elsie looks very willing to give it. Is there something happening here? I look back to Marco and he just shrugs, smiling innocently and not saying a thing.

"We did come together. I should get back to her."

"Okay, as long as it's understood you will be coming home with me and when we get there I'm going to tie you up and make that sexy fucking body of yours all pink for making me crazy. Got it, love?" His face is close to mine, his tone low, sensual and commanding.

My body trembles in excitement starting from the clench of my sex and spreading out all through me, finally making me pull my lower lip between my teeth in anticipation. He stares at my mouth as his lips part slightly.

"Give it to me." His voice is quietly demanding.

I release my lip. I stare into his face. He's eating my mouth with his eyes, and after a moment his tongue strokes it before sucking it in and nibbling on it, making me moan with desire.

"Go now, Elizabeth, or I'm going to fuck you right here in front of all these people."

And that is exactly what I would love. I turn to go back to Elsie and out of the corner of my eye I see She-devil through a group of people standing against the wall at the corner of the bar watching Marco and me. She has the most venomous and hateful look on her face. If looks could kill we would both be dead. It sends a feeling of foreboding through me.

Elsie and I are at the bar talking and laughing about how ridiculous the divas are when they are drunk, making complete asses out of themselves.

"It seems we've missed an inside joke, Brian. What do you think they're laughing at?" comes John's deep rumbling voice from behind me and Elsie. We jump, grabbing each other, looking as if we've been caught being absolutely up to no good.

"Jesus, guys, you scared us half to death. You shouldn't go sneaking up on people like that," I tell the two snickering testosterone brothers.

"You can find out what's really going on if no one knows you're coming, Elizabeth. And from the way you two were carrying on, I'd bet it was no good." John, smirks at us.

"I bet there's a lot more than meets the eye," Brian says mischievously looking at Elsie and causing a blush to spread across her face and up under her mask.

"I would definitely have to agree with you," John says as his gaze holds on Elsie a heartbeat too long. Ooh, I think this is going to get interesting.

Iggy Azalea fills the air with her popping sexy lyrics in *Beg For It*. Elsie jumps up from her position against the bar shouting, "Come on, we're all dancing!" grabbing the guys.

"We can't, Elsie, we're working but you two go ahead and we'll be there in spirit."

Elsie is almost jerked back like a rubberband, she didn't budge John or Brian when she pulled on their hands.

"Yeah, Cat Woman, you go ahead, we'll have fun watching," Brian says, quite the naughty boy.

We pop and grind on the dance floor, laughing and moving. Damien joins us on the dance floor with a friend of his. That little tattoo boy can really move for a grunge kid. After three more songs, I see Mr. Grumpy Bear Marco giving me the death glare from the edge of the dance floor. When he catches my eye, he motions me to him with his finger. I excuse myself and meet him by the bar.

"Can I have a bottle of water please?" I say to the bartender.

"Have fun with John and Brian?" Marco asks.

What the hell is that supposed to mean?

"They snuck up on us and scared us. I guess they were just checking up to see if we were having a good time."

"Come on, Elizabeth, I want to introduce you to someone if you can tear yourself away from Dr. Love over there."

I open the bottle and swallow half of it in one gulp and look at Marco like, *You've got to be kidding me!*

"Marco, may I remind you that this is a party and I have friends, believe it or not, and some of them are male. We are just having a good time." I lift the bottle to finish it off.

"I'm sorry, you're right, I'm being unreasonable. I just wish this wasn't a business function for me."

Aw, he feels left out. I'm so thoughtless. He wanted to spend tonight with me and I knew he was hurt the first time I told him I was going to be at a party tonight with Elsie.

"No, it's my fault. I'm sorry, but not for hanging out with my friends. I understand what you are saying though. I'd love to meet this person, let's go."

He leads me to this associate of his, placing his hand possessively on the small of my back. It turns me on every time he does, sending electric shocks coursing through my body.

We come up to Liana and another gentleman. They turn toward us, Liana smiles a very fake camera-ready grin and the guy at first glance seems nice and very laidback. But looking a little closer, I see his eyes are very sharp, not missing a thing.

"Elizabeth, this is Steve Mikelson, my right-hand man. His father was one of the original members of the company when it began."

Steve shakes my hand, taking it in both of his big calloused ones. That surprises me, from first glance I wouldn't think he'd have working man's hands. There is something about this guy that I can't put my finger on though, his relaxed disposition is not the man I see in his eyes.

"Elizabeth, it's great to meet you. I was wondering when Marco was going to bring you out of hiding and stop being so selfish with you."

The charm oozing from Steve is impressive and immediately disarming. He has a talent for quickly putting people at ease. I see Liana out of my peripheral vision and I can tell her nostrils are flaring. Whoa, She-devil, pull those claws in. It's very difficult for me to believe that her strong animosity toward me is jealousy alone. A grown, sane, intelligent woman wouldn't act like this just from an attraction to a man. Yes, it is Marco, but still, this is extreme.

"It's a pleasure to meet you too, Steve. Thank God Marco has you. I'm sure he'd be a mess alone."

Steve's smile is genuine, almost boyish.

"Well, someone has to keep things working." He laughs and everyone joins in.

I look through the crowd and see Brian watching us from across the room. He has a serious expression on his face, but I suppose that's normal for someone working private security with such high-profile people in attendance. I look toward the other side of the room and John is standing stone still as well looking out over the crowd. I envision them going out on some covert operation with guns and grenades strapped across their chests and knives tied to their legs. I can certainly see the military men standing here in this room regardless of what they're wearing.

"So you and Marco have worked together a while?" I ask Steve.

"We pretty much came down from New York together. The man who started the company, Vinny D'Angelo, is an old friend of my dad's. That's how my family ended up in Florida, I guess. Marco too." He looks at Marco and he nods in agreement.

"So how do you like Wilmington? It's quite an impressive project, I must say," I ask him, genuinely curious to know how this good-looking playboy likes our little city. I wonder if he feels like a fish out of water.

He smiles crookedly and answers, "It's been very, very accommodating, I couldn't have asked for better."

Interesting answer but I smile and nod. No one knows what someone else is into and who am I to judge?

I turn in the arm Marco still has circled around my waist. I stopped worrying about Liana a long time ago. I've decided I'm not wasting any more of my time and energy on that woman. Unless she crosses that line, she doesn't exist to me. Marco looks down at me and kisses my forehead.

"Are you having a nice time, Elizabeth?"

"Yes, Marco, and it was really a nice surprise to see you here. Even if we're not 'together', it's nice knowing you're here. I missed you."

His eyes twinkle and it gives me butterflies in my stomach. "Me too, baby."

He pulls me closer and places another kiss on the top of my head. I feel him sigh deeply against my chest and it warms me inside.

"Marco." Liana's icy voice breaks our intimate moment. "Don't you think you should stop being distracted and focus on what's important?"

The hair on the back of my neck has just stood on end and I turn to face her. "My dear, I think it would behoove you to pay attention to how you present yourself rather than your assumptions on what's best for others."

Her eyes widen in disbelief that I basically put her in her place. I turn back to Marco, my back rigid as I try to hold on to my composure. Why he keeps her around if he's not fucking her is beyond me. We will definitely have to talk about this.

"Liana." Marco's voice is strained. "I will be the one to decide what's important for me and I suggest you remember that." The fight to keep his temper under control shows only in the tight muscle of his jaw.

The color drains from Liana's face and her expression pinches. She's biting her tongue and it's killing her.

"I should get back to Elsie. She'll think I dumped her."

The fact of the matter is I'm not feeling exactly comfortable with Steve and Liana, especially after her snide comment.

"I'll come over in a little while. I've got some other people to talk to, okay baby?"

Yeah, to get away from these two.

"I can't wait," I say looking up into that face. I see the real man behind that mask he wears for the world, the one that says cool, powerful, calm, confident and maybe a hint of danger if you cross him. I see endearing, kind, gentle and compassionate as well. Maybe so much so that he's afraid of getting hurt.

Chapter Eleven

Elizabeth

We are in his condo in the bedroom. The lights are low and there is soft classical music playing in the background. I didn't know how erotic classical music could be until Marco took me to the symphony at Thalian Hall. That was the most sensually seductive night of my life, beginning at the restaurant and continuing all the way through the evening until I feel asleep. I know that whenever I think of that night for the rest of my life, my body will react with a deep primal need that only Marco could have elicited and satisfied over and over again, taking me to that point of maddening hunger then making me shatter in total bliss.

He comes up behind me and places his hands on my shoulders with his fingertips touching my throat as he gently caresses my face with his, breathing in deeply so I feel the rush of air against my sensitive skin.

"I'm going to pull all of your hair back, my queen. I don't want it in the way tonight," he says softly in my ear as one of his hands removes the crown from my head and places it on the table.

"In the way for what?" I ask quietly.

"I'm going to flog you tonight, Elizabeth, tantalize every cell in your skin, making it sing. But before that I'm going to put the ben wa balls inside you so every time you clench when the flogger touches you, you'll squeeze them making them massage you inside, rubbing against your walls until you finally can't let them go and you're dying to come."

Oh. My. God! I cannot say anything. My sex aches with need at his words. My mind is beginning to enter that state of erotic detachment, that feeling of being high from intense arousal. He is my poison and my antidote and I want more and more, everything he can give me, until I crumble in ecstasy.

He moves back slightly and begins to gather my hair in his hands, stroking and smoothing the thick mass into a ponytail using the tie from my braid. His touch is slow and sensual as he wraps the length of it around his hand. He pulls my head back against his chest with his fist full of my hair, opening my neck to him, licking, kissing and nibbling it. I reach back and grab hold of his hard thighs, digging my nails into them through his pants.

"Strip for me, Elizabeth," he says quietly in my ear. He lets me go and goes to sit in the chair in the corner of the room, leaning back with his gaze fixed on me. There is an intense look in his hooded eyes, his hands are stretched out along the arms of the chair and his intensity is reflected in his clenched fists. I can see the erection growing in his pants and it stimulates me more. I know that this is going to be another one of those nights.

I slide the zipper down on the gown I'm wearing then slowly push it from my arms letting it puddle on the floor at my feet as I step out of it. I raise my hands to slide the zipper down on the corset, freeing my breasts and letting them fall.

"Now the hose and the shoes, baby."

I slide my shoes off then turn to my side and raise one leg up to rest my foot on the bed. I slide the stocking slowly down my leg then I do the same with the other. Placing my feet on the floor, I turn to face Marco again completely naked.

And I wait. I wait for more direction because I know it's coming. Marco sits silently still looking at me, filling his eyes with me. I don't move as the anticipation of what's to come builds within me each passing second.

He pushes himself from the chair and stands in front of me and begins to trace the swells of the bare flesh of my breasts and I feel my nipples harden. Lowering his mouth he follows the path with his tongue then dips it between them licking the valley there. His hand slides up the insides of my thighs grazing my throbbing sex. He claims my nipples, sucking them in his puckered lips, rolling the pointed flesh between them and flicking the points with his tongue. As he straightens his body, his mouth leaves a burning trail over my shoulder and up my neck. His thumb swirls around my clit teasing that swollen nub then makes its way inside me, pushing against my walls, driving me higher. I grasp it, hold it and squeeze it with all of my need.

"Lie down on the bed, baby, I want to tie you."

His voice is gravelly and commanding and his eyes are intense.

Crawling to the center of the bed, I lie down on my back and spread my arms and legs, reaching out to the posts, waiting for my restraints, my fists clenching in anticipation. As my sex pulses I can almost see in my mind's eye my arousal being squeezed out of me from the clenching of my inner walls, my desire rising quickly.

Marco moves from the bottom of the bed to the head, grazing my body with his fingertips as he does. That light touch along the length of my body sends a ripple of shivers through me. He takes my hand and places a Velcro cuff around my wrist. Working his way around my body he fastens the other hand then my feet, always leaving a light trail with his fingertips as he moves. He comes to stand at the head of the bed again and picks up a small box that I recognize. It's something we bought at Adam & Eve. Marco pulls out two silver balls attached by a string and begins to roll them around in his hands.

"These are the ben wa balls, Elizabeth., I'm going to slide them inside you now then I'm going to blindfold you. Okay, love?"

He's going to flog me…and I know I'm going to love it!

"Yes." The excitement I feel inside is clear in my voice.

Moving back down to the foot of the bed, he holds the balls in one hand and strokes my sex with a finger from the other. Oh those incredible fingers of his, sliding, gliding, moving through my lips, my folds, around my clit, in my hole, they're making me drunk. He lowers himself and begins to slide the balls over my mound, rolling them over my clit, around and around my sex and it feels divine, before pushing them up inside me.

I don't really feel anything until I clench then it feels…yummy.

He picks up one of my stockings and comes to stand by my head. "Lift up, love."

I do and close my eyes. The nylon touching my skin is always another match to my fire, making me burn hotter. I love how my other senses instantly intensify. I feel more, hear more, smell more. I can smell Marco and he always makes my mouth water.

My focus turns to the sounds of the tempo of the music, the different notes as if played on my bare flesh and it pulses inside of me, fast, slow, high, low and I'm riding it, soaring with it.

Take me, baby, I want to soar.

Marco begins this newest experience of extreme pleasure for me. Something glides softly across my skin, over my breasts and stomach, down my legs and over my sex, making me clench and I hug the balls inside me, oh yes. Again. It begins to stroke me faster, up and down my body, then up, flicking my nipples, and then, FLICK on my sex, nipping my clit. The jolts spasm through my body as everything tenses and I grab the balls tightly. Ooooh, yes, I feel my orgasm building. There's a long moan. I realize it's coming from me.

Please, Marco, more. The words are chanting in my mind.

The licks across my skin are getting sharper, nipping, stroking, biting lightly, all up and down me, on my breasts, then a light bite on my clit, laying across my pussy like long fingers slapping me softly.

"Aaaaaahhh!!"

Yes! Yes! Yes! My mind is screaming. I'm so close, the wave is cresting almost ready to crash.

Then nothing. No movement, no sound, nothing except for the music and my heavy breathing.

"Please, Marco." There is so much need in my voice.

"Are you ready to come, baby?" His voice is very raw and deep, not like I've ever heard him sound like before.

"Yes, please, now…" My hands are grasping the straps. I'm trying to hold on, to what I'm not sure.

There's a light thump then I feel him climbing up the bed between my legs. His hands hold my thighs as his tongue swipes my sex, lapping up the juices I'm sure have seeped out of me.

Two fingers slide along my folds then slip down my cheeks and into my ass.

"Yes, Marco, please, now…" Oh, my God! He's killing me and he knows it. Almost there, so close, so damn close!

Pulling his fingers out, he opens me up more and slowly pulls out the balls. Oh, I almost came just with that. I hear them thump onto the floor. Then he's rubbing me with the head of his cock, deliciously stroking me, petting me, like velvet over my pussy.

A moan from down deep inside me reverberates through me before leaving my body.

Finally his body lowers over the length of mine. Sweet release is coming and my body sings out. His tongue licks my open lips, tracing them and my tongue meets his. He pulls it into his mouth sucking just the tip of it. The head of his cock mirrors my tongue, penetrating me and my pussy tries to suck it in the way his mouth is sucking my tongue. He tortures me like that giving me just that little bit.

His hands grasp my hips as he raises himself slightly, pulling his mouth from mine, and he pushes all the way inside me.

"Ooooohhh, yes…" I am so erotically high I'm soaring through the stars. Yes, baby, take me there, ride me through the universe until I explode into a million pieces.

"I know, baby, so sweet." He sounds deliciously intoxicated as well and it makes me smile.

Marco thrusts in and out of me, slowly, rhythmically, my sex like velvet around his silk shaft, I begin to fall and it's going to be exquisite. Two of his fingers take hold of one of my nipples as two others pinch my clit.

"OH, GOOOOOOOD!" I scream loud, long and deep. My orgasm is intense, so long and so hard. He doesn't let go, keeping me going, not breaking the pace of his slow erotic thrusts. Oh God, it's the most exquisite torturous orgasm, and it doesn't end.

Finally releasing me, his hands grab my hips tightly and he begins to pound into me hard and deep and I feel him getting harder, twitching inside me. A long, low growl comes from inside him as his fingers dig deeper into my flesh. And he rams his huge thickness into me, burying it as far as it can go, as he pulls my pussy tightly to him, connecting us, grinding us together as he comes.

He collapses on top of me, covering my face with kisses.

"How are you, baby, okay?" he asks huskily as he unfastens the straps on one of my arms then he moves to the other, rubbing the flesh to get the blood flowing there again.

"Oh, my God, Marco, better than okay." I'm still reeling from that orgasm.

"Mmmm, so you liked it," he says sounding satisfied and slightly amused.

"Don't tease me, Marco."

"Baby, I'm not teasing you, I'm just so happy that you like and want what I do to you."

I raise my arms over his head with some effort to hold him close, his heart beating hard against mine.

"Marco," I say softly, pecking him lightly on his lips, "I love everything about you."

His eyes search my face, my eyes, my lips. His smile is so big and so sincere as he kisses me with so much intensity, squeezing me tightly until I almost can't breathe.

"Me too, baby, so much," he says kissing me again.

He moves to undo the straps at my ankles then he massages and kisses them tenderly and lovingly. The action is so intimate it takes my breath away.

"Be right back, love, I'm going to get a towel." He gets up and gathers all of our toys and on his way to the bathroom, I watch that beautiful dragon moving on his broad back and, God, do I love to watch his ass. Every time I see it I want to bite it. He stops at the closet to put the flogger away, then goes to bathroom with the ben wa balls. I hear running water as he washes them and wets the towel. He comes back and places the balls in the box leaving it open to give them some time to dry completely then he begins the work of cleaning me up. I am beginning to relish these times after intimacy, the intimate way he cares for me.

We finally settle down. The restraints are gone, the toys are put away, and it's just him and me and the bright moon breaking through the misty clouds in the sky coming in through the window behind the bed. We're so close, our bodies entwined, flesh to flesh, heartbeat against heartbeat, breath mixed with breath.

"I love the way you feel in my arms, Elizabeth. You soothe me and make me feel alive."

"Me too, baby, so much." My words are whispered but the feeling is shouted.

Marco's arms tighten around me as I close my eyes and fall happily asleep.

I turn in bed and stretch my arms over my head but quickly yank them back as a dull throb shoots down them. I raise my knee and the muscles in my thighs complain to me as well. I smile mischievously reliving last night in my mind. That had to be some of the most incredible and amazing best sex I've ever had. My eyes roll to the back of my head remembering it. The things Marco does to me, with or without toys, is beyond words. I roll over only to find the bed empty next to me and a feeling of disappointment gnaws at me. The blanket falls exposing my bare body as I lift myself up on my elbows. I look around the room hoping to catch a glimpse of that beautiful naked man moving effortlessly about as his muscles flex below his golden skin. I love to watch him move as the different plains and valleys shift and tighten under the surface. I just want to sink my teeth into him.

The room is empty except for me and I don't think he's in the bathroom because the door is open.

"Brian, are you sure?"

I hear his muffled voice coming from the main rooms through the closed bedroom door. I get up and head to the bathroom to say hello the homeless woman that comes to see me pretty often in the mirror after I sleep with Marco.

Closing the door behind me, I step up to the double-sink counter.

"Good morning, and I don't care what you look like. Last night was amazing." I say defiantly at my reflection then bring home my point by sticking my tongue out at her. I'm almost forty years old, and I'm talking to my imaginary friend in the mirror and sticking my tongue out at her. What's wrong with this picture? I chuckle at the wonderfully silly action and what seeing her really means. I got fucked to the moon and back and it was fantastic!

I wash my face and brush my teeth then try to untangle the mess of my hair. Two white terrycloth robes hang on the hook behind the door, a big one and a small one. I take the small one and put it on and head out to the kitchen.

Marco's leaning over the bar in only a soft pair of jeans, barefoot with his broad back spread wide pulling the dragon taut across it, a visual image of his mood.

"And who did you talk to exactly?"

I stand silently at the entrance to the bedroom not daring to interrupt. By the sound of his voice I think it's pretty serious.

"Uh huh, and he couldn't give any specific information or names, is that right?"

A pause as Marco listens to Brian. I assume it's still Brian. The seconds seem to drag on forever. I can't help but try to hear what is being said, even from this distance. I know they've got to be discussing the situation with Marco's permits. He stands and turns and finally sees me. His brows furrow and that tiny expression makes my anxiety rise.

Oh, shit, was I not supposed to hear this? Nothing was said. Or does he not want me here? I turn to go back to the bedroom and check myself because what I really want is to run.

"Brian, hold on. Elizabeth, wait a minute, baby." He waits to continue speaking until I turn to look at him and he holds up one finger.

"Okay, Bri, yeah, how about tomorrow? We can get some coffee in the morning or something and talk about this." A pause. "Okay, I'll text you later, thanks a lot, man, I owe you."

He sets the phone down and closes the space between us in just a few long strides.

Wrapping me in his arms he kisses me gently. "Good morning, sleepy head. How'd you sleep?"

"Great, Marco. Is everything okay?"

He lets out a heavy sigh. "Yeah, actually it's good. We're starting to get a lead on the situation with the permits."

"Really? That's excellent." I feel relieved, very relieved, because it will help him fix whatever is going with that and also because of the fact that what he's upset about is not me.

He leads me to the breakfast bar and pulls out a seat for me.

"Yes, it is, but I think it's going to get worse before it gets better, babe."

"Oh." This must be bad beyond my understanding. "Really, you think so?"

"Yes, unfortunately I do. With what Brian told me just now I have a feeling where the next place it's going to lead and I was hoping it wouldn't take me there."

He looks into my eyes and I can see pain and hurt there. And the reality hits me. This isn't just about business; this is personal.

I get up from the stool and take his hand.

"Take a bath with me, Marco."

I can't take the pain from his eyes, but I can show him that he has a safe place with me.

I lead him to the bathroom and close the door behind us. Leaning over and running the water I wait for it to get hot enough before hanging my robe back on the door. He's standing there watching me, waiting. Naked I step over to him and unbutton his jeans and he leans down to kiss me, telling me how much he needs me right now to hold him and remind him that he is a good man. I push his pants to the floor following them with my body until I'm on my knees in front of him. I rub my cheek into him, kissing him in that valley where that V meets. I smell myself on him and it makes me pulse inside. Nibbling, kissing and licking him, holding his erection to my cheek I turn my face and run my teeth and tongue up his hardening shaft and suck the head in my mouth.

"Oooohhhh, baby, God, what you do to me, Elizabeth." It comes from so deep within him, the need, the longing, the wanting. And I can hear total satisfaction in it as well.

I moan as I push my mouth all the way down his now engorged shaft and I hear him suck in a hiss.

He gently pulls me up by my arms, wrapping his completely around me, and his mouth consumes mine hungrily, trying to suck me in.

"In the water, baby, I want to wash your hair."

We step into the enormous tub. Marco lies back first then he pulls me down between his legs, resting my back on his front. And we begin our erotic bath, smoothing the lather over each other's skin, letting the droplets drip over our nipples, then he washes my hair with the care of a lover adoring his muse. Our hands eat hungrily of each other with each touch, each stroke, each caress until finally he turns me in his arms and kisses me deeply as his tongue lavishes mine with the same fervor his hands did my body. He lifts me onto his hardness, pushing himself into me, filling me with all of him. Our movements are in sync as we carry each other to that cliff and we fall hand in hand, shattering together.

"Okay, Mr. Bond, I think it's finally time I cooked for you," I say hesitantly, but it's not because I want to. Yes, I do want to. I want to do things for him, I want to make him happy but I'm a little apprehensive because he cooks so well.

"Really, Miss DiStefano, I am honored." He thinks this is amusing because I'm sure he can tell I'm a little unnerved.

"Yes, it's breakfast, how bad can I mess this up?"

He howls with such a belly laugh it bounces me off his chest in the tub.

"Just don't burn the place down. I don't have insurance yet. My agent is going to kill me if you do."

"Funny, Mr. Bond. I think I can manage without starting a fire to save you from her wrath."

I begin to lift myself up when he stops me, holding me by my arm.

"One second baby, let me watch my cum drip from you."

What a wonderfully sexy dirty man I have!

Breakfast turns out pretty good, if I do say so myself.

Marco has turned the second bedroom into an office. He went in earlier to get some work done, and probably to leave me alone in the kitchen, I think so I wouldn't feel pressured with him watching me. He really is a considerate man. The spinach omelets are done, the hash browns are perfectly browned, lightly seasoned with a little onion, and the coffee just finished brewing at the same time the kettle whistle blew.

My footsteps are silent as I pad softly across the condo and tap on his office door.

"Yeah, baby, come in," he calls from inside.

I open the door just enough to peek my head inside.

"Breakfast is ready. Come and eat before it gets cold." I beam at him feeling pretty good because I think it's just about as good his.

"Thank you for cooking for me. That was really sweet of you."

He comes around the big antique desk, takes my hand and places a kiss on my lips. This is the only piece of old furniture I've seen in his place and I can see why he would have it. It's beautiful. He notices me admiring it.

Following my eyes, he asks, "Do you like it?"

"Yes, it's gorgeous." I can't hide my appreciation for the beautiful piece of furniture. It's made of thick mahogany with a deep, rich color. There are intricate carvings along the edges and curved feet. It almost looks like French design with the scroll work and four carved lion heads jutting out along the front of it. Behind it is a well-worn leather swivel office chair, the kind that would have sat behind a doctor's desk in the early 1900s.

"It was my grandfather's. My father gave it to me about fifteen years ago, after I got my shit together and I'm honored to have it. He looks back at me I can see the pride in his face.

"Oh, I have one more thing to show you." His expression has taken on a soft look. "Close your eyes."

Now I'm feeling excited. With my eyes closed I hear him take a few steps then the click of a door followed by a rustling sound. He must have gone into the closet.

"Okay, open your eyes." He sounds excited.

My jaw drops. It's a portrait made from one of the pictures Marco took of me that afternoon while I was in bed. I look stunning, sultry, exotic, erotic…a woman with longing and desire and adoration for her lover, beckoning him to come and satisfy her yearning for him. I look at him. He's waiting for me to say something, then I turn back at the picture.

"My God, Marco, I can't believe that's me." I am so shocked my voice is barely above a whisper.

"This is what I see when I look at you when we make love, Elizabeth. This woman is the woman you give me, the one I want to give immense pleasure to, the one I adore. This is you, Elizabeth, always."

I don't know what to say. There's a rock in my throat that I can't push down and tears threaten to spill from my eyes.

He turns and puts the portrait back in the closet.

"I haven't decided where to hang it yet. I want to see you all the time but I don't want to share you with anyone else."

He comes and takes my hand. I'm still mute, afraid of what I'll sound like if I try to speak.

"Come on, a beautiful woman cooked for me and I don't want to let her down."

I grab his face in my hands and pull him to me. What I can't say in words I say this way. He smiles tenderly at me, feeling the gratitude bursting from me at this beautiful gesture he's given me.

After we practically lick our plates, it was good and we both were obviously starving, I take the dishes to the sink.

"What would you like to do tonight, Elizabeth?" He sits back, rubs his stomach in satisfaction then puts his hands behind his head.

"Actually I haven't been to the movies in forever. Would you like to go?"

"Yeah, that sounds great. What would you like to see?"

I bet he thinks I'm going to ask for a romance or a girlie type of movie.

"If *The Equalizer* is still around I'd love to see that." I smile at him, waiting for his response.

"You like action movies?" Just as I thought, the surprise is evident in his expression with the wide eyes and the half smile.

"I love action movies, good ones, especially Denzel ones. He is such a bad ass."

"Okay, that's the plan then, lazy afternoon, movie and pizza."

"Perfect plan, Mr. Bond."

Leaning his head against the back of the sofa, he looks at me, thinking about something.

"What?" I ask, getting a little uncomfortable under his thoughtful eyes.

"First, I'm taking you shopping."

"Why?" the shock can clearly be heard in my voice.

"Because I don't want you to have to worry about not having anything to wear here, at least until you move in."

I choose to ignore the part about me moving in when I answer him. "You don't have to do that. I can bring some things over."

"But you won't have to if we go shopping." He gets up and reaches for my hand. "Come on, let's get ready. I really want to do this." How can I say no to a face like that?

We approach the corner of Market Street and Front Street. There are a few really cool boutiques here and I'm starting to get excited. No man has ever taken me shopping for me before. We walk in to Edge of Urge first. It's a trendy boutique catering to both the younger woman and the professional with an edge.

"Can I pick out a few things for you to try on?" Marco asks me as he's fingering through a rack, his hand poised over a hanger.

"Sure, that would be great, anything for you."

"Anything?" he asks silkily, cocking an eyebrow.

"Mmmhmm, anything," I purr back at him.

"In that case, I will remember that," he says, stealing a kiss.

After going through all of the racks in the store, Marco has an arm full of clothes and I have two items. The sales lady hasn't been able to take her eyes off Marco since we walked into the store, almost on the verge of being rude. I think she just can't help it. An amazingly attractive man dripping sexuality, and shopping, really, really shopping, in a women's boutique is something I'm sure she doesn't see often. When it looks like he's finally coming up for air and he scans the room for a dressing area she breaks her silent admiration.

"May I help you with something?"

"Yes, we'd like to try these on."

Her eyes almost pop out of her head. "All of them?"

"Yes."

"Yes, of course, right this way," she stammers.

You can't blame the woman. Marco's easily got twenty pieces of clothing draped over his arm.

"You can't really intend to buy all of those," I whisper to him on the way to the back of the store toward the changing room.

"Yes, I do, and right now I'm going to enjoy watching you undress and dress, showing off all of these things for me." He turns and winks at me, "I told you, purely selfish reasons."

The dressing room is cramped with both of us in it but Marco was not going to miss the show. I start a little enthusiastically but by the tenth item I'm getting a little annoyed.

"I've tried on everything that needs to be tried on. The rest we can judge without me having to keep pulling clothes on and off my body. Which ones do you like?" I ask him.

"I like all of them. That's why I picked them," he answers.

"Okay, which ones do you like the best so we can start putting some back?"

"I like all of them the best, Elizabeth."

Now I'm annoyed.

"Okay, well, which ones are we keeping?"

"I told you, baby, all of them. That's why I picked them." He looks at me as if I should have known this, he's already told me.

"You can't be serious." The seconds tick by in the tight square of the dressing room.

"Is there anything about me that says that I'm not?"

I stare at him. What can I say? No, you can't buy me clothes, which would be like telling him don't breathe. It's just not possible.

"Okay," is all I can manage, shaking my head as I push past him to get out of the close confinement.

We go up to the counter and place all the clothing on the counter.

"Which of these would you like?" the sales woman asks. *Yeah, lady, I asked the same thing.*

"All of them," Marco answers.

She looks at him, stopping midway through removing a hanger from a dress. "All of them?"

"Yes," he says flatly.

I can tell he had to stop himself from saying anything further. Poor guy, he just went through all of that with me.

After she rings us up and we head out the door, I decide we're not going to any more boutiques, especially if it's going to be like this. If he keeps this up, I'd have more clothes at his place than I do at my own.

Chapter Twelve

Elizabeth

It's 9:15 when we get back to the condo.

"I bet you'll never think about hardware stores the same way again, Marco."

"Definitely not, that was a great movie and an excellent idea, babe, I'm glad we went."

"Tell me something. You're in the construction business so to speak; do you work with tools and things like that?"

He pulls me down to the couch with him and we sit back. He has his arms draped around my waist and I'm reclining against him. His expression is one of reminiscing, and he looks serene, deep in the thoughts that are taking him back to another time and place.

"My dad taught me some things." He shakes his head laughing lightly. "He had my grandfather's tools after he passed away. The old sturdy kind that you had to crank to drill a hole, the old stone with the deep groove in it where knives had been sharpened on it hundreds of times, and the old-fashioned planers. You know, the ones that made the beautiful curled wood shavings." He looks at me with a sparkle in his eye at the memories.

I nod my head feeling so much for this man at this moment, this very private moment where he is exposed and the beauty that is him is brilliantly glowing.

He leans his head back against the back of the couch as his arms tighten around me.

"When I finally settle down, I want to buy a ranch with lots of property with a big white house, two stories, with wraparound porches, kind of a country house but with charm. I want to put up a tree swing and have a work shed and hang my grandfather's tools there. And one day I'll make something with them." He tilts his head back down to me and smiles. "I told you, baby, it's like art."

I can see that beautiful home, the wind softly blowing the leaves, Marco walking across the big expanse of lawn and I'm up on the porch. There's a small child running down the steps toward him with arms stretched out. I can't resist kissing him and letting some of the overwhelming emotion I feel for him right now pour into him. It's so much, I think my heart's going to burst.

When his lips leave mine his forehead rests against mine and he looks into my eyes. His lip curves up in the corner and his eyes take on that wicked look. The bad boy is back.

"And I do like hardware, and tonight I have a special clamp for you. I can't wait to see how much you like it."

My eyes widen and my mouth falls open with no sound. Instantaneous horniness.

He traces my lips with a fingertip, then slides his hands down my arms finally coming to graze his nail on the top of my shirt along my visibly hardened nipples.

"I've got a couple of phone calls to make. Why don't you get comfortable while I finish up and I'll be in in a minute?"

"Okay," I answer.

I go to the bedroom and get undressed. Along with the clothes Marco bought, he also bought a dresser just for me. We went right past the drawer to the dresser. That's impressive. Folding my clothes, I fill the drawers of my dresser and walk into the bathroom. After turning on the shower, I wait for it to get hot and pile my hair on top of my head before getting in.

My body is already sizzling in anticipation of this new toy he mentioned, a clamp. I've worn the nipple clamps a few times already so I wonder what it could be.

My eyes fly open at the realization: a clit clamp, HOLY FUCK!

I stop. The water is running over my body, the soap is swirling down the drain and I'm frozen. This will be fine. I've had a butt vibrator in my ass, I've been flogged while having ben wa balls inside me and everything he's done to me has left me mindless with ecstasy. This will be fine I tell myself. My heart is already thudding hard and my sex is wide awake. I hear the door click open then shut and all of my senses heighten. I glance in that direction and I see Marco, naked. His erection is massive standing tall, and he is stalking toward me, head slightly bowed, lips lifting at the corners with a look in his eyes that says *I hope you're ready 'cause I'm coming and there will be no mercies.* I instinctively take a step back in the huge shower and his grin gets bigger.

Stepping into the shower his presence fills what felt like such a large space just moments before. He is so overpowering, so intense, so...much. He doesn't stop moving until he's got me pushed up against the wall, his mouth crushing mine as his tongue hungrily pushes it open, devouring me. One of his hands is on my breasts kneading the swollen flesh and flicking my sensitive nipples with his fingertips as the other moves to cup my mound roughly, one finger shoving inside me with such force it takes my breath away.

"I've got to fuck you hard and fast now, love. I need you," he grits out between clenched teeth.

Picking me up by the backs of my thighs, he lifts me and slams me down on his cock in one movement as my legs wrap around him. He's pounding into me mercilessly, just as his eyes promised, slamming me back into him. I can feel the licks of my orgasm slithering up inside of me as this primal man takes what he needs from me. He twitches inside me making me dig my nails into his back trying to pull him deeper into me. My mouth comes down on his, biting down on his bottom lip, making him growl as I suck it in.

"Fuck, Elizabeth." His thrusts become more determined and more ferocious, harder, deeper, stronger.

He slams into me one final time pulling me down hard on his cock, holding me by my hips, grinding us together and throwing his head back as a long deep moan escapes him.

"Oh God yes, baby…"

Kissing me deeply he sets me down and grabs the shower head, I'm really growing to love that thing, as he turns me around to face the wall. He pulls my ass back so my back is arched and he spreads my legs.

"Here, let's clean you up," he says with wicked amusement in his voice.

I feel him lean over my back as one hand reaches between my legs and his fingers begin to play with my lips, sliding them between his fingers and pinching them, then circling my clit.

"Does it feel good when I pinch you here, baby?" he whispers huskily in my ear.

I am going into that place of ecstasy where everything is foggy.

"Yes, Marco…"

"Do you know what I'm going to put on that delicious clit of yours tonight, my love?" he says nibbling on my ear.

"Yes, Marco…"

"Do you want it, baby?" His finger slides into me, stroking me, feeding my flames.

I'm panting. "Yes, Marco…"

He shifts the sprayer to hit right on my clit while his fingers delectably move in and out of me.

"You'll scream when you come, with that clamp biting your clit, so loud and so long and it's going to feel so fucking good, I promise."

I come with his finger moving, sliding and stroking me inside and out, as that sprayer tantalizes my clit making me want more. Oh God, I want so much more!

Marco grabs my chin firmly turning my head to the side and kisses me greedily.

"Come on, baby, I'm not finished with you yet."

There is such a dark promise in his voice of sinfully delicious things yet to come. The journey I'm on with Marco, the erotic pleasures he's submerging me in, are they forbidden and taboo? I want to succumb to everything he offers me. I want to fall into that endless pit of rapture with him. I'm sure I'll follow him wherever he guides me because I know with everything in me, even though I refuse to admit it, I love him. And nothing born of love is forbidden.

He gets out and wraps a towel low around his slim waist as his still-engorged beautiful manhood pushes it up away from his body. I want to lick the water droplets off the V feeding down into that lucky towel. My mouth comes alive at the memory of his taste.

"Come here, let me dry you off."

He's holding a towel open for me so I step into the circle of his open arms. He encloses me in his strong embrace lowering his face to nibble on the wet crease at my neck and shoulders. This seductive sexual beast of a man has me in constant simmering arousal and I can't get enough of him.

"Go lie down on the bed with your legs hanging off the side," he tells me and I see his shaft growing bigger making the towel tent higher.

I have no idea what to expect from the clit clamp. I'm a little nervous knowing how sensitive my clit is. I'm afraid it will be unbearable, but I'm incredibly aroused at the same time at the idea.

I go and lie back on the bed after setting my towel down on the chair in the corner. I rub my thighs together in anticipation as I move my hands to rest on my naked breasts. Marco comes and stands directly in front of my legs. His towel is already gone and I can see he is as excited as I am, maybe even more, with his cock standing straight up almost touching his flat abdomen.

"Open your legs." His voice is low and rough but the command is definitely apparent.

I slowly separate my legs opening myself up to him. My chest is rising and falling with my heavy breathing as I imagine what he is seeing that is making his hardness twitch. Seeing the effect the sight of me has on him is so empowering.

"Play with your breasts, Elizabeth. Let me see those pink nipples rolling between your fingers. Tease them, pinch them, pull them and think it's my mouth and teeth on them."

My fingers separate, allowing the pebbled peaks to sneak through before I take them with my fingertips, twisting them and pinching them, then flicking the tip back and forth. The sensations shoot through my core all the way to my pussy making me pulse. My back lifts off the bed as my thighs begin to close searching for the friction I so desperately crave.

"Open your legs wider."

His voice is like a long hot lick along my skin making me burn more, and his words make my ache build.

"I'm going to put the clamp on your beautiful clit now."

His fingers gingerly separate my labia and I feel the cool metal sliding over my pulsing nub then grabbing it tightly. And I'm very surprised it doesn't hurt at all.

Oh. My. God. Somebody should have told me that I was going to turn into a throbbing, panting, maniacally aroused beast. This is too fucking incredible!

Marco

"Marco…" There is a slight desperation in her voice. I can hear it.

"Ssshhh, baby, just breathe." Laying my hand flat on her stomach, I try to bring her back before she completely gives in to the overloading sensations.

"I'm so…I feel so…" Her eyes are wide as the intense arousal begins to flood through her threatening to take her over.

"I know, just trust me." I hold her steady with my palm still lying flat on her stomach.

Her breathing is becoming shallow and quick. She looks into my eyes as I search her face.

"I do. Marco." God, she fucking kills me.

"Okay, baby girl." I stand back a step. "Come here and kneel in front of me."

Her eyes widen and she licks her lips as she lowers herself to the floor. Could she be any sexier?

"Take me in your mouth, love, and suck me deep in your throat." My hand is resting on the top of her head as one of hers clasp on to my ass and the other pulls my rock hard cock into that hot mouth of hers. As her lips slide down my shaft her finger runs the length of my crack finishing off with her nails digging into me. She wants to mark me and it's making me crazy. She sucks me all the way to the back of her throat as her hand moves to the front and her nails lightly score the wrinkled flesh of my balls.

"Oh God!" Fuck! So good, I push as far back as her mouth will let me. Her mouth moves from my dick to my balls sucking one in at a time while her hand hugs my shaft moving up and down. Her hot mouth claims my cock again sucking me deep as her hands go back and forth from my balls to my shaft. I don't want to stop but I have to. I want her first time coming with a clit clamp on to be with my cock deep inside of her, so I pull out of her mouth.

"Lean over the side of the bed, give me that beautiful pussy and ass of yours." I'm going to play a little bit but I hope I don't make her come.

She moans so beautifully as she bends over the bed, spreading her legs and reaching her arms out in front of her, arching her back up at me as if saying, *Here, take me, all of me. I'm yours to do what you want.*

Placing a hand on the top curve of her ass, I position myself between her legs and dip my finger into that dripping nectar of hers, just a little, skimming just the edge and not enough to push her over. Another finger joins it covering them both with her slickness. I move one up to her tight ass and tease it the same way.

"Oh God please, Marco, please…" Her pleading is so deep, her need so strong.

"Just a little bit more…" I say as I dip my fingers into both of her holes at the same time, then pull them back out immediately. She is so fucking sweet, my cock is aching.

"Oh, God…" Her moan comes from deep in her core as she tries to push back on my fingers.

"I'm going to take this ass baby, very, very soon. It's mine."

"Take it now, Marco, please. I need you!"

I know she's right on the verge of coming and she's teetering there, screaming to jump.

My fingers slide through her wetness, grazing her clit in the clamp between my fingers. My thumb pushes in to her aching pussy as I position the head of my cock at her entrance.

Slowly, so fucking slowly I push the head in and stop.

"Oh God! Oh God! Oh God!" She's screaming now.

The rest of me enters her. I have to go slow so the orgasm won't rush away from her, exploding on her like a tidal wave.

"Oh yes, so good, Marco, so good. Yes…"

She's starting to be carried away on that wave, the crest now lifting her up. And it's magnificent.

Elizabeth

Never have I been so on the brink of constant orgasm so hard before in my life. I feel like I am about to explode with it, standing at the edge dying to jump, but he doesn't give me enough to burst and it's incredible!

As he slides that big beautiful cock in me, my ravenous hunger for him begins to get sated. It is slow and sweet flowing through me, making me delirious as it lifts me higher. My beast that Marco has kept from going wild, keeping her on that leash, is lapping up this glorious serving of lust. The clamp on my clit is a powerful source of energy and Marco's cock is the cord that energy is using to travel through my body, lighting me up with nuclear wattage. Watch out. Get ready, she's gonna blow!

I feel intensely horny and orgasmic at the same time. I want…no, I need more but I feel like I'm coming. I want him to fuck me hard but I want him to be slow.

Marco feels like velvet thrusting in and out of me, caressing me inside with a soft steel. I rock back against him finally getting lost in the feelings. I'm coming. I started to come as soon as he started to move inside me. The intensity is slow, warm and fuzzy and it's endless, going on and on.

He moves a hand to slide two fingers around my clit, stroking it in rhythm to the movement of his hips then one of his fingers begins to flick it underneath.

"Aaaaaarrghh!" I scream with the power of my orgasm as it explodes.

My heart starts pounding hard, my whole lower region begins to shake, and, I can't believe this, I begin to pee.

"Oh, my God, Marco, I'm peeing." I feel it dribbling down my legs. I am so shocked. Nothing like this has ever happened before. I don't feel like I'm peeing. It's just coming out of me like a constant trickle in a leaky faucet.

"No, you're not, baby. You're squirting. Just enjoy it." He continues to gently fondle my clit with his fingers as his cock plays my pussy the way a bow plays a violin.

I keep coming and coming. My body is a slave to Marco. I have no control over myself, and the intensity of it feels like I'm being erotically electrocuted.

Finally, his fingers leave my clit and grab my hips, digging into my soft flesh. I hear something like a growl coming from him as he begins to pound into me. He's not holding back anymore. Three strokes and he buries himself holding my ass to him.

"Holy fuck, Elizabeth!" It's almost a roar and I think it's sexy as hell.

Marco collapses and pulls us both onto the bed as my legs almost give out. He covers me in soft kisses as I lie motionless, completely spent from the strength of that nonstop orgasm and stimulation, and I'm still high from it all. Marco guides me to my back, spreads my thighs and gently removes the clamp.

"Oh, no, Marco, I made everything wet," I say as I slowly come back to reality. I feel embarrassed. I don't care if he said I squirted. I've never done it before. Is it possible for someone to do it randomly without any indication that they're capable of doing it? Is it just as simple as the proper stimulation and manipulation to make it just come out? Using the clit clamp is incredible but what if this happens every time we use it? Will I be okay with squirting?

"Baby, the duration and intensity of your orgasm made you squirt. It's a beautiful thing. It's a good thing not bad. All we have to do is change the comforter."

"Really?" I am somewhat relieved but still embarrassed. I knew I was coming hard but I didn't realize how hard.

"Come, let's go to the bathroom. I'll get you a washcloth and you can clean up while I change the bed."

"Okay, I'm so sorry." I know I must look sheepish as I follow him with my head down.

"Sorry? Are you kidding me? I made you squirt, love. That is amazing!"

I raise my eyes to him and a slow naughty smile spreads across my face. "Yeah, that is pretty cool, huh?"

He laughs and pulls me to him and I can't stop the giggles bubbling up from me. My body is still highly sensitive from the intensity of what it just went through so my giggles turn into hysterical laughter as the tears begin to roll down my face. Everything I'm feeling seems to be intensified. My satisfaction turns to extreme joy just like that and I can't control my laughter, just as I couldn't control my orgasm and my bodily functions. Marco continues to hold me, stroking my body, soothing me, smiling and chuckling but I think he understands what I'm experiencing so he's continuing to keep me grounded. I have a feeling that my laughter could turn into sobs like flipping a switch. I can feel the desire to sob tugging at me but I haven't crossed over that emotional line yet. I get a grip on myself as the laughter subsides and I take a couple of deep breaths.

"Whew." I shake my head a little to clear it.

Marco pulls back a little and looks into my face.

"Better?" He's smiling but he's so sincere.

"Yes, much, I think I won't turn into a blubbering mess anymore. Wow!"

He laughs softly. "You're a beautiful blubbering mess and I'm going to turn you into one every chance I get."

When I finish in the bathroom and come back to bed he has changed the comforter and set a bottle of water on the nightstand for me. I slide in and wrap my body around his naked warmth. I don't have the energy to do anything else so my body just melts into his.

"Rest, love."

I don't argue with him. I'm feeling completely spent and wonderfully and thoroughly fucked beyond satisfaction and I wonder if there's a contented smile on my face.

Through my foggy mind, sleep is already coming to tuck me in. I hear Marco saying something to me. "I've got to meet Brian in the morning. I'll be home as quick as I can."

I try to answer him although I'm not sure my reply is intelligible.

I was already sleeping.

Chapter Thirteen

Marco

"Brian, you spoke with him at the party the other night?"

We're sitting outside at Port City Java in Porters Neck. With the information that Brian believes he has, we thought it was best to meet somewhere out of the way where there wouldn't be any crowds or anyone who would want to eavesdrop on our conversation.

"Yes, he and my dad are old friends. He came up to me and asked me about you. When he did that I thought it was a little odd, even though you are the wonderboy of the moment."

"And you're sure what he told you is valid?"

"He's the fucking mayor, Marco, of course it's valid!" Brian shakes his head laughing at my question.

"I know he's the mayor. I just want to make sure he doesn't have his dick in a knot about someone and is dragging me in it to do his dirty work."

Brian leans closer resting his arms on the table.

"I get where you're coming from but these boys used to go fishing together at the local watering hole growing up. It's good between them. I have no doubt he's not blowing anything out of proportion in order to get a leg up in his political career."

"You're right. Now it's all a power trip to see who can scale that ladder first using these guys as their players. It's obviously me against them. The teams are starting to form and the players are starting to come out on the field. It's time to play ball. They are so fucked. I don't give a shit who it is; they are going down."

I have not felt so much anger and betrayal in a very long time, but I think the betrayal is the worst. Power is one thing. Loyalty and honor are something entirely different.

"I'm calling our first player to come and join us," I say as I take out my wallet to call the councilman.

Elizabeth

What a beautiful morning, I can't remember feeling so happy before I've even woken up. I roll over to squeeze Marco but I find the bed is empty…again. What was it that he told me last night as I was falling asleep? I bury my face in his pillow and hug it close to me, breathing him in deeply. He smells so good and his scent is stirring feelings inside me making me moan out loud. I feel like Scrooge when he woke up Christmas morning. The elation I feel is almost bursting from me, it makes my heart swell. It's amazing what incredible sex can do for a person.

Releasing the Marco imposter I'm clutching, I head to the bathroom. I'm so happy today I could kiss that homeless woman who shows up in the mirror sometimes.

"It's even nice to see *you* this morning! Muuaaaaahh!" I greet my friend in the mirror, laughing at myself and this picture. I don't care; life is beautiful.

I clean myself up. As I'm sitting on the commode I look down at my clit as I hold myself open. *You are a powerful little thing, aren't you?* I think. What the hell is wrong with me? One orgasm, no, it was a constant-earth-shattering-mind-blowing-only-written-in-books-orgasm and Marco gave it to me, and I'm turning into Snow White talking to all kinds of crazy things. I want to feel him close, have him on my skin, so I decide to go in the closet and find the next best thing, one of his shirts. I might just take it hostage and bring it home with me so I can curl up with him whenever I want.

When I get to the kitchen I realize I'm alone in the condo. Then I remember again that Marco said something last night as I was falling asleep but I can't remember what that was. Looking around I see a note sitting on top of my teacup.

Good morning my sexy thing, I'm meeting with Brian this morning, be home as soon as I can. M xoxo

My first note from Marco. I feel like a kid, I want to hug myself,

Taking my tea, I step around the counter and wonder what I can do while I'm waiting for him. Maybe I can help him find a place to hang my portrait. I am speechless at the me Marco captured in the photo. That woman is a siren, a stunning passionate woman oozing desire for her lover. And that woman is me and her lover is Marco. Any woman would be passionate about Marco but I still can't get over that I could look that…beautiful.

Entering his office, I set my cup down on his grandfather's antique desk then I enter the large walk-in closet to look for the portrait. This closet is practically empty. It just contains some boxes Marco hasn't unpacked yet and some other things he has taken out of boxes but hasn't found a home for in the condo yet. There's my portrait sitting close to the front propped up against the wall on the floor. I glance around to see what other things he's got in here, taking this opportunity to get a glimpse of the Marco before me, to see this man possibly a little bit differently. I hope I'll find some things from his childhood as an image of a ten-year-old Marco comes to mind. I envision him in the front of the pack of his friends throwing stones at an old abandoned house and they get caught, and they run like the wind. What a naughty bunch of boys he and his friends must have been.

A box of identical size portraits catches my eye in the corner facing the wall. I wonder if they're family portraits. Why did Marco need things to hang on his wall if he has some right here? I walk over to them and pull one out.

Holy!

Fuck!

Everything stops and I feel the bottom drop out from underneath me. All the air has been sucked from the space and there is a whooshing sound in my head as I freeze, staring at the image I'm holding trying to register it. It's a woman tied spread eagle on a bed and wearing nipple clamps. She is beautiful, blonde and curvy, but what is most striking is the look of intense desire on her perfect features. I set it down and take out another one. Fuck! This one is a stunning brunette also tied but on her knees and elbows and she's blindfolded, her back is arched and her head is thrown back. Her mouth is open, and she's obviously in the throes of pleasure. I pull the rest of them out one by one. There are six of them in total, all of them drop-dead gorgeous women, all in different but similar degrees of bondage on a bed. One has distinct red markings crisscrossing her tan flesh, which I can assume were made by her Dom Marco. My heart stops and my knees buckle. This is the one that really hurts, the one that cuts right through me. Liana. This one makes it very real. I knew she was beautiful but this is erotic perfection. She is standing and naked, her arms are tied above her head hanging from a wrought iron hook, her eyes are half closed, and her mouth is slightly open. Her skin is flushed and her lips are pink and full, as if from heated kisses from her lover. They're beckoning to him to come and quench her hunger. She has red markings on her pale skin. These are long and thin and a bit more pronounced than the markings on the other woman in her picture. This is so surreal, I feel as if I'm experiencing this from somewhere out of my body, detached and removed.

I stand back and look at all of these beautiful women. These are some of Marco's subs. And he took all of them. Something tugs at my mind. I recognize something in the pictures. I bring my face to look at them more closely. That bed! That's Marco's bed in all of these portraits. The same one he's been making love to me in.

Six of them…then mine…me… I'm lucky number seven.

I'm just the latest sub in his little collection.

The realization washes over me and pulls me in, drowning me in the reality. How could I be so stupid? How can I even slightly expect to compete with these women? I am nothing compared to them. They are erotic, sultry, beautiful and are experienced in this world. And to think I was falling in love with him, giving him my heart, and why? He was just using me for his pleasure, probably laughing at my naiveté, what a fool I am. How could I ever think I could mean anything to a man like that? I've let myself be used again.

Oh, I don't think so, I think as anger begins to rise up within me. If he thinks I am just part of a collection, just a plaything, he's got another think coming to him. I believe I'll show him how huge the mistake is he's made.

I go to his bedroom, dragging the box of portraits with me and I turn on his music system and blast 30 Seconds to Mars's *Bury Me*, hitting repeat. It's time to get busy. I've got work to do.

Once I'm home I'm pacing the floor like a caged animal. Alanis Morissette's very pissed off voice is shouting *You Oughta Know* and I'm right there with her. I've passed being hurt, confused, livid and now I'm finally calm. I need to talk to someone about this, someone who is familiar with the other side of the story, someone who knows the needs, expectations and desires of that type of relationship. Someone who will be honest and unbiased with me.

I'll call John.

I take the card out of my wallet he gave me that first day at the gym. I take a cleansing breath before dialing, not because I'm nervous about calling him but to chase away any residual anger and pain from finding the portraits. I want my mind to be clear and my emotions to be intact so that I can be rational.

"Hello?" His voice is a little tentative. I guess he's wondering if he should have answered the phone. I know I wouldn't have if I didn't recognize the number.

"Hi, John, it's Elizabeth." Now I'm worried if I should drag him into this. I don't want to present this like a girl finding out about her boyfriend's other girlfriends. What I want is to get some understanding into a Dom/sub relationship because that's what it looked like those portraits represented. I know I'm taking a shot in the dark with John. But everything about him, all things very similar to Marco, his demeanor, the powerful confidence that oozes dark sexuality, the gaze that penetrates and commands a woman to want to submit leaving her melting, leads me to believe his a Dominant.

"Hi, Elizabeth, are you okay? Is everything all right?" It's obvious my unexpected phone call has raised alarm bells in him.

"Yes, everything is fine, John. I was wondering if we could have lunch or something today. I have some questions and you're the only person I trust who I think would have answers to them."

"Of course, just tell me when and where and I'll be there."

He's a good guy, no questions, no hesitancy. I told him I needed him and he agreed even though I'm practically a stranger to him. His generosity melts away any reservations I might have.

"How about Little Dipper downtown? They have booths, which could give us some privacy. One o'clock okay with you?" I ask nervously chewing on my thumb nail.

"I'll be there. And Elizabeth?"

"Yes?"

"I'm glad you called." I can hear genuine appreciation in his voice.

"Me too, John, thank you. See you later." I smile at him although he can't see me.

"See you in a little bit. Bye."

I believe this is going to be an interesting lunch.

I glance at my watch. It's ten o'clock. I know Marco will be home soon. In fact I'm surprised he hasn't called me yet. As if on cue my phone beeps with a text.

Good morning baby, are you up yet?

What do I do? Do I act like nothing is different? Is something different? What's different? Was I something to him besides a plaything? I need to buy some time. The question first is do I answer him.

Tick tock.

What do I do?

I finally make a decision.

Yes I'm home. Talk to you later.

Why are you home? Is something wrong?

How much do I tell him by text? He'll find out soon enough when he gets home. Right now I need some time to sort out my thoughts and get information so I can understand the situation more clearly. And I can't get unbiased information from Marco. To be honest, I don't know if I can face him right now after seeing those pictures and envisioning him doing those things and being with those women. And the worst thing is I can't help thinking there's no way I can measure up to them.

We'll talk later.

What the fuck Elizabeth?

Just stop. Later.

He's calling me, but I can't talk to him now, not until he sees everything so I let the call go to voicemail.

I hate it when you do this Elizabeth! I'm coming over.

I've got three hours before I meet John but I can't stay here.

I call Elsie, she's closest.

"Elsie, are you busy? I need to hang there for a couple of hours."

"Yeah, girl, of course, come on over. Is everything okay?"

"I'll tell you when I get there. I just have to get out of my place right now before Marco gets here. I'm on my way." I'm already out the door before I even hang up.

I decide to leave my car here so he can't see it wherever I'm at. I need this talk with him to be on my terms when I'm ready, not his.

Elsie has the mismatched antique tea set out and ready when I get there. She can tell I'm upset and the familiarity of our tea time will help calm me. She knew this and I love her for that. Before I even get seated she's on me.

"What the fuck is going on, Liz?"

So much for keeping me calm.

I settle into her gypsy couch and pour myself a coup of the Earl Grey tea I smell in the little porcelain pot.

Taking in a deep breath, I tell her what I found and what I did.

"Now I'm going to meet John for lunch in a couple of hours so that, hopefully, he can give me some insight to that type of lifestyle so I can determine if that is what Marco has been setting me up for."

Elsie lets out a whooshing breath before she says, "Girl, holy shit, did you freak?"

"Yeah, I freaked! But I'm calm now and I don't want to talk to Marco until I have all of the information I need. And I don't want to get it from him."

She shakes her head, "I don't know much about it except from what I've read but watching Marco with you, he is totally into you; he practically worships the ground you walk on. The way he watches you, Elizabeth? I don't think that kind of relationship is what this thing is with you two."

I look into her face, "El, one of the women in those portraits was the redhead who was with Marco at the party. She works with him."

The bomb has officially dropped along with Elsie's face.

"Fuck!" If there could be a silent shout that was it.

I'm already at The Little Dipper waiting when John arrives. The hostess knows I'm meeting a big sexy Indian-looking man so I'm sure she'll have no trouble finding me when he arrives, and there is no way she'll miss John. My nerves are wound up, and I couldn't sit in that little apartment with Elsie any longer. There wasn't any more I could tell her other than what I already had and I didn't want to dissect everything again.

Marco has called me about ten times and has sent just as many text messages and they're all about the same as the one I just received.

Elizabeth, let me explain, where are you? Don't do this.

He's obviously gotten home and has seen my little redesigning, then he must have gone directly to my place.

Marco

Brian and I have finally finished up what we had to discuss. Between what he's heard and what I was told, it is very evident which direction the trail points to regarding who's responsible for trying to sabotage me and my company. Sabotage. That's exactly what it is and I'm not going to let it happen. I'm torn between wanting to fucking kill the person responsible for it and wanting to say everything's fine. I know who it is, but because of who it is I have to put it in other hands.

Fortunately, it's Sunday. These types of communications, as I've learned throughout the years having dealt with quite a diverse variety of contacts, are most often best handled in a more relaxed and informal way.

I call the councilman while we are at Port City Java and he joins us for some coffee. Having money does have its advantages and knowing when best to use it is a talent. As it turns out, the councilman has a little information of his own. It seems he has a promising career ahead of him. It's so good having friends in high places.

By the time I get back to the condo, I know something is very wrong before I even get off the elevator. I can hear the music blaring as I am coming up from the lower levels. Whatever it is, Elizabeth is pissed.

I open the door to Jared Leto screaming at me in *Bury Me*, "I am finished with you!" and I enter hesitantly wondering what the fuck I did. On my way to the bedroom I stop short when I see them. How did she find them? She must have been looking for hers and looked a little further in the closet.

Elizabeth has hung all the portraits of my former subs from the canopy of my bed, dangling as if the bed is a shrine to them. And there in the middle hanging from the top of the bed in the center is hers. But she's done some work to it. I slowly step closer, cringing at the sight of it as I do.

She's painted a clown face over hers with big red lips and a bright red nose, and makeup around the eyes exaggerating her eyelashes. She's written across the front of it, "I will not be your latest toy!"

I'm shocked she could even think that's how I feel about her. I wasn't the only one there each time we were together. I have never treated her like that, never given her any reason to question where she stands with me, where we stand together. Yes, it's fucked up I have these in my apartment after I had one made of her, but it's not the same kind at all. It's obvious just looking at them. Those were purely for the image of kink. I did Elizabeth's because I wanted to look at her all the time in the throes of our passion, our lovemaking. It makes my soul sing gazing at her in that moment, just like I told her when I took the pictures.

She won't answer my calls or my texts. Her car's at her apartment and it's cold which tells me she hasn't driven it. So she's either with someone or she's close because she's walking.

The one thing that keeps me sane is the fact that Elizabeth is a mature and reasonable woman. I know she'll let me explain when she's ready…I hope.

My phone vibrates and I pull it out of my pocket. It's John.

I'm having lunch with Elizabeth.

What the fuck?! Why?

She called me.

The images of her body responding to his closeness fill my already blazing mind. And my imagination begins to see her writhing under him as he fucks her. Oh God, no!

Elizabeth

"Hi John, thanks for meeting me on such short notice."

I'm a little nervous regardless of how comfortable he makes me feel. His dominant presence commands attention, stirring something hot and sultry inside. He also has a kind face beneath all of that strength and the hints of the shadows of past pains and demons.

He slides into the booth across from me wearing camo pants and a white thermal shirt. The man is a walking sex god. There is nothing he can do to hide it. Every woman in this place turns to look at him regardless of whether they are twenty or seventy.

"Hey Elizabeth, it sounded pretty serious. Are you okay?"

"Yeah, I'm fine. I just needed an opinion from someone like you. Let's order first then we can talk."

After the poor waitress takes our order, she could barely speak with so much man in front of her, I take a deep breath and dive in.

"I need you to tell me from a man's, preferably a Dom's, perspective the logistics of a Dom/sub relationship." If that isn't matter of fact, I'm Little Bunny Froo Froo.

His eyebrow quirks at my request but he quickly regains composure. Good for him.

"Well, typically in that type of relationship it's entered into from the beginning with both partners knowing that is the type of relationship it will be, the expectations would be gone over right from the start as well, such as if there will be bondage, pain, what types, sharing, multiple partners, and if it's just sexual. Sometimes there isn't even sex. Some people look for someone to tie them up or whip them because that's all they want."

He pauses and studies my face for a moment as I'm taking this in and weighing the information to see where Marco and I would fit into this scenario.

I bring my face closer to his across the table.

"So, correct me if I'm wrong, but if a Dom is looking for a sub or has found someone who he would like to begin that type of relationship with, they would discuss it almost like a business transaction with all of the details before they even start?"

"Yes, most often it's just like that, if that is what the relationship is going to be. Never will a good Dom seduce a woman then change the relationship into a slave/sub thing. It would be misleading and would be too messy. There are too many other factors to concentrate on in that situation."

I sit quietly turning this over in my mind and everything John's saying is not fitting what Marco and I have. But I have to ask the million-dollar question.

"John, I need you to be honest with me, and you can ask me anything you'd like to determine your answer but I need your opinion."

"Okay" His expression is emotionless.

"Do you think Marco intends for this thing between him and me to be a Dom/sub relationship?"

"First of all, you should be asking him that…"

"I know and I will but I want to ask you as a Dom, and as a friend."

"Second, why do you ask that?"

I blush, averting my eyes to look down at the table.

"Well, we have played in the bedroom, toys, bondage, that sort of thing."

"That doesn't mean anything, Elizabeth. It's just exactly that, going beyond the traditional vanilla sex, adding a little kink for pleasure." He pauses for a moment. "Look at me, Elizabeth."

Another dominant assertive man who commands control. I look into his eyes.

"Just looking at the facts, the way Marco is with you, he has an emotional investment. Meaning he cares about you. If what he wants with you is a Dom/sub relationship, yes, he would be concerned about your wellbeing, but it would be more than just physical." Another pause as he searches my face. "The guy is fucking crazy about you. How could he not be? That day with Santino, he was a madman thinking you'd been hurt. That should tell you what you need to know." He sits back waiting for me to respond.

The waitress comes to the table with our fondue pot and dippers.

"Let's eat. I bet this is just going to be a snack for a big guy like you."

He laughs at my remark about his appetite and his hugeness.

My mood is much lighter. I feel like the dark clouds have cleared. But I know I still have to clean up the mess after that storm waiting for me at Marco's.

My phone has continued to vibrate in my bag the whole time John and I are at lunch. I feel a little bad for avoiding him the way I have. I just needed time and information. I know I'm ready to face him now.

Marco

She won't answer my calls. She won't return my texts. I have got to get her to let me explain. Even if she never wants to see me again because of my fucked-upness I can't let her leave me thinking that's all she was to me, a plaything. I have not had feelings for a woman in years, and even then I don't think I felt about her the way I do about Elizabeth. Elizabeth makes me feel that I can be happy, fully, completely and totally happy, not just with her but with life, with me, with tomorrow and forever. She makes me feel that anything and everything is possible. And if I've hurt her, I know that I've hurt her, but if I can at least make her see that she is so much more, that she has made life worth living for me, I'll understand if she has to walk away from someone like me but I can't let her go until I make her understand.

And knowing she could be with John right now and the things they could be doing is hell. The waiting is killing me. Each minute is torturous, going on and on and on. Every time my phone dings or every time I think I hear something outside my door I practically jump out of my skin. I want to kick myself for unpacking those damn pictures. Why the fuck did I do that?

Chapter Fourteen

Elizabeth

I know this man. He has entered into places within me, places I thought were irreparable, broken and destroyed. He's healed me and brought me back to life. It's because of this I know what I am to him, what he needs me to be. It's time for me to face him and give myself to him.

I let myself into his condo with the keys he gave me. Marco jumps when I enter. He's so beautiful he intoxicates me. Seeing him always makes my heart beat faster. He's wearing black jeans and a black T, probably the same thing he had on this morning when he left to meet Brian. It should be illegal to look this good but he looks disheveled and a little unkempt. He was sitting on the couch reading the paper when I came in and now he's standing nervously waiting for me to say something. We're quietly looking at each other, each nervous about what the other is going to say or do. The expression on his face is full of pain and worry but he doesn't say anything. He's waiting for me.

Finally, he breaks the silence. "Elizabeth…" The word is so low, choked almost.

I raise my hand to stop him from saying anything more, his eyes widen, pleading.

"You want me to be your plaything, Marco? Show me, show me how much you want it."

He looks confused and I can tell he's searching his mind for what I mean. Then I see realization beginning to dawn on him followed by his inner struggle aa he silently fighta with himself.

"I haven't submitted to a woman in a very long time, Elizabeth."

I can hear the uncertainty in his voice.

"There are no other women, Marco, only me." My tone is firm and sure, I have complete control.

He slowly lowers to his knees, his eyes never leaving mine.

"Please, Elizabeth," he says quietly, his tone sure.

I walk slowly to his kneeling body and place my hand on his hair, running my fingers through its beautiful fullness.

"Please what, Marco?" It's almost a whisper.

He hesitates before he answers, being certain he tells me exactly what he wants.

"Please take me, make me yours." There is a deep longing in his subdued plea.

"I'm going to take you, baby, but you've always been mine. Tonight I'm going to prove it to myself."

His eyes look up at me full of emotion and…gratitude.

"We're going to go into the bedroom, Marco, and I want you to strip for me. Then I want to you get out the vibrator, lube and flogger. I want you completely open for me. It's my turn to play."

His eyes widen and he licks his lips.

"Yes, Elizabeth."

"Good, now let's go."

I hold my hand out to him, he takes it as he rises to his feet.

When we get in the bedroom I see he's removed all the portraits, even mine. I take the chair from the corner of the room and move it to face the foot of the bed so I can watch him getting the items I asked for. Surprisingly, I am very calm considering I am going to flog someone for the first time. I sit back in the chair crossing my legs and rest my arms on the armrests tapping my fingernail, looking at him. He's standing at the foot of the bed waiting for my instructions.

"Remove your clothes. I want to look at you." My voice is becoming husky. The thrill of having control over this powerful man is making me heady.

He begins to slowly pull his shirt over his head and as each golden toned piece of his naked flesh is revealed my heart rate gets higher and higher.

"Give it to me," I say holding my hand out for it. He places it in my hand watching my face for clues and any indications of what I am really feeling. He's not sure if I'm serious or not.

"The pants please, Mr. Bond," I say as a tremor of excitement runs through me.

The sound of his zipper fills the air triggering pulsing in my groin. He bends as he lowers his pants down his muscled thighs and images of him at the gym throwing kicks in the cage flash through my mind. It makes my mouth water. He steps out of the jeans and picks them up as he stands, then places them in my outstretched hand. I have a satisfied smirk on my face. I'm enjoying having him on guard and not knowing what's happening.

"The underwear if you please," I say raising an eyebrow looking at him like, *you know what I want*.

His erection is already showing beneath his black briefs before he begins to slide them down his slim hips.

"Turn around." It's an afterthought, the sight of his delicious ass does wonderful things to me and I have to watch it bending over and seeing his balls hanging from the front when he does. When did I get so naughty?

And that is exactly what I'm looking at right now, Marco's glorious naked body with all of his muscles making mountains and valleys from the tops of his shoulders all the way down to his feet. He is everything male perfection, a god in the flesh brought to life but with the desires of a sinner, oozing power, masculinity, sex, and control. And he's mine.

"Look at me, Marco." My sense of control is beginning to take over. I want him in my hands to do with what I want. I want to hear him moan and sigh, saying my name in ecstasy.

He slowly turns with his underwear gripped in his hand. He's fully hard now, and his cock is flushed with the blood filling it making the veins pop up and down the shaft. I want to run my tongue along them and taste his saltiness. I hold my hand out for his last piece of clothing and put it with the rest of them on the floor next to me.

"Touch yourself, Marco, squeeze your cock."

I hear the suck of air he takes in and I see the surprise in his face. He's never heard me use that word before. It's obvious he likes it because his hard-on just flinched. He palms his shaft, begins to rub himself up and down before placing his hand at the base of the head and squeezing. Just what I wanted, some pre-cum comes out and begins to slide down the side of the head.

"Give it to me. I want to lick it on your finger."

He takes his finger and gathers it up on the tip then holds it out for my mouth. I lean into him sticking out my tongue and suck his finger into my eager mouth. His eyes never leave my face.

I stand and move the chair back.

"Now undress me. But don't touch me."

The muscles in his jaw clench. It's the only visible sign of his fight for control. It makes me smile.

He takes a step closer to me and I can feel his body heat and hear his breathing. I want to reach out and touch him but it's too soon. I want him to suffer a little. He takes the hem of my shirt and slowly lifts it up and over my head then he moves behind me to undo my bra letting the straps slide down my arms on their own before pulling it off. He comes back around to the front of me and squats to open the button to my jeans. My zipper is the only sound we hear besides the beating of our hearts and our heavy breathing. I place my hands on his shoulders so that I can step out of my pants. I feel him tense slightly under my touch. I keep my hands on him as he slides the panties down my legs and I wonder how wet they are from my excitement. He stands and places my clothes with his. And then he waits.

"Turn around and grab the posts high and separate your legs as far as you can." This is not a request but a command.

Oh. My. God. The sight of this male beast stretched out between the bedposts with his muscles taut and flexing every time he shifts is more than I'd imagined. It's going to be hard not to want to do this again and again just for this image right here alone. And that is precisely what I want to do, replace those images in my mind of those portraits with new ones. I want to burn the image of him submitting to me in my mind so that every time I think of this bed I will think of him and me. No one else.

I can't resist touching him, running my hands along his smooth flesh and feeling his body under my palms. I want to memorize every nook, groove and crease of him. As one of my hands slides up the length of his back the other slides between his legs and cups his balls, stroking the smoothness of his shaft with my fingers. His head dips back and I hear him let out a slight moan.

"I'm going to flog you now, okay?"

I feel his erection twitch again and it makes me smile. He likes the idea.

"Yes, Elizabeth." His voice is rough and strained, just like the rest of him.

I step back and pick up the flogger and run the tails through my hand. *This thing does make music on the skin,* I think to myself and smile. I begin to windmill it in the air the way I've seen him do before I move it to touch his skin. After I get the rhythm of it, I bring it to brush against his flesh, traveling down then up his body. Another moan comes from him, this one a little louder and longer. Watching him react to me, seeing his body respond and melt to my touch is the strongest aphrodisiac. It's so heady and intoxicating, I'm getting high on it. I shift movements and flick the tails across his ass cheek then move it down his leg, then to the other side and up his leg then finish on the other cheek. I drop the flogger and lightly score my nails down the length of his back watching as the red lines rise to the surface showing my mark on him. I pick up the lube and squirt some in my hand.

"Turn around, my love, and lie on your back on the bed with your ass hanging off for me."

Marco lowers his arms and slowly turns. His eyes are glazed with lust, his cock is rock hard and oozing and his fists are clenching and unclenching at his sides. Lowering his body to the bed he lies back with his ass hanging off, his balls tight and wrinkled and his erection screaming to come. And that vein is begging for my tongue.

I move between his legs and push them open as wide as they will go.

"Keep your legs open, Marco, and your arms over your head."

The power I feel from having him at my mercy is incredible. I now know what he meant when he said bringing me pleasure gives him even greater pleasure. Everything I do to him spikes my arousal higher and higher.

I take a little lube from my one hand and spread it on the other. Kneeling down in front of him, I take his huge length in my hand and begin to glide my hand up and down it, twisting and turning around him with the lube making me glide along his steel flesh. I move my other hand to run my finger along the middle of his cheeks to relax him so he will open up for me. I bring my mouth to suck on the head of his cock and take his balls in one hand as I spread the lube over his hole, moving the tip of my finger in circles around the puckered entrance. I do what makes me crazy when he does it to me. I can tell by his body he's beginning to ride that wave of his orgasm. He's in that space between here and oblivion.

My wetness has completely coated me so that my thighs glide together squeezing my pussy. His cheeks have relaxed and opened up so as I suck him deep into my mouth I press my fingertip against his hole. Up and down I move my mouth, taking him to the back of my throat while keeping my finger at his entrance. He finally opens and lets me in. First just the tip of my finger gets pulled inside him. His moaning is becoming deeper and more intense. He pulls my finger in a little more, then a little more until finally my whole finger is inside him. I begin to suck him feverishly, devouring him as I start to turn my finger, twisting, then I bend it pushing on that magic spot inside him.

"Oh God, Elizabeth!" he roars as his cum explodes in my mouth. I keep sucking him as I rub that little place inside his ass.

"Stop, baby, stop!"

Payback is so sweet.

Taking one last suck on his head, I slowly pull my finger out.

"I'm not finished with you yet, Marco."

"Oh God, Elizabeth," he moans from where he's lying on the bed.

He's still hard, and I plan to get him like steel again. I pick up the vibrator and start at his hole. I hold his legs open and keep the tip of the vibrating head at the entrance as the shaft of the vibrator rests on his balls.

"Fuck, woman!" comes another roar from the beast and it's all I can do to keep from chuckling out loud.

"Keep your hands over your head, Marco, don't move."

I hear a rumble coming from him as his erection fills with blood again and his veins bulge. I shift the vibrator so that it rests on his cock and his balls and I lower my mouth to lick up his length along that beautiful big vein.

"Slide up the bed, love. I'm going to fuck you now."

He raises his head to look at me and there is so much adoration in his eyes. He lifts his body and moves farther onto the bed. I climb up the mountain that is him and straddle him, rubbing my body along him as I go. I set the vibrator down relishing how my skin ignites against his, the feel of him against me sets me on fire. It is intoxicating. Sliding my sheath down on his cock I fill myself with him and let out a gratifying moan as I begin to move, lying on top of him, gliding against him. His chest is under my face and I nibble him, here and there, leaving little love bites all over. Sitting up I grind against him, back and forth, up and down, wanting to ride him harder and harder, and I get higher and higher with each of my thrusts.

"I'm going to come, Marco."

He picks up the vibrator and holds it against my clit and I shatter, exploding, as I ride him on that wave.

"Oh God, Marco!"

I take the vibrator from him and reach my hand behind me to place it under his balls. He grabs my hips and begins to pound me into him.

"Fuck! Fuck! Fuck!"

Slamming me into him, he comes and fills me with everything he has.

I collapse on top of him and his arms wrap around me, holding me close, stroking my back, as he buries his face in my hair. We just breathe, lying together, completely spent, lost in each other.

"It's my turn to get the towel, baby, be right back," I whisper and kiss his lips lightly.

I go into the bathroom and look at the woman in the mirror. I look the same but I feel different. I feel as if the person I was and used to be, the one who sat back and waited for things to happen, has finally let her reserve fall away exposing a stronger more vibrant woman. I feel free.

Marco comes in and joins me in the bathroom, closing the door behind him.

"Let's take a shower together, Elizabeth, please?"

I smile up at him, this strong, sensitive man. "Okay."

He turns the knobs and holds his hand out for me to come in when the water is hot. Marco doesn't wash me; he worships my body with so much affection and love, it's beautiful.

"Are you going to let me explain, Elizabeth?" His words are still laced with uncertainty.

We're in bed. So much time has passed without anything being spoken, at least not with words, just our bodies speaking to each other with a soft touch, a graze of lips, flesh to flesh.

I look into his eyes and I realize something.

"If you need to explain, Marco, then yes you can."

He might need to, not for me but for him.

Marco

When I saw her at the door I was shocked. I didn't know what to do. And when she took control and said she was going to prove to herself that I belonged to her, I thought I'd died and gone to heaven. Whatever she wanted I would do, and I'd never been happier to do what a woman wanted, my woman.

"First, I would never have had those pictures brought here if I'd known you before I organized everything for the move."

"Marco, I know this. What I want to know is what am I to you?" She swings her hand out toward them. "Am I like the rest of them, just tell me so I know where I stand." She studies my face, "You have to be honest, and if I am, it's okay, that doesn't mean I'll leave…unless you want me to. Just know that you're more than that to me." It's almost a whisper and is hard to hear but I heard ever word.

I hold her face gently in my hands so that she's looking directly at me.

"You know you're not, Elizabeth! Before you, my life was all about money, business, success. Being with a woman was only about pleasures of the flesh. That's what those pictures were about. But with you, it's like you cut me open and let the sun shine inside me and brought everything to life. You made me realize that I could be happy, that I wasn't living but I'm alive with you. I don't want you to leave me, Elizabeth, ever."

Her expression is so beautiful. Tears well up in her eyes, not from sadness but from joy and relief and hope. I kiss her hard and deep. I never want to let her go.

She pulls away from me and I can tell there's one more thing she wants to say, and I already know what it is.

"Tell me everything about Liana, Marco. All of it."

I let out a heavy sigh and pull her close. I want to be holding her just in case she tries to pull away.

"Liana and I had a fling, yes. It was a while ago, about five years ago and we saw each other for about a year. She was the one who brought BDSM into my life."

I can feel Elizabeth flinch in my arms and I just tighten my hold on her.

"Liana got off on some pain. And to be frank, I was coming out of that shitty part of my life, and it seemed that is exactly what I needed. It gave me complete control, and pleasure."

I feel her tighten again but I don't loosen my hold on her.

"She made me think she loved me. But I found out later it wasn't me she loved but what I did to her, my position in the company and the money I was making. I thought I loved her and I asked her to marry me."

Elizabeth starts pushing against me, "Let me go!"

"You asked me to tell you; now let me finish, dammit!"

She settles down but she's stiff and motionless.

"After I proposed she started to ask for things, a house, jewelry, money and then she wanted more…pain. I started to question her about it and I told her I couldn't get her all those things; a house wasn't possible yet. I gave her some things but it wasn't enough, or good enough. We started to fight and I think she thought she could do anything she wanted, that she had me no matter what she did. So she started to go out at night." I pause as I remember that time. It doesn't seem real, like it was something I watched or it was someone else.

I feel Elizabeth's hand come to lie flat against my chest as she's waiting for me to continue.

"After she'd come home with marks all over her body I decided to follow her one night. She went to a BDSM club. Apparently she'd been a member there before we'd gotten together. I filled out the appropriate paperwork to get in and signed stating I wouldn't participate in any scenes because I didn't have a clean health record on file." I let out another deep breath before I continue. "When I got in I found her in a scene with two guys after they'd caned her. One was fucking her in the ass; the other had his cock shoved down her throat.'

"Oh God, Marco, I'm sorry."

"It was a good thing, baby, because right then I realized I didn't love her and what she was doing was a huge favor for me. I didn't feel jealous over what I saw but pissed that I'd been made to be a fool." I pull Elizabeth close and finish the story, "That was Liana. I couldn't blame her for that, but I wasn't going to be her meal ticket. So I went home and packed her shit, left a note and told her I was leaving for a few days and to be gone when I got back." I look into Elizabeth's glowing face, "And that's it, babe."

"Thank you for telling me, Marco. But…"

"What is it, baby?"

"Marco, I can't be like those other women. I don't think I can be like that with you…" her eyes are searching mine, looking for something to tell her it's okay.

"Elizabeth, those women don't exist. There is no other woman but you. You're everything I want; don't ever question that, baby. Ever."

Relief is clearly evident on her face and in her body. I can feel her relaxing in my arms.

"There are no more secrets between us, Elizabeth, got that?"

"Yes, no more."

But it's my turn to ask a question now. If I don't it will eat me up inside. "Elizabeth, tell me about John."

I feel her tense against me again.

"There's nothing to tell, Marco." I can tell she's a little worried.

"Elizabeth, no more secrets. Tell me, I need to know everything, even if it hurts."

She pulls her lip between her teeth, nervously tugging on it. Oh God, no.

"I had lunch with him today." She sighs heavily with the admission. "When I found those pictures I had to talk to someone about the lifestyle, and I needed it to be someone who had no interest in our relationship, someone with a completely unbiased opinion. I just needed facts."

"Did you get the information that you needed?" I ask waiting for more.

"Yes, that's why I'm here. He helped me to see things clearly."

I suck in a breath before I ask, "Is that all that happened today with him?"

Her brows pull together in confusion. "What do you mean, 'is that all'?"

"Are you attracted to him, Elizabeth?" There, it's out.

The surprise on her face is completely obvious.

"That came out of nowhere. He's an attractive man, Marco. I'd have to be dead not to see that but no, I'm not attracted to him. I feel nothing toward him except friendship." She searches my face and I'm sure she can see the residual worry that has been eating at me all day, the uncertainty and the fear.

"Marco," she says softly, "you have healed me, made me live again, and there is no other man I ever want but you. None." She pulls my face to hers kissing me with so much emotion, so much tenderness and so much possession it melts the last bit of doubt that I might have had.

"There's one more thing, baby," I say to her.

She waits quietly for what else I have to say.

"I liked that Dominatrix in you. Do you think she could come out to play again?" I say as a wicked smile curves my lips.

The blush creeps quickly over her cream skin but she can't stop the slow naughty grin spreading across that beautiful face.

"Well, Mr. Bond, I'm sure she will have to to remind you who's really in control."

"Like I said, baby, you're the best kind of bad."

My hard-on is pressing into her and her body answers it, our need calling to each other, wrapping itself around us, entering us and we succumb to it, getting lost in each other, mouths, hands, tongues, fingers. We ride that wave together climbing higher with nothing to stop us now and we crash together lost in each other. No kink, no binds, nothing but desire joining us, becoming one.

I fall asleep with Elizabeth in my arms and I feel like life is just beginning and it's magnificent.

Chapter Fifteen

Elizabeth

"Mr. Wu," I'm on the phone with him, a client, "I appreciate the offer to make me dinner, but I'm sorry, I can't."

This is the fifth time this widower has asked me out and he's not even a sugar daddy!

"If there is anything else we can help you with…" I pause as he asks me about Medicaid benefits. "Yes, when open enrollment comes around give us a call and we can review some other options for you. Have a great day, Mr. Wu, bye." I wait until I hear the word bye from him then I hang up.

I groan, "Oh my God, again!" and I hang my head.

"What's the matter, Elizabeth, Mr. Wu proposing to you again?"

Carol loves this; I can hear her practically rolling on the floor laughing at me.

"My God, the last time he did this he called me here every day with something or other and came in to the office three times that week. What is it, does the man have mating cycles like women have periods that get him all worked up? He's a sweet old guy but he's driving me crazy!"

Now the whole office is in an uproar. I'm not going to live this one down for a while.

Thankfully the front door chimes announcing a visitor and hopefully putting an end to my Mr. Wu torment. I get up to greet them and stop when I see Marco. He's got a huge bouquet of yellow roses in his hand.

"Ms. DiStefano, how is your day going?"

His smile brightens up the whole room and his voice still makes me want to swoon.

"Mr. Kastanopoulis, it's much better now that I see you again, although I'm afraid you're too late. Someone's already proposed today." I tease him as his arm goes around my waist pulling me to him.

"Oh really?" I feel him tense against me and it makes me giggle.

"Yes, dear Mr. Wu, he's asked to make me dinner again tonight." I'm a terrible person for making fun of the old man's sweetness, but I mean, really?

"Ah, I see, well, I understand. I cook for you all the time."

All three women in the office yell out at the same time, "You do?!"

He laughs at the extra ears before answering. "Yes, I do, breakfast, lunch and dinner, but she's worth it."

"Don't spoil her too bad, Marco, she's hardly tolerable as it is," Carol says coming out of her office, smiling from ear to ear.

He loosens his hold on me but doesn't entirely let me go. I'm totally crazy for this man. I just want to scream it out sometimes!

"Hi, Carol, actually it's you I came to see today."

The surprise is evident on her face as her eyes widen and her mouth falls open while her words get stuck in her throat.

"You did?" she finally mutters.

"Yes, and these are for you. The mayor told me about the lunch you and his wife had." He moves his hand from my back and reaches out to give her a small hug. "He said his wife was asking him questions about my project and wondering why it hadn't begun yet. She told him how it would be such a shame if anything got in the way and what a disservice it would be to the community…and to his re-election."

If I thought I was surprised before, I know I am now. Carol quite demurely used her connections to gently suggest in an ear that most certainly would have the greatest effect, the mayor's wife's, that maybe something was amiss with Marco's project. It was quite brilliant really. It was informal, I'm sure a comment made in passing, probably sounding more like an afterthought than a formal complaint. A talk between two old friends, much the same way they would talk about the latest fashions. Brilliant.

Carol blushes, I have never seen her blush before, and she lowers her head, smiling bashfully.

"Leonora and I used to go line dancing together when we were kids. She's an old friend of mine. She is the most regal women I know today but back in the day, wooey, she was a hellion. That's probably why the mayor scooped her up so fast."

"Well, after she questioned him on it, he did some checking. That little conversation of yours and Leonora's was a big part in my finding out what was going on with my permits. And for that I am forever in your debt, my dear." Marco bows slightly before handing Carol the roses.

"Aw, honey, what are friends for, come here you big ole teddy bear." She gives him an eye-popping hug. Now it's Marco's turn to blush.

By now everyone has come out of their offices and are watching the emotional, yes it's emotional, display. I can't believe we're all not in tears. I know I feel them welling up threatening to fall. This must not be easy for Marco. He's not an open man especially with such personal and business matters. But this is Carol, and he must have felt her genuineness.

"You didn't have to do this, Marco, but they're beautiful, thank you."

"It's the least I can do, thank you for caring; it doesn't go unnoticed. Now, if Ms. DiStefano has some time, can we review that timeline again and maybe make some revisions according to the latest updates? We can start to move forward now." He turns back to Carol. "Did you see what Elizabeth showed me?"

"Yes, I went in and she gave me a peek one day, she was holding the goods out on me until it was ready, and I was very impressed. This is going to work very well for you and your company."

"Yes it is. I couldn't be more pleased." Turning back to me he gets a little glint in his eye. "Can I have you for a few minutes, Ms. DiStefano?"

"I'm all yours, Mr. Bond. Shall we go?" I smirk at his naughtiness.

When we enter my office I decide to close the door. I can't wait until we get home to find out what's going on with KMD Enterprises. I want to know now. Taking my seat across from Marco, he's his usual classic business gentleman who never shows any signs of stress, I jump right into the questions.

"So, what's going on, Marco?"

"Actually I can't discuss everything yet. I promise I'll tell you all of it tonight though. I haven't addressed the entire situation this morning but I had to come and see you and I wanted to give Carol a little thank you present, so I decided to kill two birds with one stone." He's so cool and relaxed and it's killing me. I'm dying to know.

"All right, I suppose I can wait a few more hours, but you promise you'll tell me everything tonight, right?"

Dropping his head back and laughing at my childish behavior he laughs. "Yes, I promise, now let me see that prospectus again."

"Absolutely, Mr. Kastanopoulis, and there are some other things I'd like to discuss with you. I understand you might have some concerns if you should have a fire in your home," I tell him as I put on my glasses and begin clicking open some screens on my computer.

His fingers begin to drum on the arm of the chair as he's looking at me.

"Have I told you, Elizabeth, that I want to fuck you with your glasses on?"

Fuck.

Marco

"Mr. Kastanopoulis, there are two gentlemen here to see you," Christine pops her head in my door. Her eyes are wide and her face is serious.

I remind her again to call me by my first name. "It's Marco, Christine, and I'm coming, thank you."

I can hear the nervousness in Christine's voice and I can see the apprehension in her expression. It's completely normal. Vinny and John always make people nervous. It's gotten them to where they are today.

I walk out to the lobby and find Christine stealing glances at the two imposing men talking quietly together. I'm sure she's never met anyone like these gentlemen before. If you're not from the "neighborhood" then you don't meet this type of people. Vinny D'Angelo is a bear of a man in size but his presence is even more commanding, it's intimidating and you can feel a dangerous element about him. John Mikelson, Steve's father, is a bit more outspoken but is also every bit as intimidating. He's usually the one who speaks for the both of them. His talents lie in his verbal manipulation and he always gets what he wants. Steve gets this gift from him. There is not a person who was ever able to say no to John. If they did, it was handled. Both Vinny and John are in custom-tailored suits and designer Italian shoes. There isn't a hair out of place and their nails are manicured, looking like the epitome of business polish, almost old-school style.

"Marco, my boy, come here." Vinny sees me first and opens his arms to embrace me. I know I have a special place in this man's heart, Vinny and my dad were childhood friends. Once when they were kids they were involved in something that could have gotten Vinny into a lot of trouble with the police but my dad took the rap for it. Because my dad didn't have anything prior on his record he was released. At that time people knew each other in the neighborhood. They looked out for each other. Families would come and sit on the front stoop after dinner and socialize while the kids played together. No one messed with the people from the neighborhood, nobody. After a time, while I was growing up and the older generations died off, people started moving away, things changed, and that's when Vinny moved to Florida. But he believed that you take care of the people who take care of you so he made the offer to my dad, along with John, to come with him. My dad wanted to stay close to the rest of his family so he refused. Vinny wanted to give my dad a chance to get out too so he lent my dad the money to open the restaurant upstate. We left the neighborhood and started a new life. It was a good life, my parents did well, and maybe all because of that day my dad and Vinny got into trouble.

Vinny has never forgotten this favor even after lending my dad the money and that's why he gave me the opportunity to go down to Florida and learn the business with him. When I first got started in it, I immediately loved it and learned everything I could, absorbing whatever these two had to teach me and anyone else who would talk to me.

Vinny holds my face in his two hands and kisses me on both cheeks. When he releases me John pulls me in and does the same thing while patting me warmly on my back. His look is a bit more serious than Vinny's. I'm sure this is not a trip he wanted to make.

"It's good to see you, Marco. We miss you down in Florida but you're doing a great job here on your own," John tells me warmly.

"Well, to be fair, I'm not really alone."

"Yes, you are. But we know what you mean just as you know what we mean," Vinny says.

"I understand." I turn to Christine to introduce her to these two men. I know she's dying to know who they are.

"Christine, I'd like to introduce you to Vinny D'Angelo." I turn to her and nod indicating it's okay, he's not going to bite.

"It's very nice to meet you, Mr. D'Angelo." Her voice is a little high showing her nervousness.

"Thank you very much for keeping our boy straight, Christine." He is charismatic and endearing. There is no denying it.

"And this is John Mikelson."

She looks at me with a question in her eyes. "Mikelson?"

"Yes, this is Steve's father."

"I am very pleased to meet you, Mr. Mikelson." She doesn't seem as nervous to meet John, maybe because of Steve and how amiable he appears to be. She might not feel this way if she knew what this man has done.

"You are a very lovely young lady, thank you for all of your hard work with these two boys." He's a bit of a charmer like his son.

"Christine, these men are the M and the D in KMD Enterprises. Vinny is the man who started it all in Florida and John made the baby grow. They're like fathers to me. They're my mentors and partners in the business."

Her eyes are as wide as saucers. I think she's afraid to make any assumptions. Good girl.

"I need you to call Liana and Steve in, Christine. Tell them Vinny and John are here." There is nothing else that needs to be said. She nods her understanding.

"Come, let's go inside so we can talk. Would you like some espresso? Christine makes a delicious cup."

"Really? Of course, three cups please. Just like home, Marco, that's a beautiful thing." Vinny beams.

We go into my office and close the door. The two men take the seats in front of my desk and I sit behind it.

"Things look really good here, Marco. You're doing a great job."

"Thank you, Vinny, I appreciate it."

John speaks next. "So you know why we're here then." His expression is somber.

"Yes, how long have you known?" I look back and forth between the both of them.

Vinny speaks up. "Probably since just about the beginning. The contacts I reached out to when we first started discussing this project caught wind of the situation as soon as things got held up and as the other 'relationships' were being made."

"I see," I say wondering why it took me so long to find out.

Vinny continues. "We knew you'd find out on your own and would handle things so we didn't want to interfere." He pauses and looks over to his old friend John. "And maybe we were hoping that things would right themselves before it went too far."

"The situation has been taken care of and things are moving forward. Now that you're here, they'll realize the entire situation and the attempt to sabotage it are exposed and stopped," I reply.

"Yes, and I'm glad you made local connections on your own, they will be very useful to you, as you've already found out," Vinny answers.

Christine knocks on the door and I get up to let her in with the tray of our three cups of espresso and sugar on the black lacquer tray.

"These look perfect. Marco has taught you well. You would make a fine wife for a good Italian boy," Vinny says. Some things never change.

"Thank you, Mr. D'Angelo," she answers, blushing then turns to me. "I spoke with Liana and Steve. They'll be here as soon as they can."

"Thank you, Christine, let me know when they get here before they come back, and close the door behind you when you go, please."

She looks at me with a puzzled expression before saying, "Yes, sir," and turns to leave, closing the door behind her as instructed.

I turn back to Vinny and John and ask, "The question is what do we do now?"

John sighs, sitting back in his chair, as Vinny answers. "This is an unusual situation. Normally, as you know, the person would already have been taken care of, but in this instance we've decided to wait until we speak to them directly before moving forward."

I let out a deep sigh. This is what I've been dreading.

"I appreciate it being handled this way. I just can't believe it's actually come to this." I can't help but feel torn. I wanted to "take care" of this person myself but my personal feelings outweigh all of my anger.

"Well in the old days it wouldn't have come this far but thank God things have changed a little."

I fill them in as to the progress we were able to achieve even with the problems we had getting started and I show them the timeline Elizabeth prepared for me. It's useful in getting Vinny and John up to date on the situation. I even tell them about the Bid On a Date function I'm doing and, God knows, I haven't heard them laugh that hard in years, which is a good thing because we all need a good belly laugh.

The phone rings, breaking the light mood. "Yes?"

It's Christine and I can tell she's tense. "Liana's here."

"Excellent, have her wait to come in until Steve gets here. And don't worry, sweetie, everything's fine. Okay, Christine?"

"Ok, Marco." She sounds a little less tense.

"Good girl."

I look to the men sitting anxiously quiet across from me. "Steve's not here yet."

They each nod in understanding.

The minutes are beginning to drag by loudly.

My phone alerts me with a text from Elizabeth. I can't help but smile as I read it and I'm relieved at the brightness it brings to a very bad moment. I don't know how this is going to work out. The fate of the traitor is not up to me finally but up to these two men. And they did not become the well-respected powerful men they are by being nice and complacent.

Hi Sexy, was just thinking about you ☺ Elizabeth's text reads.

Vinny asks, "Is that a girlfriend, Marco?"

I look up at him. "Yes, it is. We've been seeing each other about a month. She's the one who prepared the timeline I showed you. Her name is Elizabeth DiStefano."

He looks at me and the corner of his mouth turns up as his eyes uncharacteristically soften.

"A nice Italian girl, this will be the one you will marry, Marco. I know that look. I remember when I first had it, so many years ago." The look in his eyes is one of nostalgia for long ago memories of a new love.

He's just knocked the air out of me. Me, married? No fucking way! But even as I try to deny it the idea alone warms my heart. I push it aside not wanting to think about that now. I don't want to fight with myself about the possibility that I could feel like that about Elizabeth, finally.

"I don't know about that, Vinny, but she is an amazing woman." I can't stop the smile from spreading across my face at the thought of her, picturing her face, her voice, her smile, her laugh, the way she smells and bites her lip when she gets nervous or turned on.

"Vinny knows. He gets that sight from his grandmother. She knew who all of us would marry as soon as she saw our faces. He should have been Cupid or something," John states, testifying to Vinny's words.

The absurdity of these two tough guys talking about marriage and Cupid and hearts and flowers is too much to resist and we all have another good laugh at the idea of Vinny dressed up in a red leotard with a bow and arrow and wings. Holy shit, that's funny!

The phone rings again and we all stop, getting jerked back to what is going on and why we are all here.

"Yes?" I answer it again.

"Steve's here now," Christine states. I can tell she's nervous again. She's probably picking up on the tension in the air.

"Thank you, bring them both in together if you please, Christine."

She lets out a little sigh before answering, "Okay." She does not want to be a part of this. Even though she doesn't know what 'this' is, she can feel something is going on.

The three of us sit and wait silently for the door to open. The few seconds seem to drag on forever.

There's a light tap on the door before it opens, initially just a crack then it slowly opens all the way. Steve enters first, his jaw clenched tight and his brows pulled together above his eyes that are shooting back and forth from each of us. He steps to the side and allows Liana to come in from behind him. She of course has her nose up in the air and saunters in, daring anyone to confront her.

"Hi, Pop, good to see you," Steve says to his father. "I didn't know you were coming up. You should have called me, I am your son."

John sets his glare on Steve warning him not to push it.

"Because you're my son is why I'm here, Steven. For no one else would I have come for this."

I see Steve's nostrils flare. At least he has the common fucking sense to keep his mouth shut.

"Hello, Zio, you should have told me you were coming," Says Liana to Vinny.

Vinny is Liana's uncle, zio means uncle in Italian. She has always used this term of endearment to get what she wanted, almost to the extent of abusing the fortunate position she had nothing to do with.

"I love you, Liana, but you will not be receiving any special treatment from me; this you are well aware of," Vinny warns her before he continues. "Now, sit, both of you. You know we have much to discuss."

Vinny speaks with the mannerisms of the old times, not giving in to slang. His position as the head of our family is one that was established many generations ago, following his father as the head of the family before he came over on the boat and was dropped off at Ellis Island in the early 1900's. We all sit and wait for him to begin, showing our respect.

"Now, Steven, why did you do it?"

"I don't know what you're talking about."

Is he a complete fucking asshole? He did not just insult Vinny's and his father's intelligence by denying he bribed a governor. His plan to get the local offices to stop my permits with a promise of large financial support to the governor during his re-election is now common knowledge. Steve also promised favors to him with some very strong political backing, connections he did not have. He'd attempted to use his father's and Vinny's power to persuade the officials to support the governor in order to gain control over my business and project.

John leans forward in his seat and speaks calmly, putting his hands together, "Steven, we're going to ask you one more time, only once, and if you're smart, you'll tell us everything." He sits back in his chair and takes a deep breath before continuing. It's so quiet in here I can hear the fabric rubbing as we shift in our seats. "Why did you do it?"

John stares into his son's eyes for a long moment before Steven opens his mouth. "Because this should have been my project. I'm your son. Marco's not even blood and you offered him this opportunity, put him in charge of the first expansion. He doesn't even have the business education. I'm the one with the certifications. How could you do this to me, Pop?"

I'm torn between wanting to destroy Steve, physically and professionally. If he was anybody else, I would already have done it. After he dragged his ass up from the beating I would have given him he would never be able to show his face again. The anguish, hurt and resentment pouring out of him is breaking my heart. I want to get up and leave the room, I feel so guilty. I feel as if I'm responsible for taking his opportunities away from him, that I punched him in the face and left him there to suffer. We've been friends for a long time, or at least I thought we were.

"Steven." John is not an emotional man but his tone is endearing right now as he speaks to his son. "Yes, we offered Marco the opportunity to make this expansion happen. And he formed this company. We are involved, but minimally. This is all him. But you should have come to us and asked us what we had planned for you. Do you think we would not have done anything for you as well? And do not insult Marco by saying he's not blood. He's part of the family, just like Vinny and I are family. And what you did here, you did to the family. That cannot go by without being punished somehow."

Steven's expression has just become one of mortification. He knows what's happened to those who have wronged the family in the past.

Vinny turns to me and asks, "How much did this cost the company, Marco?"

"Approximately $10,000," I answer calmly. He asked me this earlier so I've calculated the fees due to delays and other incidentals.

Vinny turns Steven. "You will write a check to KMD Enterprises for $10,000 to correct the financial loss incurred. It hasn't been decided what's going to happen with you but for now, you're coming back to Florida with us. Go home, pack your suitcases and be ready to leave. We'll call you to let you know when the flight is. And don't say a fucking word, Steven. You're lucky you're getting off this easy, and you know it. Now go. I'm so disappointed with you right now I can't see straight. What you did to the family, you should be ASHAMED of yourself. And you made us look like fools up here with these politicians and the local rednecks, putting us against each other. How do you think we look in terms of strength as a company? As soon as we get into town you start fighting for power, fucking disgusting! Now go!" He bellows so loud, the door shakes.

Steven has the decency to look ashamed with his head bent and a flush on his pretty boy face. He stops at the door and turns to me. "I'm sorry, Marco," he says quietly then turns to leave.

"Steve…" He's my friend, I can't help it. Never, never would I have imagined he would betray me like this. The pain I feel is deep.

I don't know when I'll see him again. What happened breaks my heart but it doesn't break the bond I have with him. It goes too far back. Money, power and greed turn people into monsters, using and betraying the ones they love. It's so sad.

Vinny turns to Liana who, unbelievably for once, has been sitting quietly.

"Liana.," he says to her.

"Zio…"

"Thank you for calling me when you thought something was not quite right. Your keen senses never let you down. I'm grateful for your attentiveness. It does not go unnoticed."

"Of course, Zio."

I am shocked!

"You knew? When?" I ask Liana. I have no doubt the surprise is evident on my face.

"I had a feeling something was up. I overheard some conversations Steve had on the phone and something seemed off but I couldn't put my finger on it. Sometimes being thought of as a bimbo can be used to your advantage. People think you're stupid."

The insinuation succeeds in making me feel like an asshole. Then something dawns on me.

"So every time you came into my office…" I let the sentence trail off as the realization comes together in my mind.

She picks it up. "Yep, I was checking to make sure Steven hadn't gotten into any of your documents or hacked into your computer." She looks relieved that everything is finally out.

"Holy shit, I can't believe it. I'm sorry, Liana, if I've ever insulted you, I would never want to do that." My apology is genuinely heartfelt.

"Marco, regardless of what you may think of me or feel about me, I would never do anything to jeopardize you or your business. But we can discuss that privately if you'd like," she purrs at me, right in front of Vinny and John.

"Liana, behave yourself. Marco is taken, stop that," Vinny chastises her.

"I know, Zio, but it's so cute to aggravate him and watch him get all flustered." So she's been playing with me all of this time, that little pain in my ass.

John has been sitting quietly through this whole conversation until now. "Marco, you're going to have to get a replacement for Steven immediately," he points out. "Now that things are moving again, you need someone with experience to oversee what's going on out on the project."

"Yes, you're right, John. I've already spoken to a friend of mine who does have experience and he agreed to help me out until a full-time replacement can be found." I look back and forth between Vinny and John. "And if you have any other ideas or suggestions we can discuss it."

"Liana, you can go now, my dear. As always it's lovely to see you." Vinny stands pulling Liana up with him and puts his arms around her.

"Thank you, Zio, give Mama and Papa a kiss for me, okay?" she says as she kisses both of his cheeks.

"Of course, my dear, and don't make any plans for dinner, we're all going out, even Marco's girlfriend. Send Christine in on your way out."

Vinny has a very elegant way of dismissing people. And I can't help but think that Elizabeth is absolutely going to love this. She's going to kick my ass.

Christine knocks tentatively at the door.

"Come in, Christine," I call from behind my desk.

When she enters she looks at each of us and can tell that the air in here has cleared. Her posture immediately relaxes. It's wonderful being able to read a woman, no matter who it is.

"Christine, make reservations for us for dinner tonight at…" Vinny turns to me for a restaurant.

"Circa 1922," I interject and smile.

"At Circa 1922 for seven o'clock for, let me see…" He counts the number of people in his head. "Six people, okay?"

"Certainly, Mr. D'Angelo." She even appears not to be as afraid of him now.

"And, Christine, call Elizabeth at work, the insurance agency, and let her know about the reservation and that I'm tied up in meetings with Vinny and John. Explain why I'm not calling her, please." I know I have just appeared totally pussy-whipped in front of Vinny and John but I don't care.

"Yes, Mr. Kastanopoulis, um, Marco." She steps out smiling to herself. Even she thinks I'm a pussy. Shit.

Vinny and John look at each other.

"Yep, you are so fucked, Marco, better just cut your balls of now and hand them over to Elizabeth in a nice little Tiffany's box with a pretty ribbon wrapped around it," John says busting the last nut I've got.

Chapter Sixteen

Elizabeth

I'm a nervous wreck and have been since I received the phone call from Christine at work. She was babbling about two men arriving today, and Marco and these men are locked up in his office having a meeting, and how she doesn't want to go back in there. And that I was having dinner with them tonight at seven at Circa 1922. If I didn't understand anything else about that conversation I do know it's good news because we're eating at "our" restaurant and if it's there, it's got to be good.

After I hung up with Christine I didn't know what to think. I didn't want to call Marco because, obviously, he's extremely tied up or he would have called me himself. He always calls me, and I don't want to text him because I don't want to distract him from whatever's going on. So I decide to not worry about it, apparently everything is fine and he will either pick me up or if he's not here by 6:45 then I'll just meet them there.

It's 6:15 and I'm trying to ignore my nervousness, fake it until you make it, and I'm faking being calm. When I'm alone, I tend to have elaborate conversations with myself, taking on both sides of an argument. The argument going on inside my head at the moment is about why Marco is throwing me in to a den full of lions tonight, two that I know of, without giving me any information about them. This is really quite unfair. It could be anyone really, like Brian and John or the councilman and another politician. There is no way of knowing without speaking to him. On the other hand, he wouldn't knowingly put me in an uncomfortable situation without giving me fair warning, would he? I stand at the open door to my closet in a black bra and panties with my thumbnail sliding between my front teeth as I'm trying not to chew it, not really looking at anything, completely lost in my thoughts. Then I hear the front door click open.

"Baby?" Marco's voice floats to me from the foyer.

"Thank God you're here!"

My body instantly relaxes just knowing he's here and I let out the air I guess I was holding.

He strides toward me and the room is suddenly filled with him and it thrills me and calms me at the same time. His presence wraps around me like an embrace pulling me toward him and holding me close.

"Hi, baby." His arms are around me and his lips are on mine forcing my mouth open and he kisses me as if he's starved and I am his only sustenance.

My hands bury themselves in his hair as I kiss him back, my hunger for him matching his, ravenous and starved. He continues to walk us, holding our embrace, until my back comes in contact with the wall. His hands slide to my waist and he lifts me as my legs wrap around him and I hug him with my legs. He holds me against the wall with his body as his hands fumble with his belt, button and zipper of his pants.

"Marco," I pant into his open mouth.

"Sshhh, baby, I need you... Right. Now."

Desire courses through me with his need. I feel it in his body, I taste it on his tongue, and I hear it in his voice.

I hear his pants drop to the floor the instant my panties leave my body, ripped off with both of his hands. They move to my breasts taking handfuls of them, squeezing them tightly before pulling them out of their confinement of the bra, exposing them to his hungry mouth. He growls as he feasts on me, penetrating me with his rock-hard erection, filling me completely and I cry out with it. His hands tightly on my hips, his mouth sucking and biting on my tits, he's fucking me like a mad man, wild and primitive and fierce. And it drives me wild. I dig my nails into him, begging for it, demanding it, pushing him on. We explode, screaming and biting and digging into each other like animals lost in the heat. He embraces me quietly with our foreheads touching, just breathing, coming down, and holding on to each other, he sets me down gently and brushes his lips against mine.

"Come on, baby, let's get cleaned up and I'll fill you in." He pulls up his pants and takes me by my hand and leads me into the bathroom. I can feel our cum dripping down my legs as we walk.

Lifting me into the tub, grabbing a washcloth and wetting it, he begins to clean me and begins to tell me what's going on. "Okay, here's the short version of it: Steve was responsible for having the permits stalled. He was trying to sabotage me so he could take over. I think those were his plans. He was doing it by bribing a governor. I found the trail when I spoke with the mayor. Actually Brian spoke to the mayor at the Halloween party, then I met with the councilman while having coffee with Brian on Sunday. That's what the councilman wanted talk to me about that night at the restaurant. You still with me, babe?" He looks up to see if he's confused me yet.

"I'm good, go ahead." I nod for him to continue.

He wipes himself before tucking everything in and zipping up his pants, then lifts me out of the tub and carries me back to the closet.

"We're having dinner with Vinny D'Angelo, he started the company in Florida years ago, and John Mikelson, Steve's father, who is Vinny's right-hand man, also considered an owner of the company as he was integral in its growth. Still with me, babe?" He steals another look.

I nod after he hands me a new pair of underwear then he leafs through my closet finding something for me to wear. He pulls out a black jersey body-hugging dress, simple yet elegant.

"If you keep ripping my panties, I won't have anymore," I scold him

"The only reason I'm going to buy you new ones is because you look so good in them and I like ripping them off." He leans toward me and pulls my lower lip between his teeth giving it a quick suck.

He continues. "Liana—" I roll my eyes. "Just listen, Elizabeth. Liana got a feeling a while back that something was up when she overheard Steve on the phone. She's been keeping an eye on him for a month. She called Vinny as soon as she thought Steve was up to something."

"Are you kidding me?" I can't hide my surprise. I was certain she had something to do with the problems.

"Well, it won't be as much of a surprise when you know that she's Vinny's niece."

My jaw has just hit the floor. The boss's fucking niece, isn't that just lovely.

"But what you really need to know is who and what Vinny and John are, well, mostly were." He pauses after he's pulled the dress over my head letting me arrange it on my body.

"Are you going to tell me or am I going to have to guess?"

"I can't really tell you but what I can say is they are from the neighborhood with the power of the family behind them."

I stand there staring at him not really believing what he's just told me. I open my mouth to ask and he just nods.

"That's why Christine was so freaked out. She's never been in contact with anybody like that. Jesus, Marco, you should have prepared the poor thing!"

"I know but you also need to know that Liana and Steve are having dinner with us tonight."

I can see him almost cringing delivering that wonderful piece of news to me. I know he was not looking forward to that part.

I square my shoulders and pick out my sexiest shoes and walk to the bathroom telling Marco over my shoulder as I go, "Thank you for letting me know, I have to put on my war paint."

I hear him laughing behind me as I close the door.

It's seven o'clock exactly when we walk in the door of Circa.

"Mr. Kastanopoulis, so good to see you again. Your party has already arrived. Right this way please" Mr. Maître D greets the local celebrity who is my boyfriend and turns with his chin up already walking toward our table.

Marco slides his hand down to the small of my back with his fingers splayed open in that wonderfully possessive way that I love. I lean into him and whisper, "Do I have to get used to being with someone who's a celebrity?"

His grip becomes firmer on my back pulling me closer as he answers, "You're damn right you do. You're mine, and I'm not letting you go anywhere. So get used to it." He kisses me, sealing his declaration as the entire table with Vinny, John, Liana and Steve watch.

The joy I feel bubbling up inside me is almost bursting. I am so happy, even a dinner with Liana can't ruin it.

The gentlemen stand as we approach and Liana looks almost…civilized. My eyes return to the two imposing, er, gentlemen, standing in front of me. They are striking, there is no doubt about that, and everything about them reeks of money, from the perfectly styled slicked back hair down to the fine round laces threading delicately in and out of the holes of their very expensive Italian leather shoes. Experiencing the sense of power and simmering danger lurking below the surface emanating from both Vinny and John is like hearing a sonic boom off in the distance and then being rocked by the tremors of its aftereffects. You know if you get in its path, it will throw you on your ass. No wonder poor Christine was so shaken up and couldn't even speak. She couldn't process everything that was happening and maybe couldn't understand it but she obviously felt it.

"Vinny, John, I'd like to introduce you to my girlfriend, Elizabeth DiStefano."

Vinny speaks up first. "Elizabeth, it's a pleasure to meet the woman who has made our Marco settle down. And I can see why. You are stunning." He holds me by my shoulders then kisses me on both cheeks. His New York accent is still evident but is not very heavy. I can tell this man has worked very hard at becoming who he is today going from that slick kid running the streets of Brooklyn and evolving into the dapper well respected business man in front of me now.

And you know what I'm thinking? I'm wondering if I should bow and kiss the ring on his finger. Is that what's expected? This man is power personified, strength, charisma, fear, envy and success.

"I'm honored to meet you," I say as I return the kisses on each of Vinny's cheeks, "and I don't know about making Marco settle down, though, he is a very stubborn man." I steal a glance at him.

He's smiling, he looks so happy being with his "family". And I'm being welcomed into it. I simultaneously feel a little apprehensive and happy about it. We've all heard stories of entering into the family. These men are connected and very close to the top. I wonder if Marco is considered a made man. I look at him trying to imagine him in the mafia. He doesn't fit any of the stereotypes I'd always envisioned. Yes, he's a very good business man and I think that's where the extent of his involvement lies. I believe he is involved with a business that was made by money and support of the family, a legitimate business that is doing a very good thing. This thought alleviates some of my concern.

"Elizabeth." John takes hold of my shoulders. "Welcome, it is an absolute pleasure to meet you. If you ever get tired of Marco just call me. I'll come save you." He kisses both cheeks, laughing as he does, and I smile kissing his as well.

"I will keep that in mind, John, and if Marco gets out of line I will let you know." I almost flirt with him. One must be careful what one says to a man like this. You don't want to offend nor do you want to over promise, even playfully.

John's eyes are sharper than Vinny's. Make no mistake though, Vinny misses nothing. He is the lion, sitting regally still all the while taking everything in. John is more like an eagle. His view is more lasered and swift. I almost want to shiver under his touch from the ice running through his veins. Where Vinny will incinerate and obliterate you, John is lethally cold. They are the complementary opposites of each other, making the perfect dangerous whole.

I turn to Liana and Steve as I take the seat Marco is standing behind waiting for me to sit down in. "It's good to see you both again." I decide it's best I pretend I don't know what's going on. "The party went very well the other night, don't you think?" I ask them trying to keep the conversation light.

"Yes, it was great and your friend's costume was amazing," Liana says. I can't believe she is actually being pleasant. I wonder if the shock is showing on my face because I am not believing this actual turn in her behavior is for real.

"I know; she made it. She's a designer and has been in charge of wardrobe for various movie productions for years now. Her talent is incredible." I answer her pleasantly but I'm still waiting for the bitch Liana to peel off this imposter's skin.

"Really, that sounds fantastic. I'd love to talk to her sometime. She must have some interesting stories."

I cannot believe Liana is talking to me as if she wants to be friends, please don't let me fall of my chair! Maybe I should warn Marco to watch out and be ready to catch me just in case.

Steve asks me, "Did you have fun at the party, Elizabeth? It looked like you did."

Sitting this close to Steve now I can see the many likenesses to his father and other interesting characteristics about him that I missed the other night. But I have to wonder if my opinion of him is being tainted or if it is a clarification in light of the newest developments in the attempted sabotage of KMD's project. As I look into Steve's eyes there is nothing but coldness in them. They're flat and without emotion. What I thought was a flirtatious laidback guy appears to be a cold, callous, unfeeling shell of a man.

"Yes, it was the first party like that I've been to. Fortunately, I knew some other people there besides Marco and Elsie."

"Marco," Vinny cuts in, "you'll have to bring Elizabeth to visit us in Florida, and we can show her around."

"Actually, I thought we might go up to New York and visit the family up there around the holidays," he says smiling at me.

I am speechless. Marco just said he wants me to meet his family, his real family, mother and father and any sisters or brothers. This is a huge step. This is the one that screams long-term commitment. I want to throw my arms around him and smother his face in tiny butterfly kisses. Thankfully the waiter approaches our table with water glasses saving me from making a blubbering idiot of myself in public.

During our meal I study Vinny and John through the veil of my lashes. I see no depth of emotion in their eyes, no sense of love or compassion. There is a fondness, yes, that they've exhibited to their family members at the table but it seems life has forced them to put this impenetrable stone veneer over their hearts. I glance at Liana and catch a glimpse of unguarded emotion on her face. She's lonely and my heart instantly hurts for her. Finally I turn to Steve and all I can think about is the poor little boy who was starved for the love of his father, and I pray that it's not too late for him. Marco's hand comes to rest on my thigh and his touch fills me with warmth and comfort. I look up into his face and the happiness and joy I'm filled with by his touch is looking back at me in his beautiful deep dark eyes.

The evening passes so beautifully, like family and friends with no worries, no conflicts, no hidden agendas. We're just enjoying our time together, making memories and giving smiles. Even Steve and his dad seem close sharing inside jokes that only they know. This is about as close to Norman Rockwell as we all get, the extent of our white picket fence image. Even on the surface we're different from most people, our little group of misfits, but we fit and tonight we're about as normal as everyone else. The only difference between us and them is we wear our dysfunctionality proudly. It makes us who we are.

Marco

Elizabeth has amazed me tonight. I was pretty certain she wasn't going to go running for the hills when the last bit of my past came roaring out of the closet. I was hoping to keep it locked up for at least a little while longer. Everything is out on the table, all of my fucked-upness and sick shit. When I tied her up and flogged the shit out of that beautiful cream skin of hers, she begged for more. And now she has seen my backbone and the backbone of my company and she didn't bat an eye. On the contrary, she stood tall smiling in everyone's face and proudly said, *Bring it, I can handle all of you and more.* This woman is totally fucking amazing.

And what I realize, what I know is the absolute truth, is that she doesn't want anything from me. She expects and demands nothing and because of that, everything within me flows and runs over into her endlessly. She accepts me for who I am, for what I am, and that allows me to be open and relaxed and completely free with her. With her acceptance she gives me freedom and with that freedom she gives me herself. She was always there, open and waiting for me, waiting for all of me to be shown to her so she could give her everything to me, her heart and soul.

Tonight all of our facades are gone, all of our closets are open and those skeletons are thrown out never to be hidden again. Tonight we stand before each other completely naked, stripped of all personas and labels and names. Tonight we will come together raw and truly uninhibited, bare and exposed, able to lose ourselves in the purity of it.

We've just walked into the condo after dinner. I feel like the weight of the world has been lifted off my shoulders. I hadn't realized all of this, the problems going on with KMD Enterprises and Elizabeth not knowing everything about me, were actually pressing so hard on me. I feel like I can breathe deeply and not worry about anything or anyone being ripped from me or crumbling within my grasp.

I look at Elizabeth and I can tell there's something on her mind.

"Marco," she says tentatively.

"Yes, baby?" I knew this was coming, the last brick to that wall.

"I have to ask you something." I can hear the hesitancy in her voice.

"Anything, baby, and I'll be completely honest." She deserves it after everything we've been through and all that she already knows.

"What about you... How much are you, um, connected?" It took balls to ask me that, but she's got bigger balls than a lot of men I know.

"I'm not, baby. I just have the backing. I run a company that is an extension of one built by the family. If I wanted to sell my portion of KMD Enterprises I could and have no affiliation, although I hold the largest part. But it's my baby. Vinny and John only contributed for investment reasons and quite frankly, I used them and their company for prestige. Having those connections and that reputation backing me is very advantageous. My plan is to buy them out when I've built a solid enough foundation under KMD. At the completion of this project, I believe, that will be the time. But I'll always be indebted to them for giving me this opportunity. Without them, I'd never have gotten to where I am today as quickly as I did." I wrap my arms around her, "Okay, baby?" I can feel her melt into me.

"Yes, Marco, but I don't know if it would really have mattered to me."

What she's really telling me makes my heart swell. She would have accepted me anyway, even with the risk of all of that, the family, as a constant threat to us.

The emotion welling up inside me is almost more than I can take. "I can't wait any more, Elizabeth!"

I grab her and throw her over my shoulder like a fucking cave man. It seems like she likes it though, by the way she's laughing and squealing.

"Marco! What are you doing?"

"I'm taking what I want. You know how selfish I am," I say swatting her ass next to my cheek, an ass I can sink my teeth into, turning to bite that beautiful round cheek.

"Stop it!" she squeals swatting my back.

"No, it's mine, I can do whatever I want." I'm so happy I laugh.

When we get to the bedroom I slide her down the front of me holding her tightly. As her feet hit the floor my arms wrap around her small body. I want her close, but I need more, flesh to flesh is not enough. My mouth takes hers, slowly, hungrily, wanting to pull her inside me, my yearning for her is so intense. Our hands begin to undress each other slowly, adoring each piece of skin intimately and thoroughly as it is exposed, imprinting each inch to memory, burning the images seen through our hands in our minds, hearts and souls. We don't need spoken words; our bodies are speaking loud enough. With every soft moan, with each slight turn of Elizabeth's body she tells me what she wants and what she needs. I know the language of her body. It speaks to me even in my dreams, haunting me by day and by night. Our mouths and tongues follow our hands and fingers, tasting, licking, and biting each other from the tips of our fingers to the ends of our toes.

It's time for her pleasure. I want to drown her in it. I want the whole house filled with the cries of it as it rings in my ears.

I turn her around and press lightly against her back between her shoulders blades motioning for her to bend over the bed.

"Bend over and spread your legs for me, love, open up to me," I tell her and I notice my voice is rough with the need that is so evident in my raging cock.

She does and I bend over her back sliding my hands down her back, over her ass and through the slick wet folds of her pussy, grabbing it in my palm.

"I'm going to get a surprise for you love, stay just like this," I tell her quietly next to her ear and nip her shoulder before I move away from her.

She doesn't say anything but I can tell by her heavy breathing she's excited.

I walk to the closet and pull out our little bag of tricks. Ah, here is what I want, the anal beads, butt plug and lube, vibrator and wrist restraints.

I stand behind her bent form admiring the vision in front of me. I put some lube in my hand closing a fist over it to warm it up, stroking her skin as I do. I massage the lube between my two hands and apply it over her tight asshole. Tonight I'm going to take it. She's begged me enough with her actions, constantly pushing it back on me begging for more when I'm fingering her there. I'll use the plug to get her ready first. My cock aches with the thought of it.

I begin to slide two fingers through her velvety slick wet folds, teasing her clit and sliding in and out of her sex. With the other hand I take the beads and coat them with the lube in my palm. I begin to work her back hole, circling it and teasing it with my finger, watching it pucker anticipating my entry into it. I push the tip of my finger inside as two fingers thrust into her pussy. God help me to last because this is fucking exquisite. Her ass is ready for the beads, loosening up and opening with my fingers. I begin to push them inside her one by one, pop, pop, pop, pop. When they're all in and she's a squirming little kitten under me I guide her to stand, turning her to face me.

I lower my mouth to hers, teasing her, licking her, sucking her lip. I feed the strap attached to Velcro restraints onto the wrought iron hook on the bedpost. I take one arm and lift it, sliding the cuff over her slender wrist as I watch her hands close over it, holding it tightly. Kissing her arm from the inside of her wrist then her elbow, and following it down, I bring her other arm up and fasten it in place. I begin my feast of her with her breasts, sucking, biting, and licking the globes and the nipples. I love the moans Elizabeth makes when I flick my tongue back and forth on the pebbled tips. Moving down to my knees I bury my face between her legs, pushing up on her clit with my nose and thrusting into her hole with my pointed tongue. I suck, lick and nibble on the whole of her pussy and her clit, alternating between fucking her with my tongue and my finger. I know she feels the beads inside her when she clenches. These aren't as large as the ben wa balls but they don't have the same purpose either. When I feel her walls beginning to close in on me, grasping me tighter, and I know she's about to come, I slide one finger inside her and curve it, rubbing that spot inside. I take her clit between my lips and roll it between them. The first spasms of her orgasm hit. Now I start to pull out the beads. Pop.

"Oh God!"

Pop.

"Oh, God, oh God, oh God!"

Pop.

Pop.

Pop.

Pop.

"OHGODOHGODOHGODOHGODOHGOO OOOOOOOOD!!"

I smile to myself. That's right baby, let me hear you SCREAM!

"Marco!"

I chuckle with her clit still between my lips as the vibrations press into her.

"Aaaaagghhh!"

All the anal beads are out so I remove my finger from inside her, then place a soft kiss on her still pulsing sex. I want to cover her in kisses, shower her with devotion and affection. I am consumed with a need to please her, pleasure her, protect her and care for her. And suddenly I know, it is in her submission that I am her slave. On my knees, I wrap myself around her bound body, bowing my head, consumed by my burning love for her.

Even with that orgasm, she hasn't had enough so I stand and release her arms, rubbing her wrists and kissing her deeply. She's breathing heavily and her nails are scoring my back.

I can tell she's hungry for more.

"I'm not finished with you yet, my love, turn around and give me your ass. Tonight it's mine."

My cock jumps against her torso with my words and a little smirk lifts a corner of my lips. Her eyes widen and her mouth opens in nervous anticipation. I don't give her time to think about what I've just said, guiding her to turn and bend so I can start to play with that ass again the right way.

Picking up the lube and the butt plug, I put some in my hand to warm it again and apply some to the plug. I think about the last time we used the butt vibrator and my cock throbs with aching need. That was absolutely incredible for each of us. We both screamed.

I lower myself to my knees behind Elizabeth and I begin to lick her with long lapping strokes of my tongue as my hands reach under her taking both of her breasts in my hands and grasping her nipples between my fingers. I roll them before putting the tip of my finger at the crest of each one and begin to flick them. Her hips begin to squirm under my tongue ever so slightly. I pull one hand away and move it to her clit to mimic the movement on her nipple there. She's pushing her ass into my face. I take the plug and place it at the entrance of her rear hole and hold it. She begins to open up to the plug and it easily slides in. Her movements are becoming stronger and more demanding now with the plug filling her ass.

I stand behind her and pull her up.

"Sit on the bed, baby." My voice is ragged now with lust.

She looks unsure but she does it, squirming when she sits down and her eyes shoot up to look into mine. A big smile spreads across my face when I recognize the glaze beginning to cover her eyes. Oh yes, she likes it.

"Good girl. Suck me, Elizabeth." It comes out almost as a plea, my cock is aching, it's so hard.

Her mouth begins to work its magic on my hard-on but her sucking me off is not my intention. I focus on her face and her body to see how she's feeling with that plug pushing around on her hole. I can see she is beginning to ride that plug in her ass, writhing and squirming around in circles. She's sucking me hard and deep and I know I have to stop her now or we're both going to come. I want my cock inside her when we do.

Pulling my cock from her oh-so-wonderful, lips, I guide her to her feet telling her through gritted teeth, "Get on the bed, all fours, chest down."

How the fuck I have the willpower to stop is beyond me.

After applying some lube to my shaft, I follow her onto the bed and position myself between her legs behind her, putting the vibrator within arm's reach. I begin to slide my cock over her pussy, rocking us back and forth, titillating that electric nub with the head of my cock. I slowly ease the plug from her ass and watch in fascination as the hole stays open as if waiting for my cock. With the last amount of lube on my hand I rub it around the rim of her hole and place the head of my hard shaft at its entrance. Fuck, I can almost blow my load now with the anticipation of her tight, tight ass. I begin to tease her pussy, sliding my finger in and out, twisting and turning it, rubbing her walls. Her hole begins to open up more for me and I ease in slowly as it does. A little farther, a little farther, the head is in.

Fuck yes!

"Oh, God, Marco, it hurts," she moans underneath me.

"I know, baby, but I'm in and it's going to stop hurting now and feel so good. Hold on, my love."

My head is back and the drunken stupor is beginning to flow through my body with the beginning of my orgasm. She doesn't realize it but she's pulling me into her and I feel like I'm falling into bliss. I look down and she's taken almost all of me and I'm shocked. I hold still letting her get used to the feeling of me inside her. The moment the pleasure starts to take over her I know it, I see it, I hear it, and I feel it. I begin to move slowly in her tight grip. It won't be long. I know it. I've been waiting a long time for this. I reach around and pinch her clit between my fingers making her ride that wave with me, rocking back and forth. I reach down and pick up the vibrator, turn it on and put it on her clit, then hold tightly against her.

"Oh God, Marco!"

Her movements are stronger, pushing back on me making me fuck her harder and faster. I've got one hand on her hip and the other holding the vibrator on her clit and she's starting to buck against me.

"Oh yes, yes, yes!"

She slams back on me grinding her ass into me as she comes.

"OHGODOHGODOHGODOHGODOHGOD OHGOD!"

I keep thrusting and holding the vibrator right there. I am not letting her stop any time soon.

"Oh, God, please, Marco!"

"Not yet, baby, you're not done!"

"FUCKFUCKFUCKFUCK!"

I feel the first trickle of wetness and I fucking explode.

"ELIZABETH!"

My hand is dripping from her squirting on me, and I fucking love it! She doesn't exactly squirt. It doesn't come shooting out, but she just leaks a lot.

I throw the vibrator on the floor and pull her down to the bed with me, we're both completely sated and spent.

But there is one thing more, one thing I haven't given to her. I'm not done yet.

I turn her in my arms and cover her face with little kisses.

"Open your eyes, baby."

Her eyes slowly open. They are the most beautiful shade of hazel, just like a cat's eyes, and I can't help but stare into their depths getting lost in them.

"I love you, Elizabeth, with everything in me."

The first teardrop falls from her eye, then another.

"I love you, Marco, so much."

Epilogue
Five Years Later

Elizabeth

It's Christmas Eve, my absolute favorite day and night of the year! You would never guess it by the weather though. The sky is a soft blue with gentle puffs of clouds floating slowly past and the sounds of birds fill the sixty-five-degree air. Even a hawk can be heard close by.

"Marco, don't let them do that! It's too dangerous for them yet!" I holler from the porch.

That man is going to be the death of me. He is more of a child than the children. They're three, and it's him I've got to keep an eye on. The twins at least think about what they shouldn't do. Marco just does it. He's got both of them on the four-wheeler right now and I can hear their peals of laughter as he drives through the fields. I wonder who was responsible enough to remember to put on the helmets, him or the children. I'm the more uptight one of course. I'm the mom.

We moved into this house four years ago. It's a new two-story white plantation style house on a fifteen-acre horse ranch with wraparound porches with rocking chairs, porch swings, fans and screened-in areas. There was an older home on the property, which we did some renovations to, and the property manager and his family live there now. There's also a barn, stables, work sheds, gazebo, pool house and pool, and now a playhouse. Marco has his work shed which he dabbles in sometimes. He had his grandfather's antique hand tools professionally matted and hung so they hang in the family room with all of our family photos and memorabilia.

When the children were babies I'd bring their bassinettes out on the porch and sing to them, read to them, and just talk to them and watch them sleep. As much as I love the babies, Marco adores them, he worships the ground they walk on but Carmela has him wrapped around her little finger. He was lost to her the second he looked into those same deep dark eyes as his with her thick curly brown hair. Her brother Marco, who is older by fifteen minutes, is one of the sweetest, naughtiest, most loving and witty boys in the whole world. He will get caught doing something but charm his way out of it with those big hazel eyes of his and those beautiful long lashes. The pregnancy was a very difficult one. When I was three months along I lost my plug. I was so afraid

I was going to lose the babies. The doctors ordered me on bed rest for the duration of the pregnancy, which I did under the guard dog Marco's threats. He was always at my side. When he couldn't be there he enlisted the help of Elsie, Janie and Christine along with some other wonderful people Marco hired. I was already a high-risk pregnancy because of my age and we knew that going in. I was a beached whale when I was pregnant, with twins growing inside me, and ordered to be on bed rest, along with my love affair with Snickers and Reese's Peanut Butter Cups, all this did not amount to minimal weight gain. The babies were two weeks premature which isn't much, but enough that their lungs were not fully developed. They had to stay in the hospital a little bit longer and it was the worst two weeks of my life. Marco and I were at the hospital around the clock. One of us was always there, if not both. This was when I missed my mom the most, when I sat next to the incubator watching my children with breathing tubes shoved down their throats and needles stuck all over their skin.

When the babies were finally able to come home, Marco's parents came down for a week to help out and I was extremely grateful for that. His mother and father accepted me as one of their own children, always making me feel appreciated. When they were here last year we discussed building a cottage for them on the property since they've been talking about moving from the Northeast. They're finally sick of the snow storms, high taxes and congestion.

I think it would be great having them here. I don't have either of my parents and Marco has finally laid all of his past demons to rest. He has come to terms with everything, embracing both his past and the future of our family, making today the best it can be. I also think that seeing me without my parents has brought him the realization that his parents won't be around for much longer. I believe he doesn't want to have the same guilt I do once they're gone. My family was very close growing up, my brother and I still are, and the kids having their grandparents here to spoil them and to save them from those dinners they hate would be great for all of us.

"Mommy!" Carmela calls to me as they speed by, her little arm waving in the air, and she's smiling from ear to ear. I am going to kill that man, I swear it. Her brother is more the strong silent type, but to be honest I don't think he gets a chance to speak, she's always doing the talking for both of them. He's the thinker, the introvert, the one who wonders why and how instead of where and when. Right now he's also got the Cheshire Cat's grin on his handsome little face, loving the joy ride. But the biggest grin has definitely got to be Marco's. He is living his second childhood with the kids and he is having a hell of a blast.

As I stand here watching my family my heart wants to burst with the love and happiness I feel and I wonder every day, how did I get this lucky? Marco has made every single day the best day of my life. My God, I remember the day I told him I was pregnant. He held me as I cried tears of joy, my beautiful strong, powerful, controlling husband. I think he wanted to cry as well. He didn't say a word for a few minutes, I think because he had such a huge lump in his throat and he didn't trust his voice to keep from cracking. He called his parents and they cried, then I called my brother and I think he wanted to cry. Then we invited our friends over, Elsie, Janie, John and Brian and broke the news to all of them over dinner. These four people turned out to be completely invaluable during my pregnancy and the dearest and kindest individuals in the world, taking turns babysitting and waiting on me, and the babies really, while I was forced to lie on my big fat ass for almost seven months.

Another loud screech and that's it, I can't watch anymore so I decide to go inside to make lunch for the four-wheeling maniacs.

"You stay here, Zeus, and watch them. Call me if anything happens." I look down at the faithful white pit bull sitting beside me on the porch. I think he's actually smiling at me while thumping his tail on the wooden planks as if he's answering me, *I got this, you go ahead.*

"I know you do, big boy, that's why I love you so much," I tell him, scratching him on his head between his ears. His smile just got bigger as his tongue falls out the side of his mouth. "Crazy mutt," I mutter as I go inside letting the screen door slam behind.

After I finish everyone's lunch, I walk out the back door to call in my crew and Zeus is right where I left him, turning his head to look at me with his tongue hanging out panting away. I just hope they can hear me over the roar of the engine of the four wheeler.

Ding ding ding!!!

Nothing.

I climb down the steps with Zeus at my heels trudging across the yard although it looks more like a football field than a yard. Half way across they see me, thank God, and I start waving to them to come on in. When they signal to me that they understand I turn and head back towards the house.

About half way there, they pass me and all three of them yell, "We're gonna beat you!!" followed by the cackling of the three kids in the race they decided we're in.

I yell to the backs of their heads, "Wash your hands!!"

When I reach the house the kids have already gotten half their lunch finished, which is a pleasant surprise, I don't have to goad them today, but Marco's at the sink cleaning up the dishes.

I come up behind him sliding my hands around his waist and ask, "So Mr. Bond, what's the secret weapon you used to get them to eat so well?" laying my cheek against the warmth of his back, squeezing him tightly. I love this man so much. Still.

He turns in my arms and looks down into my face wrapping me in his arms and with that million dollar smile on his face, he kisses me lightly.

"Who's Mr. Bond?" Marco Jr.'s voice cuts into our moment. We both can't hold back our laughter at the innocence of his question.

Pulling away from Marco I take his hand and lead him to the table so that we can sit and eat lunch with our children. In our house, meal time is family time.

"Mr. Bond, Marco, James Bond, is a secret agent in the movies, a very handsome one too, and very smart. All the ladies love him." I look over to Marco, and he's shaking his head laughing, so I continue, "When your father and I first met after our, um, first date, I didn't think your father would call me…"

"Your mother was completely wrong!" Marco cuts in.

Carmela's eyes shoot open and her mouth opens up full of a bite of her triangle sandwich. Marco Jr.'s brows furrow together, they are completely shocked and confused.

"You didn't want to go on another date with daddy, mommy?" the poor baby really looks sad.

"Of course I did, but let me finish, he had it already planned you see, he called me a few days later. That was a secret agent move, so since then I've always called him Mr. Bond," I finish the story and the children look very pleased with the antics of their father.

Carmela jumps up and down in her chair excitedly, "Daddy! Daddy! Tell us about the time you met mommy again!" Marco Jr. looks up at us as well with a smile on his precious little face. My children are hopeless romantics, like their parents. He takes after me more than he does his father, with the far-away look in his eyes, his gentleness and patience but once he's reached his limit, there will be hell to pay.

Marco gets that dramatic edge to his voice as he begins to tell the children about our first night, the G rated kid friendly version.

"I saw your mother from across the street from the chair I was sitting in, and your aunt Janie, I didn't know her yet, was standing with some other friends of hers and she started yelling hi to someone. When I looked, I saw it was your mother and that was that exact moment I fell in love with her." He looks at me and the sincerity of his words are so evident in his eyes, I know I'm glowing with my love for him as well. He continues, "I watched her all night long with her friends, even as she danced with another boy," he makes his tone firm looking right at the kids.

Both Carmela and Marco Jr. look at me shouting, "MOMMY!!"

"I didn't even know your dad then!" Then I tell Marco, "Don't make it seem like you were Mr. Innocent." I don't want to tell them that Marco had this blonde bimbo pouring out of her dress hanging all over him.

"Now, kids, it's ok, your mom knew that it was me she belonged to so she sent all of those other guys away with their tails between her legs. And I knew she was disappointed I didn't come and talk to her before she decided to leave," and he gives me a sideways glance smirking at some private joke.

I give his arm a swat, "You, Marco, are horrible!"

He laughs, "I didn't want to scare you away too fast, Elizabeth!"

The children are laughing at our pretend little squabble as Marco continues, "I noticed your mom was saying good bye to Aunt Janie and the rest of her friends and I wasn't going to let her leave without making her mine. So you know what I did?" He looks at Carmela and Marco Jr. wide eyed, he's got them totally hooked even though he's told them this story a hundred times. This was a bedtime favorite for years.

"YOU FOLLOWED HER!!" they shout in unison.

He laughs with his beautiful eyes scrunching, pearly whites gleaming, dimples showing chuckle, the one that makes all women's panties go up in flames. And he's mine, all mine.

"Yes, I followed her, but that doesn't mean it's ok to follow strangers, it could be very dangerous, but this is our story. Now, where was I?" he pauses for moment for dramatic effect, tapping his cheek with his finger, "Oh, yes, I started to follow your mother down the street. She walked about a block and when I finally caught up to her it was right at that moment her heel got stuck in the sidewalk and she almost fell flat on her face right there in front of God and everyone. And do you know what I did?" He smirks knowing what's coming.

"YOU CAUGHT HER!!" They shout in chorus again.

"Yes, I caught the woman of my dreams in my arms and from that moment we started to live happily ever after." He looks at me and leans over smiling softly and kisses me gently. The kids erupt in loud applause just like they do every single time Marco tells this story.

"Tell us about when you asked mommy to marry you, daddy!!!" Carmela squeals, clapping her hands and bouncing in her booster seat. Marco Jr.'s going right along with her with his hands hitting the table.

Marco turns to the kids and brings his face very close to them, "What is tonight, kids?" he almost whispers.

"CHRISTMAS EVE!!"

"That's right, mommy's favorite night of the year, right after your birthday, so, we are going to be extra good and after lunch you're going to go pick up your toys and maybe tonight after The Night Before Christmas I'll tell you that one. Now, Santa's not going to be very pleased if you don't finish your lunch."

"But I'm not hungry," Carmela pouts crossing her arms in front of her but Marco Jr. digs in.

"Alright, princess, how about a little apple sauce then I'll let you up?" Marco coos to her.

"Ok, daddy, just a little," and she knows she has him right where she wants him.

That night after the children have been bathed, their story read to them in front of the Christmas tree in the family room, and have been tucked in with Marco telling them again about when he asked me to marry him we finally get a moment to ourselves.

Marco is sitting on the loveseat in our bedroom where my portrait, the one he took of me, hangs over our bed. He had another copy made when I promised not to destroy this one.

"Come here, baby," Marco lifts his arm beckoning for me to come and rest my head there.

I go and sit with him leaning against his chest just soaking in the feeling of him. He kisses me gently on the top of my head.

"We still have presents to wrap, don't we, my love?"

I sigh heavily remembering those other two bags of toys that still need to be wrapped in our closet.

"Yes."

"Go get me the ribbon, baby, I'll start now," his voice rumbles through my body.

I get up and retrieve the bag of ribbons and scissors and tape from the closet.

I stand in front of him setting the bag on the table then I start to turn to get the paper.

"Stop, Elizabeth." His voice has dropped and become firmer.

It's that voice, the one that makes my sex leak. I suck in a sharp breath instinctively just from the sound of his voice, licking me in my most intimate parts.

"I want you to strip for me, baby, then I'm going to tie you up like my Christmas present and play with you. Take your clothes off, my love, let me look at my beautiful wife."

The End
Keep going, there's more…

without them, we get lost in the great cyber abyss. Those reviews, and when you tell your friends about us, are what bring us to life in the world. Without your help, we can't survive.

I can't tell you how much I appreciate your taking the journeys with me through the worlds in my stories. My greatest wish is that I can bring some of the love I have for my characters to you in the pages.

Because, really, that's what makes the world a sacred place. Love.

With my love,

~ N.M. <3 xoxo

Keep going, there's more....

I hope you enjoyed *STRANGER* and *SWITCH* as much as I enjoyed writing them and I hope you will take a piece of Marco and Elizabeth with you. <3

Next in the series is *KINK, it's exactly what you think and so, so, soooo much more.*

Elsie leans against the wall while the bass pumps through her small body, the beat so hard you can almost see her breasts jiggling inside the vinyl black Cat Woman body suit she's wearing. Even if she does say so herself, she looks pretty damn hot wrapped tightly in that shiny black second skin. The Halloween party that UE Movie Studios threw tonight is a huge success. Everybody who is somebody is here tonight including her best friend Elizabeth's boyfriend, Marco Kastanopoulis, apparently the newest celebrity in town. It looks like the poor guy is stuck working tonight, having to talk to all of the boring old stuffed shirts in town like the councilman and newspaper editors and anyone else Elsie would probably fall asleep talking to. Right now he has broken away from his watch dog, She-devil, and his sidekick, Pretty Boy, to get some much needed alone time with Elizabeth. Which is why Elsie is sitting by herself.

Out of the corner of her eye Elsie sees John Wolfe walking toward her. He should have been named John Bear, the man is as huge as one and almost as formidable at first glance. She becomes a blithering oozing pile of female hormones whenever he comes into view. Tonight he's shirtless, which is completely killing her. That big wide torso ripples with all of his muscles every move he makes, dressed in just Indian style fringe pants and moccasins with a band tied around the bulging muscles of one his upper arms. On the other side is a tribal tattoo starting on his shoulder coming mid-way down the upper part of his arm with a band of some sort of design at the bottom. It feeds down his shoulder blade on to his back leading to a beautiful wolf. On his upper chest is a pair of wings with the Sacred Heart of Jesus in the center and a star on his other shoulder. And the man doesn't walk, he stalks, everything about him shouts predator and I'm-gonna-take-whatever-I-want. The very thought of it makes her mouth drool, how she would love to be his prey, hunted and stalked by him until he takes her, devouring her, leaving her completely breathless. She shakes herself, trying to snap out of her thoughts, the outfit she's wearing doesn't leave room for unnecessary moisture.

From her other side she sees Brian Daniels coming towards her as well. He's the other end of the spectrum of John's dark and intense, he's drop dead good looking blonde and blue eyes with a disarmingly sweet smile, six foot laid back elegance. These two together are lethal and she knows she's in trouble, the simple act of speech will be nearly impossible with them.

"Hi Elsie," John's melted caramel voice envelopes Elsie, making her heat rise and her heart race.

"Hi John," is all she can manage which is out of character for Elsie, her tongue is razor sharp and ready to shred at a moment's notice.

"All alone?" Brian comes up on her other side and her temperature sky rockets even more.

"Yeah, um, Marco came over and pulled Elizabeth away from the dance floor for a little while, I think he was lonely with those two with him," she lifts her chin in the direction where her friend is standing.

"Well, Elsie, we've made it our mission to make sure you're ok," John takes another step closer to Elsie, just on the verge of being intimately close.

"Oh?" is all she can intelligibly say, his body heat and his completely he-man delicious smell is fogging her brain with erotic images and she doesn't trust herself not say something that might come out sounding like, 'yes, please push me up against the wall and rip my clothes off.'

"And our missions are always completed with the utmost satisfaction, Elsie," Brian takes a step closer as well, his panty melting smile working his magic on her, making her squirm from the pulsing deep in her core.

"You don't mind if we make you our mission, do you Elsie?"

Brian's voice licks her with fire, igniting her, as images of both of them taking her, getting her lost in oblivion and she's instantly ready to cum at the mere thought of both of their mouths, their hands, their cocks all over her body. She gasps fighting the urge to lean her face against John's bare chest and licking him from where that happy trail starts, then dipping her tongue in his belly button listening to his breath catch from the wet touch, to finally sucking on those tight little nipples of his.

Elsie's face lifts to look into both of theirs. The promises of erotic delights beyond her most intimate imagination are being offered to her without words, without a touch, without so much as a whisper but they couldn't be any clearer. And there is no way she can resist.

She is so screwed.

Yep, still more...

ABOUT THE AUTHOR

N.M. Catalano is an Amazon best-selling, multi-published author. She spent many years in the corporate world, and owned several businesses. Having been fortunate to have such varied exposures, she had many opportunities to be exposed to different societies and cultures. After years of studying people and lifestyles, her fascination comes to life in the pages of her stories.

"I am just a woman, like many of you, who has lived through beauty and ugliness, happiness, (sometimes extreme), and sadness, (sometimes heart wrenching), and have grown to love life and myself even more. I write because I love the characters, I am madly and hopelessly in love with them and want to share them with the world. Life is beautiful and is meant to be enjoyed day by day, sometimes you have to pick out the good stuff with a magnifying glass like a needle in a haystack, but enjoyed none the less. The stories that I put on paper, I think, help us to find that enjoyment a little bit more.

I am just a woman who is in love with love............<3"

Connect with her at:

Blog: https://nmcatalanoauthor.wordpress.com/

Facebook:
https://www.facebook.com/nmcatalanowriter

Twitter: @nmcatalanowriter

Pinterest:
https://www.pinterest.com/catalanoauthor/

Fan Group, (where the giveaways happen and news is posted, along with other awesome stuff): nm catalano's book babes.

Newsletter, (to receive notices of giveaways, and chapters of upcoming releases nowhere else available): http://eepurl.com/bpEW9X

Coming up, Other Works…

OTHER WORKS

STRANGER, Book 1 Stranger Series
I couldn't resist submitting to him. I still can't, no matter the cost.

I thought I was fine, I thought my life was ok. Until I met him. One night of erotic abandon blew open the door to the prison of my life and there was no way I wanted to lock it back up. I couldn't, not when he kept coming back. But I knew there would be a price to pay. There always is, I had been warned. The past always comes back to haunt you especially when it promised it would.

Your body is my playground and I want to play.

Life is good. I have control, I like having control. Until I met her. I thought that one night of her deliciousness would be enough to satisfy me. I was wrong. I wanted more, there was something about her, she was different. And now I was losing control, there was no way in hell I was going to lose.

** This is book is meant to be read as a stand alone but is the first book in the STRANGER series. No cliffhangers.

**Disclaimer: explicit sex scenes, be prepared to

sweat and your heart rate to accelerate, intended for mature readers.**

SWITCH, Book 2 Stranger Series

Life can change in an instant.

Betrayal. Just like that everything I had built, my entire life, was falling apart. My world threatened to collapse from under me, everything was slipping through my hands, and it looked like there wasn't a damn thing I could do to stop the destruction. I was going to lose everything but the worst part was, I was going to lose her.

A second chance.

Fate smiled down on me and gave me a second chance. And it was so much better than I could have ever imagined. He worshipped my body, he made me feel adored. Until that day. The day I found them, the day his skeletons came pouring out of that closet he thought was so well hidden. He made a huge mistake if he thought I was naive. It was time for me to take control. Can he SWITCH to get it all back?

KINK, Book 3 Stranger Series

She's a damaged girl hiding behind a tough façade and a razor sharp tongue, afraid to open up to him and trust him. Her wounds are deep, the scars are many, some are visible, and others cannot be seen.

He thinks he doesn't deserve her, that he doesn't deserve to be happy. The demons he fights are loud and strong, some are real, while others are not. But he wants her. And he'll have her.

He'll share her. They'll plunge her into the most erotic oblivion she's ever experienced.

**Warning, this book contains very strong sexual content, BDSM, menage, and a scene or two which could be a trigger containing sexual assault/rape. 18+

PERFECT, Book 4, Stranger Series

Brian Daniels has life by the balls. He's gorgeous, so much so, it hurts so good to look at him. And his dominant sexual skills leave the women he's with in a state of complete erotic delirium for days, knowing exactly how to bring her the most pleasure. The dark and dangerous beast inside him, the one that was born in the Marines, is released in the cage when he fights, and in the bedroom when the women are tied and begging for more. He is absolutely perfect. But he's miserable, empty, and hollow, wondering if this is all there is to life.

Everything about Brooke stops traffic. Her perfect body and face have men following behind her like a trail of whimpering little puppy dogs. And she hates everything about herself, because it destroyed her. She lives with its curse every day, one that will never allow a man to get close to her heart. She's a brilliant Marine Biologist fighting against the clock amid brutal shark attacks, trying to find a way to stop the animal before it strikes again. But she's defenseless against the monster inside her.

When Brian and Brooke collide, it's an erotic war zone, one that Brian will not lose.

Can he save her from her demons? Can she finally submit and let Brian free her from her hell? Or will tragedy strike first and rip Brian from her, destroying any chance they have at love?

THE ROOSTER CLUB, The Best Cocks In Town

We all have that first true love, the one we never forget, the one that makes our heart hurt, even today.

This is their story. It spans decades.

This is his story....

All wrapped up in the decadence of the '80's:

Sex (lots of it).

Drugs (almost as much).

Discos (where it all happened).

How it all crashed in the 90's.

And today, how it found her once again...

BLACK INK, Part I, Black Ink, Part II, Black Ink Part IIIThe BLACK INK Trilogy

In Part I we met the man,

Alexander Black
Ruthless. Powerful. A prick.
Intoxicating, intriguing.
He took, he claimed, he possessed.
In Part II,
He owned.
I a world of seduction,
Danger,
Darkness.
In Part III,
The beast is unleashed.
In a deadly race against time,
The only thing he wants is
Blood,
Revenge,
Annihilation.
In a dangerous race against time,
Will it be too late?

HIDING, Book 5 in the Stranger Series (Rico's Story)

Warning: It is passionate, it is suspenseful, it'll blow your mind. There is darkness, you have been warned, now enter at your own risk...

Secrets, they entice you, they bind you, they hold you captive. A challenge whispered to you luring you closer. Will you delve into their darkness? Would you go? Or would you hide...

I had rules. They protected the fortress of my darkness.

My secrets.
I allowed myself certain distractions, but nothing permanent.
It wasn't allowed.
If I slipped, then I'd fall.
That was one thing I couldn't afford.
Until her.
She was secrets wrapped up in a challenge. Tied with a big bow of sensuality.
I was about to take the biggest fall of my life.

I'd found complacency in my nightmare.
A comfort in normalcy.
I was surviving.
It sucked, but I was safe.
Until he crashed into my world.
He had secrets.
Lots of them.
He wasn't the good guy, not at all.
But was he what I needed?

She's hiding from her future.
He's running from his past.
When they collide it's explosive.
Danger is a persistent predator.
It seeks until it finds.
There is no past, and no future.
There is only now, and right now danger is coming.
You can run, but you can never hide.

Made in the USA
Columbia, SC
29 July 2022

63979470R00228